One Night Seduction

Katelyn Taylor

Playlist

eyes don't lie by Isabel LaRosa
Daddy Issues by The Neighbourhood
Out of My League by Fitz and The Tantrums
Summer by Calvin Harris
Mount Everest by Labrinth
I feel like I'm drowning by Two Feet
Guys My Age by Hey Violet
Make You Mine by Madison Beer
Older by Isabel LaRosa
You're The One That I Want by John Travolta, Olivia
Newton-John

Trigger Warning

Please carefully review these triggers before continuing. This book is forbidden by nature with a complicated and somewhat taboo relationship between a woman and her mother's ex-husband. The triggers inside this book are but not limited to: Age gap, Dom/Sub dynamics, ass play, impact play, spanking, sharing, body shaming (by the evil twat mother), kidnapping, violence, alcoholism, graphic sexual scenes, graphic language and more.

Dedication

We all know it's technically frowned upon, but how could
something so 'wrong' be
so delicious?

Chapter One

Arianna

My fingers twist against the smooth strings of the silver masquerade mask in my hand. I thought about not coming so many times tonight. Not because I'm a prude or anything; honestly, I'm far from it. But the idea of actually going to a sex club seemed…intense. Intimidating maybe?

Normally, I like my encounters to be of the drunken and never see you again variety. I guess this place has the same allure since the club's theme is masquerade. Everyone is required to wear a mask, whether to provide anonymity or just amp up the kink factor. It provides a sort of sense of comfort, though.

I'd probably be scrolling on my hook-up app tonight or at the bar just down the street from the university if it wasn't my best friend's birthday. Usually, twenty-first birthday parties are spent doing pub crawls, going to dance clubs or raves, but oh no, not my best friend.

Cassi decided that she wanted her and her closest friends to celebrate her milestone birthday getting railed in a club together. I mean, when you put it like that, I guess it doesn't sound terrible. I can't believe we even found this place. It doesn't even have a name. Literally. There's no sign outside, no name when you look up the address, and their website is extremely vague, promising only anonymity and a night you'll never forget. A senior Cassi was hooking up with handed her this black card when she was talking about her birthday plans a few days ago. It only had an address on it, but he swore we would love it. Let's hope he's right, I guess.

So, we all rented a hotel room to share in case the place was weird, and if we didn't feel comfortable, we could head back to the room and eat the whole minibar. To be honest, this night seems to only be capable of good times.

Still, I can't help but feel a rush of butterflies as we walk up to the nondescript door before Cassi excitedly knocks. She plays with the gold mask in her hand as I glance to see our friend Naomi doing the same with her red one. She looks excited too, but she has a flicker of hesitancy as well. She's always been the meek one of our group. She's also a virgin, so the fact that she agreed to come tonight shocked me.

An imposing man opens the door, giving our group a once over before staring at us expectantly.

"Gratify," Cassi says, a smile full of mirth playing on her full lips as she pushes her red hair to the side, a complete contrast to my near pitch-black hair or Naomi's bright blonde.

Where Cassi is every bit the spunky redhead with the perfect number of freckles dusting her cheeks, I'm her polar opposite. My sleek black hair, blue eyes, and resting bitch face typically earns me the group's resident bitch title. I'm okay with it, though. After all, I got it from my mother, apart from the eyes, and at forty-five she looks better than most twenty-one year olds I know. Men certainly think so, at least.

The bouncer looks to Cassi, giving her an approving nod

before taking our ID's. After he hands them back, he gestures to our masks before stepping aside.

"Masks on, ladies, and welcome to paradise."

We lace up our masks before I run a hand down my black cocktail dress. I stared at my closet for a solid forty-five minutes before deciding there was literally no right or wrong thing to wear to a sex club, they don't exactly have a dress code stamped on a website anywhere. So, I figured the classic LBD would be perfect.

I might have made an oversight in the shoe department. My heels are so tall, I'm ready to snap an ankle at any given moment. Hopefully, I won't be vertical for much of the night anyways.

The doorman guides us down the dark hallway behind him, the barest glow of light leading us deeper into the club. Just as I almost roll my ankle for the third time, the darkness gives way, revealing something akin to a seductive, depraved wonderland.

There is a large bar pushed to the back wall as soon as you walk in. Lights flash and dance from the ceiling, dozens of chandeliers scattered around the room, amping up the elegance of the place.

At the bar, I see several people in...unique attire, chatting to the person beside them, grabbing a drink, or passionately making out. In the center of the room, a lounge area is filled with various couches and loveseats, people enthusiastically taking up every inch of them.

My eyes snag on a gorgeous blonde who is between an older man's legs, sucking his cock like it's the best thing she's ever tasted. Another woman is sitting completely naked on a man's lap reverse cowgirl style, her tits bouncing with each thrust he gives her.

Now, I identify as straight, but if you can look at a great

pair of tits on a beautiful woman and not get a little turned on, then I'd straight up call you a liar.

"Fuck," Naomi mutters in a husky voice.

"I told you guys, right?!" Cassi squeals excitedly. "I wonder where the bondage demonstrations are."

Her eyes flit around the place before she scurries off to explore. Naomi follows after her, a confident little sway in her hips. Good. She deserves a little fun, even if she says she won't be losing her v-card tonight.

Instead of following them, I decide that I definitely need a drink first. I don't even know where to begin in a place like this. There are no rules, no expectations. I guess you just find the first decently attractive person and whip their cock out? Yeah, I'm going to need to sit back and observe for a minute.

When I get to the bar top, a gorgeous blue-eyed, blond haired bartender smiles at me.

"What can I get you, sweetheart?"

"Tequila, please. Better make it a double."

"Same for me," a deep voice rumbles from behind me.

I look over my shoulder to see a large man standing only a few feet away from me. His shoulders are wide, arms corded with huge muscles, and hair a deep chestnut brown. He's wearing a black dress shirt with the sleeves rolled up his forearms in that sexy way that all good looking men seem to do. His black mask takes up most of his face, but I can see the shape of his Roman godlike nose, a trim beard and full pink lips. I also can see those eyes, deep set and dark. They're so intense, so focused, and trained directly on me. College guys don't look at you like this, fuck, college guys don't *look* like this.

My breath stalls in my chest and my mouth dries up at the sight of him. Or maybe it's because of the way he's staring at me. Either way, even if I can only see a third of his face, I already know without a doubt he is one of the best looking men

I've seen in my life. I can tell by the way he carries himself that he's gotta be older. Later thirties at the minimum.

Right now, ask me if I care.

Interrupting our mutual eye fucking, the bartender sets down two glasses in front of us.

"Put it on your tab, sir?" the bartender asks the masked man.

He dips his head, not removing his eyes from my own as he reaches for our glasses, handing mine over before clinking them together. I try to say thanks but come up short on words, mainly because I'm not sure I remember how to speak. Fuck, he's gorgeous.

I watch as he lifts the glass to his lips, his eyes hooded as he tips back the clear liquid. My eyes are laser focused on the way his throat works the tequila down. Shit. Can a man taking a drink really soak my panties just like that? You'd think it's been years since I've last had sex, not days.

This is different, though. So different. This isn't some frat boy trying to buy me cheap beer in the hopes of getting laid. This isn't even a nice respectable guy that I meet at a coffee shop and then fuck in his car before I go to class. This place, this man, the energy. Everything is heightened. The sexual tension from this entire atmosphere is so thick you can choke on it, while simultaneously craving more.

When his eyes come back to me and he sets his drink down on the bar top, I remember that I'm still holding my drink, staring at him like an idiot. So, I lift the cool glass to my lips, allowing the sharp burn of the tequila to prick my taste buds before running down my throat. The warmth I feel is immediate, and when I tilt my head forward again, I find the mystery man in front of me staring at me with the same amount of intensity as before.

Setting the glass on the bar top beside his, he reaches out

his hand to me. It's a large hand, though it looks smooth and strong. Like he doesn't have to use them for physical labor, but he could do some serious damage with them if he wanted.

Or deliver a dizzying amount of pleasure.

My hand slides into his before I even fully decide that I want to go wherever he is taking me. It's like I'm not even in control of myself as his fingers lace through mine, gently guiding me through the club.

Chapter Two

Arianna

I take careful steps, making sure not to break an ankle or trip in these fucking heels as the gorgeous stranger guides us through this labyrinth of a club. We go up the stairs, turning down a few hallways before he pulls me to a stop in front of a doorway. I look up at him and meet his gaze before he pushes the door open and pulls me inside. As soon as he closes the door behind us, the sound of a lock engaging echoes through the room. Something about the sound of that lock sends a shiver down my back and sets my pulse racing. Fuck, this is beginning to feel like some Dateline shit. This place is safe, though, right? I mean, anyone can come in here as long as they are over twenty-one and have a password, but it's still safe. Right?

When he turns to face me, though, I realize that none of my typical internal alarms are going off. I don't feel unsafe, I don't feel trapped. I feel...nervous. What the fuck is the matter with me?

My eyes dance around the room, in complete awe. The room has a large bed draped in black satin sheets, the walls are adorned with every toy or tool you could imagine for the bedroom. If I didn't have this absolutely captivating man in front of me, I'd probably be interested in taking in my surroundings more. Instead, I find myself far more interested in how he prowls towards me methodically, like he's allowing me time to back out.

His chest presses against mine, the strong smell of his clean cologne filling the space between us. God, of course he smells amazing.

"What's your safe word?" his low voice rumbles.

"M-my what?" I pant.

"Safe word," he repeats, his head cocking to the side slightly as he watches me.

"Banana," I say.

His lips slowly start to curl upward in a smile before lifting a hand to cup my jaw. A zinging feeling rushes through me at his touch, and I happily sink into it. He lifts my head to accommodate our six inch height difference before speaking again.

"Use your word whenever you feel you need to, but trust that I'll do what's best for both of us in here."

I swallow at his words before nodding obediently.

"Have you ever had a Dom before?"

I shake my head. I'm not overly well-versed in the kink/sex club world, but I know enough. Jerry Andrews trying and failing to boss me around in a fast food parking lot definitely doesn't classify as a Dom/Sub relationship, I know that much.

Shaking my head softly, his fingers continue caressing my face, a pleased look filling his gaze.

"A Dom and a Sub's relationship is complex. It requires balance and trust, even if it's just for a night. You have to be willing to put your trust in me, give yourself over completely, and know that I'll take care of you the way you need, but maybe not the way you expect."

His words excite me and relieve me all at once. It's like he's taking all of the pressure out of this, the uncertainty. He's taking control, and all he's asking from me is to go along with it. There is also this comforting familiarity sound to his voice. Like I can trust him, like he will have my best interests in mind.

"Can you do that for me?" he asks.

That's a hell of a lot to expect out of a stranger, but his strong and steady demeanor has me agreeing easier than taking my next breath.

I nod my head softly, not trusting my voice.

"I need your words. I need to hear you commit to this night, to me."

My stomach flips in anticipation as I clear my throat.

"Yes. I can do it."

A pleased smile lifts his mouth, and it sends an odd feeling of gratification running through me as he leans forward, pressing his lips to mine. It starts out gently at first, like he's testing the waters. The softness of his lips pulls at my own, and I can't help but savor the lingering taste of tequila and something uniquely him.

Reaching out my hands to his shoulders, I wind them around his neck to pull him closer. My act of comfortability, of craving, seems to do something to him because, in the next moment, I'm being tossed onto the bed, his large body quickly following, covering every inch of me and trapping me against the mattress.

Our kiss turns savage, desperation for one another lingering on each other's lips as he tears at my dress, lifting it as high as it will go before stopping just above my breasts. Luckily for both of us, I decided to skip the bra tonight and he takes full advantage of it, his mouth latching onto my nipple before sucking it into his mouth.

Fuck, that feels so good.

His large palms are running along the length of my bare

skin before he winds his fingers around my panties. He yanks them off with a single tug before tossing them across the room. I feel his mouth release my nipple with a pop before he switches to give the other one the same level of attention. I can't help but moan as his tongue flicks against me, teeth grazing as his hand cups my now bare pussy.

He doesn't say anything, and I think that's what makes this all the more exciting. There is no awkward chit chat or fumbling foreplay. This man knows exactly what he wants, and right now, what he wants is me, and fuck, I have never been wetter in my entire goddamn life.

The heel of his palm grinds against my clit a few times, forcing a breathy moan to escape my lips before he begins trailing his mouth down my body, stopping when he pulls my thighs over his shoulders and buries his face into my pussy.

The way he eats me out is like nothing I've ever felt. It isn't even like he's trying to give me pleasure, it's like he's eating to survive. Like he'll die without my taste on his tongue. The dizzying high from it all is too much, and I fall apart with the barest of efforts, shouting and moaning as I grind my pussy against his face.

When my legs stop shaking, he slowly sits up, trailing his fingers from my wet slit to my asshole. I feel his finger probe me gently, causing me to tense as he hushes me softly. He runs his finger back up to my pussy, dipping inside of me and coating himself with my juices before returning to my ass.

The initial feeling of him pushing inside my tight hole is almost too much until he finds that perfect spot that has my body relaxing almost instantly.

"Your cunt tastes like heaven, and your ass is the tightest thing I've ever felt. How will I choose what to take first?" he muses.

"Both, anything, just fill me up. Please," I babble pleadingly.

A satisfied smirk crosses his face as he pulls his finger out of me, slowly standing to his feet. Disappointment consumes me. If he's a sadist who is into denying me whatever I ask for, I'm gonna be fucking pissed.

Thankfully, he returns within moments with a shiny jeweled butt plug. I've used them once or twice before, so when he squirts some lube against the cold steel and presses it against my waiting hole, I'm not the least bit surprised at the feeling. It's almost like a relief. He makes a low sound in his chest as he pushes it all the way in, like he's as desperate to fill me as I am to be filled by him.

Once the plug is seated in my ass, I expect him to line himself up to my pussy. Instead, he comes up to the side of my head, slowly pulling down his pants before revealing a beautifully thick and pierced cock. It's just a single double barbell piercing at the head, but it's enough to have me more than excited. I've always wanted to be with a pierced man but never had the opportunity.

"Suck," he commands as he rubs the head of his cock against my lips.

I open my mouth instantly, allowing him to push into me as I widen myself and relax my throat to take him fully. Fuck, he's huge. He keeps pushing until I gag, and then he pushes further. I wince, and he slowly pulls back before thrusting back in, forcing me to gag once more.

"Good girl. Choke on my cock," he encourages as he does it again and again.

I take steady breaths through my nose as I do what he says, enjoying the feeling of his smooth length thrusting in and out of me.

When he pulls almost all the way out, I let my tongue run against his piercing before pushing against it slightly. His movements pause as his body shudders. I look up to see his eyes snap to mine, his lips pressed together though his chest is heaving, silently begging me to do it again and again. My tongue flicks against him languidly, teasing and sucking on his tip as I graze my teeth against the piercing. At my continued teasing, he lets out a muffled curse before tipping his head back, staring at the ceiling as he cups either side of my face and begins vigorously fucking my mouth.

When I reach between his legs and grip his balls, he lets out the sexiest groan before quickly pulling out of my mouth. I blink hazily, trying to track where he's going before he's back on me, this time kneeling between my legs. I watch as he rolls on a condom in record time before pushing inside me without a single warning.

I gasp at the sudden intrusion, a burn tearing through me at his width combined with the plug in my ass. Fuck, I don't think I've ever been so full in all my life. Slowly, I begin adjusting to him. I say slowly because he doesn't pause for a single second before his hips begin viciously, almost feverishly, snap against me as his hands dig into my hips.

"Oh fuck, oh my god," I gasp, my nerves lighting up at the dual sensations of the plug and his thick length.

"Look at you, all full and a fucking mess from my touch, my cock," he grits between clenched teeth as his hand reaches up to my throat.

He doesn't grip it yet, shortly pausing, I assume for me to use my safe word. Fat chance in hell. I reach down, gripping his hand and forcing it around my throat. That must have been exactly what he was craving, because his eyes roll into the back of his head as he pushes deeper inside me, picking up a new pace I didn't even know was possible.

My heels dig into his back as I wrap my legs around him,

causing him to release a soft grunt at that. Like he loves it. I dig them in further, testing the theory, and when he gives me another grunt and a steady look, I know without a doubt, I'm being good for him.

Fuck, why is that such a turn on?

His hand grips me perfectly, not restricting too much airflow at first as he pushes me closer and closer to the edge. I'm a fucking hoe for some good breath play. The problem is, no one ever seems to do it right. Instead of teasing, testing the limits of your capacity, forcing you to float in that space between conscious and not, they usually end up crushing your trachea. Definitely not sexy.

My gorgeous masked man needs no instructions, no time for adjustment. He knows exactly what he's doing. Being cradled by this man, held down while he fucks me hard, is literal perfection. All I can do in response is *feel*.

I feel my pussy begin spasming, and though I'm desperate to hold off this orgasm, to make this feeling and moment last as long as possible, it's pointless. His hand squeezes tighter, forcing my intake of oxygen to almost stop altogether. A heavy feeling begins pounding in my head, desperate for air. As soon as my vision begins to spot and my legs tremble, he releases me, allowing a wave of oxygen to slam into me at the same moment my orgasm rips through me like a tidal wave.

A scream that hardly sounds human tears through me as I moan and squirm against him over and over again until his cock begins to swell, and he follows me right over the edge. His body covers mine, a feral groan escaping his lips as he wrings out every ounce of his orgasm, thrusting into me slower and slower before stopping. He blows out a labored breath after a moment, pressing a delicate kiss to my collarbone before rolling off me and onto his back.

We both lay there for several moments, quietly floating

around in a blissful hazy state before he stands up, disposes of the condom, and slips on his pants. I expect him to walk out the door, mission complete style, but he surprises me by coming to my side of the bed, carefully parting my legs before removing the butt plug and setting it aside. I gasp as he pulls it out, suddenly feeling incredibly empty.

He leans down, cupping my jaw before bringing me in for a searing kiss so intense it makes the entire room spin.

When he pulls away, he lets his lips ghost over my own as he holds his hand out for me.

"Are you ready for more?"

My eyes nearly burst out of my head at that. More?! He's kidding, right? I don't think I could even walk right now, let alone go for another round. But there is something about that look in his eyes that has a newfound energy filling me, so I take his hand.

He gives me a pleased smirk like I did the right thing, and I can't help but react to it, for some reason wanting more than anything to please him.

"Would you like to stay in here? Or use another room?" he asks.

"What kind of room?" I ask.

His head cocks to the side curiously as his fingers continue stroking my skin almost mindlessly.

"Is this your first time here?"

My teeth sink into my lower lip as I nod shyly. He dips his dead in response as his hand begins roaming over my naked skin.

"Do you have any hard limits? Things you've tried and aren't interested in?"

My brain stalls at his question. I don't know. I can't pretend to be an expert in the world of kink. Outside of a little choking, butt play, or some toys, I can't say I've done much of anything.

But the prospect of dipping my toes into the kink world instead of skirting around the edge has a thrill running through me.

"No," I say softly. "Not that I know of."

His tongue runs over his lip, considering my answer before holding out his hand for me. I take it, standing up as he pulls down my dress until I'm fully covered. We move to the door when he stops, bending down and picking up my panties. I hold out my hand for them, but all he does is cock an eyebrow, slipping them into his pocket like they are his property now. Fuck, why is that so goddamn hot?

He continues leading me toward the door without another word, and like a moth to a flame, I follow.

Chapter Three

Logan

My hand engulfs her petite one as I lead her through the darkened hallways of the club. I'm by no means one of the club's most frequent members, but I'd be lying if I said I didn't visit often, especially over the last year or so.

I've met plenty of women within these walls, all who have been beautiful and more than pleasurable, but nothing more.

Nothing like her.

As soon as she stepped into the club, I felt this pull to her. My eyes were swinging to her before her friends could even abandon her side. I wanted to approach her immediately, but she looked easily spooked, definitely out of her comfort zone, despite the aloof exterior she was trying to portray. So, I kept my eye on her, watching as she glided through the room, all eyes gravitating towards her while she remained blissfully unaware of the effect she has on others by simply existing.

I didn't anticipate her to accept my invitation so willingly, nor did I expect her to open up for me so easily. It was as if my touch allowed her to shed all of her insecurities and hesitations and let her simply live in the moment. The power that gave me was indescribable, and after one taste of her, I knew this night couldn't be over in that room. I needed more of her, all of her, and like the perfect woman she is, she seems to want that too.

She said that she has no limits, at least none that she knows of. Something in those words made the beast inside me beat his chest, salivating at the chance to rise to that challenge. I want to see her bend, to see how far I can push until she breaks, revealing the true person behind it all.

I could have taken her to a million rooms, thrown her into the lion's den, and made her question her sanity in giving a random Dom this much control of her. But I'm less interested in seeing what I can *make* her do and more so in seeing what I can get her to *want* to do.

When we round the corner, I notice that the door I'm looking for is open, indicating that it's available.

Perfect.

I step to the side, allowing her to walk in first before closing the door behind me. She freezes in place as she notices the large glass wall where two rows of plush seats are placed in front of it, giving a perfect view of the king size bed. A few people trickle in, taking their seats by themselves or with their partners.

Her beautiful blue eyes swing to my own, fear splashed across her face despite the mask hiding most of her features. I close the distance between us, cupping the nape of her neck as I hush her softly.

"Don't be frightened. They're just here to watch."

"Watch us?" she whispers.

"Yes."

She bites her lower lip, a tell I've already been able to gather is her sign that she's thinking it over.

"I've never done anything like this before," she admits.

"I assumed not. You don't have to do anything you don't

want to," I say, my fingers slowly rubbing against the sensitive part of her neck. God. Her skin is intoxicating, like silk beneath my touch.

She stays silent for a few more seconds before she looks back up to me, giving me a small nod before I pull her in for a kiss. I keep it light at first, allowing her discomfort to melt away before I deepen the kiss. With each passing second, I can feel her body slowly relaxing until she's pliant in my arms.

I run my hands down her silky dress, slipping the straps off her shoulders this time before finding the zipper in the back. I gently pull the zipper down while stroking my tongue against hers until the smooth material pools at her feet, leaving her completely exposed.

She breaks our kiss, just for a moment as she looks at the growing room of spectators. The size has easily doubled since we stepped into the room. I expect her to run, to take off for the hills after making direct eye contact with our voyeurs. To my surprise, she does the opposite. She pulls my head down to her neck, arching into my hold while keeping her eyes on the crowd the entire time.

My cock throbs at her reaction, and I can't stop myself from pushing her backwards until her legs hit the edge of the bed, and she falls onto her back. I don't cover her immediately, allowing the spectators to see her first as I undo my pants.

The beauty's eyes are locked on one woman in particular in the front row. She's older but still beautiful with two men on either side of her. They all seem to be entranced by the gorgeous woman beneath me.

She truly is a sight.

"Do you like this?" I ask.

"What?" she asks, almost breathlessly.

"You like them watching you? Feeling seen? Desired?"

"Desired?" she echoes.

Since the room has microphones that play through speakers in the other room, the throuple in the front all collectively smile salaciously, hungry looks in their eyes as they reassure her. I take a step closer to her, skimming my hands along her smooth inner thighs before I press on them slightly.

"Open up. Show them how pretty your little cunt is."

She hesitates only for a moment before she does as I say, letting her legs fall open and causing several members of the audience to groan or adjust themselves in what is no doubt obvious pleasure.

"You're beautiful," I encourage as I allow my hand to trail over her pussy, slowly pulling her open to give our voyeurs a show they'll never forget.

One of the men from the throuple practically presses himself to the glass as he watches me run a finger through her soaked slit before plunging inside. She moans her approval as I begin pumping in and out of her before adding another.

"Anyone of those people would switch places with me in a heartbeat if I allowed it."

Several heads bob at that, causing her eyes to snap back to mine in surprise before I continue.

"Unfortunately for them, I saw you first, and this is the closest I'll get to sharing tonight."

"Tonight?" she asks curiously, forcing a crooked smile to pull at my mouth.

I add a third finger, causing her to cry out.

"T-too much. It's t-too much," she whimpers.

"Do you want to use your safe word?" I ask as I continue slowly easing my fingers in and out of her.

She shakes her head instantly, closing her eyes and controlling her breathing.

"Good girl," I praise. "Deep breaths."

Her pussy begins to relax around my fingers, allowing me

to push deeper until I brush against that spot that sends her eyes flying open.

"Oh god!" she cries out.

Her orgasm comes like a freight train, crashing into her and sending her over the edge before I can even do anything to prolong it as her pussy throbs and her body trembles. Fuck, she's so beautiful when she falls apart like this, so perfectly obedient. Like her body already knows how to obey me, how to please me.

I brush some hair out of her face as I cup her jaw.

"Ready for more?"

This time she doesn't hesitate. A spark lights up her irises as she agrees eagerly.

Good fucking girl.

Chapter Four

Arianna

I've never considered exhibitionism. Ever. But god, what a high. At first, I wasn't sure I could do it, having all of those people staring at me, judging me, picking me apart until I was left feeling raw and exposed.

Instead, I felt seen, appreciated, *desired*. The beautiful woman in front was the first to put me at ease. When I locked eyes with her, she gave me a soft smile before her eyes raked over my naked body, lust quickly filling them and causing my entire body to shiver. It's nice when a man thinks you're attractive, but when a woman does, it hits differently.

Between the looks of awe from the voyeurs and the praising words out of Dom's mouth, because what the hell else am I going to call him, every fiber of my being was buzzing with anticipation. It only took a few touches from him to send me over the edge embarrassingly fast.

Dom suddenly pulls his hand away from my jaw, encouraging me to get up as he speaks.

"Hands and knees."

I obey all too eagerly as I quickly spin, adjusting myself so

I'm positioned across the bed, giving our audience a much better view. Something about that idea sends a rushing feeling through me. Like not only am I the one getting pleasure, I'm giving it too.

I feel Dom step up behind me, running the head of his cock between my wet pussy, but not penetrating just yet. His cool piercing sends a shudder running through me, my pussy throbbing in anticipation of feeling him again.

The pressure of his head against me increases just slightly as I feel him attempting to restrain himself.

"Fuck. I need to get a condom on."

"I'm clean," I blurt out, hating myself as soon as it slips out.

You're in a sex club, Arianna. It doesn't matter if you're clean. He probably isn't! How reckless could I fucking be?

I feel more than hear the growl that reverberates through him as he pushes his head in a little more, resting just at the line before penetration.

"I wish. Maybe someday," he grits out.

With that, he pulls away, moving to the side table beside us and reaching inside to reveal a stockpile of condoms before grabbing one, rolling it on, and returning to his position behind me.

This time he doesn't hesitate. He pushes into me with one smooth move much like he did in the other room. You'd think my body would have adjusted a bit since then, but no luck. My back bows, and a cry escapes me as I attempt to take all of him. His thick cock is stretching me to the point of pain as he slides in, inch by inch, until he is fully seated inside me.

"Goddamnit," he barks, his hands coming to my hips, squeezing so tightly, they'll no doubt leave bruises tomorrow.

"A-are you okay?" I say in between deep breaths.

A gruff chuckle leaves his chest as he slaps the side of my

ass cheek and winds his other hand around my hair, pulling back sharply.

"Peachy. Now be a good girl and bounce on my cock."

I begin working my hips, forcing myself to move up and down his length, his piercing rubbing against my g-spot with each thrust. Fuck. I will never fuck a man that isn't pierced again. This is fucking heaven.

I glance to my side, noticing that the beautiful woman from before is still seated, but the man from her left is now between her legs, eating her pussy, while the man to her right has her top pulled down, exposing her breasts as he sucks on one. All the while her eyes are on me, on us, eyes drenched in lust and pleasure. It sends a tingling shiver running through me and spurs me on to move faster and deeper.

Dom's grip on my hair shifts slightly before his body pauses, his movements stop, and he seems to almost freeze. I look over my shoulder to see him staring at me intently, jaw clenched and mouth in a flat line.

"What's wrong?" I ask.

"Your ear."

"My ear?"

His jaw clenches again. "Your tattoo."

It takes me a second to realize he's talking about the tiny sparrow tattoo that I got just behind my ear my senior year of high school. God, my mom came absolutely unglued over it, but I can't lie, her reaction gave me a small amount of joy. Part of the reason I decided to get it was to piss her off, but the other was because, to me, it was a sign of freedom. I was moving out, going to college, finally on my own and away from her. But since it's behind my ear, I forget about it from time to time.

"You afraid of birds or something?" I tease.

His eyes bore into mine for several slow beats. He stops for so long my brows knit in confusion. It's just a tiny tattoo. What? Are tattoos deal-breakers for him or something?

Slowly, his hold on my hair releases, that same hand sliding around to my neck and pulling me back further before crushing his lips to mine. It's a bit of an awkward angle, but the feeling of his smooth lips on mine and his tongue running against my own is enough to make me forget my own name, let alone a little discomfort.

I feel his thrusts pick back up, a new vigor to them than before. I try to pull away, but he doesn't allow me to, keeping my lips smashed to his even harder than before.

His cock begins to throb, and I feel my pussy begin to spasm as he finally tears away from my lips, whispering into my ear as he pushes deeper and deeper into me.

"Come for me, Sparrow."

Something about that nickname, or the way he says it, sends me shattering apart. I buck and scream as his hold on my throat tightens slightly before releasing completely, allowing a fresh wave of oxygen to rush into my lungs. The thrumming in my head only intensifies my orgasm as his cock swells inside me, pleasure filled grunts filling the room as he finds his release.

It takes a few moments for our breathing to settle, and once it does, Dom slowly eases out of me, leaning down to press a tender kiss to my neck. I look over to see most of our audience has begun to dissipate as the show is now over.

"I never thought I could do something like that," I say more to myself.

"Something like what?" he asks stiffly.

"Something so...exposing."

I roll onto my back to see Dom already getting dressed, holding out his hand for me to stand. I slide my hand into his large palm, a ripple of something satisfying running through me at the feel of his skin on mine again.

He pulls me to my feet before cupping my face with both his hands, cradling me like I'm something precious as his eyes look through that mask at me.

"You did beautifully. You're capable of so much."

"You mean that? I mean, will you, um, show me?" I ask, internally cringing at the sudden uncertainty in my voice. God, who the fuck have I become behind these doors? This is not me, I'm not some bumbling amateur. I'm sure as hell not an innocent little virgin like Naomi. So why am I acting like one?

He watches me carefully for a few moments. He seems to be weighing his options, like he can't decide if I'm worth seeing a second time. Okay, maybe those are my own insecurities about not being enough, but still.

I open my mouth to say something else, to tell him I was joking, fucking anything that doesn't make me look as pathetic as I feel. But he surprises me when he leans forward, pressing a kiss to my forehead, his fingers holding my chin in place as he speaks against my skin.

"Meet me here next Saturday, nine o'clock sharp. If you're on time, I'll reward you well."

"And if I'm not?" I test.

His grip on me tightens slightly.

"Then I'll punish you."

Why does my pussy pulse at the prospect of either scenario? Both sound good to me, but then again, the way his gruff voice rasps it out, I'm not sure if I can handle his idea of punishment.

Yet.

Dom releases his hold on me, scooping up my discarded dress before slipping it on over my head. I lift my arms, helping him so that he can slide the straps onto my shoulders. It feels like his form of aftercare, like he's trying to restore me to the way I was when he found me. Unfortunately, the effort is futile. I don't think I'll ever be the same after tonight.

He slowly pulls the material down until the hem meets my thigh. His fingers trace over my skin once more before he pulls the zipper up and takes an abrupt step away. I frown at the sudden move, watching him reach out to run his hand through my hair in what seems to be an effort to tame the chaos before dropping his hand. He gifts me with one last scorching glance that heats me from my head to my toes before he slips out of the room without another word.

Next week it is.

Chapter Five

Arianna

My fingers drum against my bare thigh as the car moves through the Saturday night traffic. It feels like I was just here, yet it also feels like it's been months instead of days.

Excitement buzzes through my veins, sending butterflies fluttering through my stomach as that familiar corner comes into view. I thank my rideshare driver quickly before stepping out of the car and up to the entrance. I lift my shaking hand to the door, knocking when the doorman from last week opens it. I already have my mask on, but he must remember me.

"Welcome back," he says, opening the door and guiding me down the hallway. Glancing at my phone, I notice the time. 8:58 PM.

The thought of being late crossed my mind for a moment. I debated if it would be worth losing whatever reward he planned for me in place of a punishment I would more than likely enjoy. I didn't feel like taking that risk. Something in me didn't like the idea of upsetting him, irritating him. I want him to be happy when he sees me. I want him to be pleased by my presence and punctuality.

That's if he even shows up. When I told Cassi about my night on her birthday, she was ecstatic, begging me for a play-by-play, but when I told her he wanted to meet me again, she got a weird look on her face and told me not to get my hopes up too high. I couldn't tell if she was saying that out of envy for not receiving an invitation back from the man she ended up spending her night with or out of genuine concern for my safety. Maybe a little of both?

Naomi wouldn't give us much detail on how she spent the night. When I texted them that I was heading back to the hotel after Dom left, because honestly, I knew no one was going to compare, they both responded, saying they were staying for a little while longer. Apparently, the man Naomi was with gave her a ride back to the hotel. The only thing she would tell us was that she's still a virgin. Seems like we all had an interesting night.

I've been trying to keep my feet on the ground all week, keeping in mind the very real possibility that Dom won't be there tonight. Even if he plans to, life happens, things come up. At least, that's what I keep telling myself, so if he doesn't show, the blow doesn't hurt as bad. The eagerness I feel when I step into that lavish lounge area has all remnants of sensibility floating away, though.

My eyes scan the room, attempting to be discreet despite knowing I fail miserably. My heart sinks when I don't see him. Granted, we didn't discuss a meeting spot or anything, but it's now 8:59 PM. If he were waiting for me, he'd be down here. Right? Maybe I should look around in the rooms? See if he is there.

Fuck. No. You already exposed how out of your depths you are in this world. No need to portray yourself as a clingy psycho on top of it.

Despite how many times I mentally prepared myself for

this feeling, it doesn't temper the sting that comes from rejection. Maybe he didn't have as good of a time as he thought. Maybe he got here early and found someone more appealing, more experienced, just...more.

Slowly, I make my way to the same bartender from last week. He smiles at me in recognition before laying down a napkin in front of me.

"What will it be, sweetheart?"

"Tequila, please?"

He reaches for the tequila and a glass as I fidget with my red dress. I decided to switch it up from last week. This is one of my all-time favorite dresses because it has a built-in bra that easily adds two cups to my breasts. Pulling my hair over one shoulder, I can't help but let out a disappointed sigh. Damn, I really hate how high I actually got my hopes up.

The bartender slides the glass in front of me, at the same moment, I feel a heady presence at my back. Two large hands cage me in, his firm chest pressing against me and a familiar deep voice rumbling in my ear.

"You're here."

My breath hitches before I look up to see Dom smiling down at me. My heart hammers in my chest, hope and excitement flooding me. He's wearing the same black mask from last week, a similar black dress shirt, and black slacks. His brown hair is perfectly in place, and that delicious cologne is rolling off him, giving me an instant hit of dopamine.

"So are you."

He slides his black card to the bartender who sets my drink down, all while keeping his eyes on me.

"You don't have to do that," I say with a shake of my head.

"Grab your drink and follow me. I have a surprise for you."

I do as he says, grabbing the glass before Dom reaches out his hand and laces it with my own, leading me down a hallway

I haven't been down before. We come up to a silver elevator just around the corner, and with a wave of a key card, the doors open and allow us inside. He presses the "L" button just as the doors close, taking us up what feels like several floors.

When the doors open, my eyes widen as I look around the expansive room. One side of the room has a large bed, larger than even a king, with a shelf beside it stocked with every type of toy you can imagine. On the other side of the room is a Saint Andrew's cross, a crazy looking sofa that looks like the perfect height to be bent over, and a pole in the middle of the room.

"Do you like it?" he asks as he watches me.

I blink in awe.

"It's amazing."

He comes up behind me, brushing a piece of hair off my shoulder before he presses a kiss to my neck.

"Only the best for you."

I lean into his touch, arching into his lips as a feeling like nothing I've ever felt runs through my body. It's as if his touch is pure electricity coursing through my veins.

"Lay down on the bed. Dress off," he murmurs against my skin. A thrill shoots through me as I turn to face him, slowly removing my dress, allowing it to pool at my feet, and leaving me completely naked besides my panties and heels. His eyes roam over my exposed flesh hungrily before he makes a sound of approval.

I sit down on the edge before lying down in the middle. My heart is racing as he takes several purposeful steps towards me before pausing to look at the shelf beside the bed. It doesn't take him long to find what he's looking for before he plucks a black satin blindfold from the selection.

He turns to face me as he lifts the blindfold in a silent gesture of permission. I dip my head as he moves to place it over my eyes.

"Do you remember your safe word?" he asks.

I nod my head again.

"Words, Sparrow."

I feel my skin erupt in goosebumps at the nickname.

"Banana."

"Good girl," he rumbles, lowering the blindfold until my vision goes black.

It takes a moment to get used to the loss of a sense, which he seems to anticipate, waiting several moments before he touches me. He doesn't touch me with his hands, though. The touch is light and soft, like a feather. I feel him trail it along the column of my neck, then between my breasts, circling around my nipple before making its way down my stomach.

"What are you doing?" I ask breathlessly as goosebumps race over my skin.

"Relax for me," he answers.

Swallowing roughly, I do as he says, forcing myself to focus on how good the light touch feels. When it runs between my thighs, it sends a fluttering into my stomach that I've never felt before, and I feel myself wiggling against the smooth bedspread.

"Have you ever played with sense deprivation?" he asks.

I shake my head.

"Take away one sense, and it heightens the others. Feel the difference?" he asks as one of his fingers traces through the slit of my pussy, slipping inside with ease.

I didn't even realize I was getting wet, by a feather of all things, but now that he is so easily pumping in and out of me, I fully grasp that I'm fucking dripping.

"Oh god," I moan.

"Mhmm," he hums lowly as I feel his body reach to the side before bringing over something new.

It's cold, smooth, and instantly has my nipples hardening, a chill running through my body.

He runs the cool, metallic feeling object on the inside of my thigh before running it up my stomach and over to my breasts, tracing soft lines around them before gently brushing against my nipples. I let out a shuddering breath as his fingers increase their efforts. Fuck. I don't even know what he's using, but it feels amazing.

Moving the chilled object from my breasts, he pulls it away, pressing a soft kiss to my lips. I try to kiss him back, but he is here and gone the next moment. I hear the sound of a lighter striking in the otherwise silent room. We sit there for what feels like minutes, his fingers languidly pumping in and out of me. Not nearly fast enough to make me come, but just enough to keep me engaged, to keep me on edge.

"Stay still," he says.

Before I can question it, the hot burn of what feels like wax stings my stomach. I hiss in surprise before the pain slowly eases.

"You're doing beautifully," he says almost reverently before he does another small drip of wax.

It doesn't hurt as much this time, in fact, the pain is beginning to morph into pleasure as he drips more wax over my stomach and breasts. He does this repeatedly, alternating between fast and slow drips, keeping me on edge, waiting for the next drop.

"Fuck," I breathe out as he curls his fingers inside me, rubbing against my g-spot and causing my legs to tremble.

"Not yet. Not until I'm inside you," he says before pulling his fingers out of me and, from the sound of it, setting down what I'm assuming was a candle. I hear the tear of a condom wrapper, then the soft jingle of his belt hitting the ground.

In the next moment, he's pushing inside me. It feels so

intrusive, so forceful, it nearly takes my breath away. I feel his hands grip my hips tightly as he lifts me to meet his movements.

"Yes," I moan, reveling in this newfound experience. "Dom."

"Dom?" he questions on a thrust.

Embarrassment flashes through me. Definitely didn't mean to say that out loud.

"It's not like I actually know your name," I say with a shy smirk and a shrug.

His movements pause for a moment before he picks up his pace once more. I feel one of his hands move from my hips to my throat, holding me tight as he fucks me deeper. Without my sight, everything feels so intense, so overwhelming. Instead of watching him, I just feel him. I feel everything. I feel the throbbing of his cock. I feel the steady grip of his fingers nearly cutting off my air, his practiced control as he literally holds my life in his hands. That kind of power...it's indescribable. I smell the crisp, filtered air of the room with a subtle scent of musk that I know belongs solely to him. I hear his labored breaths, and the sounds our bodies create together. Skin against skin and the whimpered moans I don't even try to temper as each moment and each touch becomes more and more intense. His thrusts suddenly become more jerky and uncontrolled, his breathing labored.

"Fuck. Come for me, Sparrow," he says as his piercing rubs against my g-spot, sending me falling apart on command.

"Arianna!" he growls, finding his own release.

I shout my orgasm so loud I'm sure someone downstairs will overhear. Wave after wave of pleasure crashes into me as my pussy spasms for what feels like hours. Oh my god! Fuck! Shit! It's all so overwhelming, so satisfying, I almost miss the small but very important detail.

My name.

Breathing heavily, I slowly lift my blindfold to find him watching me intently, his chest heaving in an attempt to catch his breath as he obviously waits for me to process what he just said.

"Y-you know...how do you know my name?" I ask carefully.

He swallows roughly but doesn't speak, instead just licking his lips as he eases out of me. I expect him to speak but he doesn't. Instead, he reaches for his pants, discarding the condom before fastening his belt and tucking in his shirt.

He knows my name. Knows me. There is no way he could have found out any other way, and now he's trying to walk out just like that? Fuck that. I jump to my feet as quickly as I can, reaching for his mask before yanking it up and over his head.

He spins to face me, probably in an attempt to stop me, but it's too late. The mask is clenched in my hand tightly, and my eyes widen at what I see. Horror crawls through me as any and all words die right there on my tongue.

What. The. Fuck.

Logan Cunningham. It's Logan. Dom is Logan.

Oh my god.

I fucked my ex-stepdad.

Chapter Six

Logan

Fuck. This is not how I wanted her to find out. I didn't want her to find out at all. I wasn't sure how I wanted to play this all out. From the moment I figured out that my perfect beauty was Arianna, I told myself it had to be a one-time thing. I told myself we had already crossed a line, that me denying us both the pleasure we deserved wouldn't change anything. We'd find the mind-altering pleasure we were capable of with each other and go our separate ways.

But then she asked me to show her. So vulnerably. So beautifully. It was like she reached inside my head and spoke the one thing that brought my inner Dom to his knees. This beautiful, perfect girl wanted to learn, to explore, and she wanted me to be the one to teach her. How could I have possibly turned that down?

I told her to meet me back here tonight which was so fucking stupid. I talked myself out of coming so many times throughout the week. I know how wrong it is, sick maybe, but the mental images had been burned into my head from that night with her, the noises she made, the way she responded so well to me.

It was addictive, and I needed more.

Don't worry, I berated myself up, down, and sideways when I realized the woman I was lusting over was none other than my ex-wife's daughter. My ex-stepdaughter, I suppose. Arianna was fifteen when I met Kelly, so it's not like I raised her or anything.

Still, I know her well enough to know that I'm going to fucking burn in hell for this.

I know her enough to know that she doesn't like the taste or smell of coffee. I know that she has to eat breakfast in the mornings, or she'll get sick. I know that she has always had a desire to be a photographer, even if her mother tried to squash those dreams every chance she got. Above all, I know her sparrow tattoo that she came home with during her senior year. Her mom nearly had an aneurysm over it, and they didn't speak for days.

The horror on Arianna's face tells me that despite our insanely powerful chemistry, it isn't enough to wash away what we are to each other, or at least what we were. Still are? Fuck, I don't know. But she looks ready to bolt now that the mask has quite literally been ripped off.

"L-logan? You...and me...oh my god!" she gasps as her chest begins to heave.

I watch as she looks around frantically, her breathing becoming choppier and shallower. She always used to get the worst panic attacks, and it looks like she's teetering on the edge of one right now.

Going against my better judgment, I close the distance between us, cupping her face with my hands as I force her eyes to look at me. I push away the silver mask she was wearing, revealing her perfect porcelain skin. Something hits me square in the chest when I look at her without her mask. Like the two versions of her are colliding before me. The Arianna I know, and the Sparrow I met inside this club. Two totally different women, two totally different feelings for each. All of it melding before my eyes. I feel my own heart rate spike as I allow the gravity of our situation to sink in.

Her breathing is still labored, but her eyes are on mine as I slowly brush my thumb over her lower lip. I don't mean to, but for some reason, I can't stop myself. The softness of her lips, the full shape, and beautiful color has me mesmerized.

It takes me a moment to realize her breathing has steadied and her body is less tense. Something like pride fills me that I was able to bring her back, even if I didn't really do anything but touch her.

"How long?" she whispers.

"How long what?" I ask with a small frown.

"How long did you know?"

I roll my lips against each other before answering truthfully.

"Your tattoo."

Her eyes widen slightly as understanding passes across her face. She still hasn't pulled away from me, so that's a good sign, right? Do I want her to pull away from me? The answer should be yes. Hell fucking yes. I should be repulsed, disgusted. I should be begging her to run far and fast, to take her and her alluring body as far from me as possible. She's twenty-five years younger than me, she's my ex-wife's daughter, she's...Arianna.

It's fucked up, so fucked up, but when I tighten my grip on her face and I feel her press against my touch just slightly, it has something primal in me coming to life. Then, as if she's been snapped out of this spell between us, she's gone. Running. Sprinting away from me. She barely has enough time to gather up her dress before she darts into the elevator, quickly slipping it on before the doors shut, leaving me with a disgusted and almost disappointed look to remember her by as she disappears.

I'm staring at the screen in front of me, but my brain refuses to compute the useless words no matter how hard I try to focus. It's been two days since I saw Arianna. She ran like hell, and I let her, because what the fuck else was I supposed to do? I had no right to chase after her, to want to. Hell, I had no right to have her in the first place, but I already had. Couldn't take that back if I wanted.

Not like I would.

Call it what you want, an obsession, a distraction, a sick addiction, it doesn't matter. I've never felt so connected, so fulfilled with anyone in my life, her mother definitely included. It wasn't just sex, it was everything. It was the way she moved, the way she carried herself, the way she spoke. She's so beautiful, so flawless, so full of potential. I can't help but want to test her limits, push her past her breaking point, and show her what it's like to really live.

Fuck.

No.

I have to let it go, have to let her go. Things inside the club seemed so perfect, so easy. Outside those walls is an entirely different beast. Hence the forbidden appeal.

"Mr. Cunningham, I have Mr. Langford on the phone?" my secretary Debra says through the intercom.

Christ. He's the last person I want to talk to right now. He's one of our best clients and is basically keeping this firm afloat with his business alone. I don't have the patience or focus to deal with his eccentricities today, though.

"I'm out of office," I say back to her, my typical code for I don't want to be disturbed.

She doesn't respond, likely already getting rid of him for at least the day. I dig my fingers into my hair, trying to banish the look of bright blue eyes popping into my head, her slim neck, silky black hair, and flawless skin.

Goddamnit. I'm not hard up for women. I've been with plenty before her, and I can get anyone I desire with the snap of my fingers. Whether it's thanks to my obscenely large bank account, my classical good looks, or my power as Seattle's top defense attorney, it doesn't matter.

People are attracted to power, and I'm just as powerful in the bedroom as I am in the courtroom. I know I sound like an arrogant ass, and maybe I am. The problem is that I'm used to getting my way, to getting what I want.

I tap my finger against my desk, my restraint waning before I slam my fist against my desk.

Fuck.

As if some sick twist of fate, my phone buzzes to life, a text from Kelly, of all people.

Kelly: I rented the lake house for the week, just like old times. You should come. I miss you.

She has been trying to get back with me ever since I caught her with one of her clients. She is a real estate agent, and when one open house seemed to be going really well, I got out of court early and showed up to lend a hand. Imagine my surprise when I found her bent over a baby grand piano, moaning like a goddamn porn star. I filed for divorce within the hour and never looked back. She hasn't been able to do the same, though.

She drunk dials me often, telling me she's still in love with me and she will never love again. I don't believe a goddamn word she says. She misses the money and the sex, but there's nothing else to it. I should have blocked her years ago, but at this moment, I'm glad I didn't.

Temptation sits there, so close I can nearly touch it. Before I know what I'm doing, I'm responding to her.

Me: Who will be there?

I love that house, I really do. We had some great times on the lake. It's about an hour outside of Seattle, and the place is like a little slice of paradise. We used to rent it every spring break and go up there with my brother, her sister and husband, and...Arianna.

She responds almost immediately, no doubt shocked that I've responded for the first time in over eighteen months.

Kelly: The usual. Marissa and Tom, their kids, and Ari.

Ari.

Fuck. That should be reason enough for me to pass, so why the fuck is it the reason I'm wanting to go?

Kelly: Please come, Logan. It will be a lot of fun. No pressure.

I'm not an idiot. If I say yes, Kelly will take the opportunity to seduce me every moment she can. She'll try to get me into bed with her and hope that I'll just forget the betrayal. The problem with her plan is that I realized once the ink had dried and the divorce was finalized, I never really loved her. I loved the idea of her. She was good for my ego, a beautiful trophy wife.

I was a different man back then. I've grown, changed, maybe for the worse, since the only reason I'm even interested in allowing her back into my life is so I can get just another moment with Arianna.

With all the red flags waving wildly in my face, I'm responding before I can stop myself.

Me: I'm in.

Chapter Seven

Arianna

I still can't believe it. I fucked Logan Cunningham. My mom's ex. My ex-stepdad. Fuck, I think I'm gonna be sick. It's been three days since I found out who the man behind the mask really is, and I still can't get over it.

Logan? Seriously...Logan? I just...I'm speechless. He never gave me weird vibes or made me uncomfortable while he and my mom were together. He was always pretty checked out, hyper focused on his work. It's one of the reasons my mom used to rationalize why she started sleeping around.

He was always a good guy, a kind man. He spoiled my mom rotten and tried to do the same for me as well. I didn't accept his generosity as willingly as my mom did. Was that his way of trying to get to me? Was he attempting to...fuck, I honestly don't know.

The fact that he knew it was me while we were fucking, and he still kept going, is fucking insane. I'm still trying to process what was going on in his head.

Probably the same things that were going on in yours.

Despite how horribly wrong and disgusting it was, in the

moment, it felt great. When I didn't know who he was, it was perfect, *he* was perfect. Together, we were just...

Closing my eyes, I wince as I shake my head. I just need to forget it ever happened. I'm heading up to the lake house my mom rents every spring break in the middle of nowhere. Plenty of space to relax, de-stress and not obsess over the fact that I fucked my goddamn ex-stepdad.

And loved every second of it.

I'll definitely take that small piece of information to my grave.

Shaking off this weird funk I've been in over the last few days, I decide to just let it all go. There isn't great cell reception up here, so I can avoid Cassi and Naomi's questioning, though they both seem to have gone radio silent lately. We all need a girl's day soon to catch up. After I figure out how the hell to process what I've done, that is.

When I turn the final corner down the dirt road and park in front of the lake house, nostalgia hits me. We've been coming here for years. It's a home away from home. Even though it's not ours, it feels like it. There is something special about this place. I used to spend hours running around the woods and the dock, taking pictures until my camera was out of storage. It's where I truly fell in love with photography and where I made the decision to major in it.

As I shut off the car and step out, the crisp Washington air fills my nose, and I smile. It's been unusually nice lately. Typically, April is nothing but never-ending rain, but we've lucked out with a small break. It's supposed to be sunny and high 60's to low 70's, which is scorching for April.

Pocketing my phone, I grab my backpack filled with my essentials for the week and walk up the grand deck. Of course, my mother would never dare be caught dead in anything less than a mansion. She's lucky the market has picked up lately. I wasn't sure how she was going to maintain her high-end life-style when Logan left her. She got way too used to being a millionaire's wife. Considering her last serious relationship was with my father, a deadbeat mechanic who couldn't leave the state fast enough when he found out she was pregnant, Logan was certainly a step up. Until she fucked everything up.

Shaking my head at my mother's "extracurriculars," I look up at the two-story lake house before me. It's huge, with crisp white paint with black trim. It looks so out of place in such a heavily wooded area. It belongs at the end of a long winding cul-de-sac with an HOA fee equivalent to most people's mortgage. Still, I have a lot of memories here, and I haven't seen my aunt, uncle, and cousins in a while, which is the only reason I said yes.

Pushing the front door open, I find my aunt Marissa and Uncle Tom unpacking the groceries while my younger cousins Brady and Melanie sit on the couch watching a show.

"Hi guys!" I greet.

The twin fourteen year olds turn to look at me over their shoulders, giving me 'too cool to be excited' head bobs before focusing back on the TV. It's hard for me to remember that they aren't the same hyperactive kids I've grown up with.

"Hi, sweetheart!" my aunt smiles. "Was the drive okay?"

"It was fine. Tons of traffic, of course."

"We live in Western Washington. You couldn't escape traffic if you tried," my uncle says gruffly.

I laugh at that, shrugging my shoulders in agreement.

Quick footsteps echo down the stairs as my mom pops her head around the wall, looking around the room frantically.

"Is he here yet? I haven't finished my hair!"

My aunt rolls her eyes in annoyance.

"No, Kel. He's not here yet."

The tone of my aunt's voice is a clear indicator that this is my mom's fifth time asking, minimum. She gets just as fed up with my mom's shit as I do. Hence why she's my favorite. I didn't ask for her as a mother, just like she didn't ask for her as a big sister. We bond over our mutual irritation like any normal family does.

"Who isn't here yet?" I ask as a heavy knock sounds at the door.

"Shit!" she hisses, rushing back upstairs to presumably finish her hair.

I scoff and roll my eyes.

Hi, Mom. Nice to see you. Yes, it has been three months since I last saw you. Oh, yeah, school is doing great. I missed you too.

I have to have these conversations with her in my head because if I don't, we'd never have them.

Wow, that sounded just as pathetic as it feels. It's bad enough to grow up without a dad. I really had to drive home the childhood trauma with a shallow, complacent mother.

Crossing the living room, I make my way to the door, allowing in whatever new infatuation she's brought along for this family vacation. It's like she doesn't know how to be alone. She has to constantly have someone smothering her with attention, or she will combust. Poor bastard doesn't know what he's in for.

Pulling open the door, my attempt at a warm and welcoming smile drops as my entire body tenses.

What. The. Fuck.

Deep brown eyes are staring straight at me. Eyes I've been trying to permanently scrub from my mind...along with other parts of him. What the fuck is he doing here? He hasn't been around my family since the divorce. I'd say myself included in that, but...you know.

"Arianna," he says, his tone not exactly stiff but not warm either. More like careful.

I don't respond. I'm still trying to decide what the best course of action is. A door slammed in his face, a kick to his balls. Something.

"Ari, let Logan in." My aunt laughs.

I stay in place for several more seconds, and Logan lifts an eyebrow like he's wordlessly checking to see what my next move will be. His calculating gaze unnerves me, and I step to the side, allowing him and his black duffel bag inside.

"Why are you being so rude?" my aunt scolds, shaking her head as she wraps her arms around Logan. "It's been forever. How are you doing?"

Logan hugs her back before she pulls away.

"I'm good. How have you guys been?"

"Better than you. You sure you're ready to board that shit show again, my friend?" Tom snarks, gesturing upstairs to my mom.

Logan laughs, but it's more sarcastic than amused. His large hand scrubs at his jawline as my aunt smacks her husband's chest.

"I'm just here to hang out, decompress a little. I love this place," he says, his eyes pausing on me for half a second before quickly moving back to my aunt and uncle.

"That's fine, Logan. It's none of our business," my aunt says, casting a side eye to Uncle Tom, who holds up his hands in surrender but has an amused look on his face.

"Just trying to give the man one last chance to run. She's your sister, babe. I've known her for over twenty years. You got out, man, don't look back now."

"Tom, shut the fuck up," my mom hisses as she glides down the stairs, shaking her hips like she's a runway model and strutting through the kitchen towards Logan.

Her dress, because of course she's wearing a dress at the lake, is low cut and revealing. It has spaghetti straps and a lace bodice that transitions into a silk black skirt. She's also wearing black heels with her hair in loose, sexy curls paired with a bold red lipstick, practically pointing an arrow to her mouth.

I can't help but glance at Logan to see how he reacts, and to my surprise, he doesn't. His posture is stiff, hands curled tight into fists at his side as his eyes stay on hers. Apparently, I'm in the way of her catwalk because when she gets near me, she shoulder checks me out of the way. I stumble for a moment, righting myself and seeing Logan watching me with furrowed brows.

"Logan," she croons, wrapping her arms around his neck as she presses every inch of her body against his.

He hesitates for a moment before breaking our gaze and wrapping a single arm around her, releasing her almost immediately. She doesn't get the hint, though, and continues to hold on like a monkey around his neck. The entire room glances at each other as an awkward air settles around us before my mom finally pries herself off him. The entire interaction is cringey at best, and I actually feel bad for her at Logan's lack of attention. I mean, what did he expect would happen showing back up here after all these years?

"I have to say I'm surprised you showed up. I wasn't sure you'd actually come." My mom smiles.

Logan's unwavering gaze yet again comes to me before he speaks.

"I wasn't sure either, to be honest."

He finishes his sentence by turning that dark gaze on my mom.

"Well, we're so happy you're here. Are you hungry? We could run into town and grab some lunch?"

His eyes rake over her, and she preens at the attention, but the indifferent expression on his face is, I'm sure, more than a little disappointing for her.

"I think you might be a little overdressed, Kel. Looks like there is plenty of food here. I can cook," he offers.

My mom's smile falls at the clear brush off, but she masks it quickly enough.

"Yeah, it was just what I had on. I was going to get changed. I'll be right back."

She struts back towards the stairs, albeit with a little less swagger in her hips this time.

"We were just planning on making some sandwiches for lunch if that's okay?" my aunt asks Logan.

"Sounds great. How can I help?"

She waves him off. "We've got it handled. Ari, help Logan find a free room. Unless you're staying with Kelly…"

"No," he quickly intervenes. "I'd like my own room if there's space," he says.

My aunt gestures for me to show him the way to the stairs. Hesitantly, my feet begin moving. Not sure why I have to show him, it's not like he doesn't know the house as well as I do. Not to mention, I literally just got here. I haven't even grabbed a room for myself yet.

Grabbing my bag, I start up the stairs, almost missing the second step because I can feel him closing in on me. His heady presence is suffocating me on this staircase, and I want nothing more than to get to the hallway already.

When I finally make it to the top, I feel like I can breathe again. Well, that lasted all of two seconds until he's behind me once more. I glance over my shoulder at him, coming to a stop when I see that the two empty rooms left are right beside each other.

Great.

Turning to face him, I awkwardly point.

"You can have whatever room you want."

He shrugs his shoulders. "You pick. I'm good with whatever."

I shrug. "Me too."

We just stand there, staring at each other for several seconds before he speaks.

"That one has a bathroom attached. You take that one."

"No, it's fine."

"I insist," he says.

"Why?" I question.

His eyes close, and he lets out a frustrated breath.

"Just take the fucking room."

I lift my eyebrows in surprise, shaking my head and stepping into the room. Another exasperated breath escapes him before he follows me into the room, throwing the door shut behind him.

We stare at each other for several seconds, the silence almost deafening.

"I'm sorry. I just...why do you have to be so difficult?" he says on a heavy exhale.

"Why do you think you have any right to order me around like—"

My words die on my tongue as Logan's head tilts in curiosity, staring at me intently as he takes slow, measured steps towards me.

"Like what?" he asks.

For a moment, I lose my nerve. Why, though? Rolling back my shoulders, I lift my head a little higher as I stare at those chocolate brown eyes with enough contempt as I can muster.

"Like you're in charge, like I have to bend to your every whim. Like..."

This time, I let my words hang between us, because too many words and thoughts are flickering through my head. Ones that I have no right to be thinking. Ones that I don't want to be thinking.

"Finish that sentence. I dare you," he challenges, a trace of mirth swirling in his eyes. Is he enjoying this? Does he think this is cute or fun? Spoiler alert: it definitely isn't.

I stay silent, my eyes flicking back and forth between his for several seconds before I lower my tone.

"What are you doing here?"

He lifts his shoulders. "I was invited."

I roll my eyes, backing away from him and creating much needed distance.

"Oh, please! You've been invited for years. Why have you suddenly changed your mind?"

Logan stares at me for several seconds before slipping his hands into his pockets.

"You're a brilliant woman, Arianna. I think you know."

My head rears back, completely blown away by his audacity.

"You're...disgusting! Are you fucking serious? You were married to my mother," I whisper, though it's coming out more like a shout.

"I know," he says.

"You were my stepfather."

"I know."

"You...fucked me," I say as I glance around like the walls are listening in on us.

His lips mash together in a tight line as he stares at the ground.

"I didn't know," he says.

Logan's eyes come to meet mine as he continues.

"I would have never approached you, never touched you,

never even looked at you if I knew who you were. Then, by the time I figured it out I..."

He pauses, his head dropping in defeat.

"I didn't *plan* this, Arianna. I didn't *want* this. I'm not some predator that's had my eyes on you for years."

"It sure as hell feels that way." I laugh bitterly.

He shrugs. "You can believe what you want, but it's the truth. When I touched you, I wasn't touching my ex-stepdaughter, I was—"

"Ew, you know what, stop. Just stop," I say with a wince, shaking my hands. "Hearing you say it out loud is so much worse. Just...stop. It's done, it happened, and maybe one day, if we're both lucky, we can scrub the memory from our brains."

His eyebrows pinch together, but he doesn't speak as I continue.

"You're here. There is no way in hell my mom is going to let you leave now. Let's just...keep our distance and get through this week."

Turning away from him, I walk through the doorway into the bathroom, sitting on the edge of the tub and hoping he will get the hint and leave.

"Is that what you want?" he asks from the doorway.

"Hm?" I ask.

He takes a few steps in, keeping his tone even and emotionless as he speaks.

"You want to scrub the memory from your brain? Want to pretend it never happened?"

I frown, looking over my shoulder at him.

"Of course. Don't you?"

His face is impassive and cold as his posture stiffens.

"Of course."

With that, he slips out of my room, shutting the door a little harder than necessary. As soon as he's gone, I can finally catch my breath. A sinking feeling settles in my stomach immediately after, though. A foreboding feeling from what has happened or what's to come? Does it really matter which?

Chapter Eight

Logan

I slam Arianna's door shut harder than I intend as I storm into the empty room beside hers. Tossing my bag onto the bed, I dig my fingers into my hair. What the fuck am I even doing here? This was such a mistake. A stupid, impulsive, desperate to see her and test if the connection was real or something I conjured in my head at the club, mistake.

Test concluded.

Just two minutes alone with her, and all suspicions are confirmed. It wasn't a fluke. It wasn't a lust induced one-off or twice-off, I guess. Being near her sets my skin on fire. It has my mind clouding, my heart racing. She puts me on edge, and I'm like an adrenaline junkie flirting with the cliffside, torn between staying safely where I am and free-diving straight off.

What a fucking ride it would be.

Clearly, that isn't an option, though. Despite the obvious morality conflicts, there is one larger hindrance I didn't account for. She wants absolutely nothing to do with me.

I'm not going to say that it hurt when she spoke about our moments together, as if they sickened her. Mainly because that would make me seem weak, which I am most definitely not. Her response was...upsetting, to say the least.

I'm not exactly sure what I was expecting her reaction to be when I showed up unannounced to her family vacation. Is it too delusional that I hoped she'd be a little excited? That she'd feel that small sense of relief wash over her when she saw me like it did for me when I saw her?

Fuck.

Listen to me, I'm losing my goddamn mind. I can't be this strung out on a woman after two nights spent together. We've barely even spoken to one another in years. It was sex, just sex.

It was more than that, though. I know it, and she does, too, even if she's not ready to admit it yet.

I'm standing in the middle of the empty room, contemplating getting in my car and driving back to Seattle, because this is clearly a terrible fucking idea. My spiraling thoughts are interrupted by the sound of my phone ringing.

Glancing down, I see it's my younger brother Tyson. I almost don't answer, but I know that he will just keep calling until I do. He's annoying as fuck like that.

"What?" I snap.

"Geeze, that's not a very nice way to answer the phone," Tyson lightly scolds.

Blowing out an irritated breath, I lift my head to the ceiling.

"What do you want, Ty?"

"I came by your place to see if you wanted to grab a beer, but you're not here. I called your office, and your secretary said you were out of office for the next week. Since when do you take a vacation?"

"Since now. Wait, are you in my house again?"

"You really need to update your security code, bro." He laughs.

Shaking my head, I move to the window in the room,

looking out over the lake. Tyson is twenty-eight, but you wouldn't know it. He's stuck in the immature 'I have no responsibilities' phase of his life. I keep waiting for him to grow up, find a girl, get a job that he's actually passionate about. Something. Instead, he's more content bobbing through life, living off his inheritance our parents left, and bartending on the weekends. I think the bartending is just so he can have an easy selection of hookups.

"So, where are you?" he asks.

"The lake house," I answer quietly, like maybe he won't hear me or be interested enough to ask more questions.

Of course, neither happens.

"The one out on Lake Roseiger? Where you and Kelly used to vacation?"

"Yep," I say stiffly.

The line is quiet for a few moments before he laughs.

"Holy fucking shit. Don't tell me you're with her right now."

"Not just her," I add in quickly, like that makes the situation any different.

Yes, my ex-wife is here. No, it's not just her and I here alone. No, she is definitely not the reason I came.

I can't share that piece because, as judgment free as my brother is, telling him that I fucked my ex's daughter *twice*, and have been thinking about nothing else but doing it again and again, tells me I'd warrant some judgment.

"The whole family is there? Why the fuck wasn't I invited?" he pouts like he's genuinely upset.

Rolling my eyes, I sigh into the phone.

"I gotta go. Get the fuck out of my house."

"Whatever. Have fun fucking your gold digging bitch of an ex," he says as the phone goes dead.

Ty was pissed when everything went down with Kelly.

Almost more so than me. I think a small piece of me knew before I actually found out. I was always away, and she needed constant attention. She was good for my ego, a pretty face and fairly sweet. We never quite...fit, though. I was approaching forty with a large fortune but nothing to truly show for it. I wanted a wife, a family, and Kelly offered both to me in a pretty package. It was easy to fall for the charming, beautiful woman, or at least I thought it would be.

The honeymoon phase didn't last long. My hours at work became longer, my work trips became more frequent, and eventually, I found myself not missing her at all. That's probably when she started fucking around, maybe even before that. I guess I don't hate her because I don't really blame her. We never had that spark, that connection. We were never truly in love with each other. More like we just were mutually using one another for different things in life. Things we thought we needed to feel fulfilled.

Our marriage and divorce left me with the resounding feeling of failure, something I was not accustomed to. Thanks to my iron-tight prenup and her clear violation of the infidelity clause, it financially cost me nothing. Something she was furious about, hence Tyson's gold digger comment.

Tossing my phone onto the bed, I run my hand down my face. I hate who I've become. I'm restless, irritable. All I can think about is...her. It's fucked up and irrational, but here I am, sharing a vacation home with my ex-wife, her sister, and the woman who has quickly become the entire center of my attention. What could possibly go wrong?

Chapter Nine

Arianna

I pretty much barricaded myself in my room last night. My aunt tried to get me to come downstairs and have dinner with everyone, but I told her that I was tired and going to go to bed early. You could tell she didn't believe me, but she didn't try to stop me either.

I just didn't want to deal with Logan. I contemplated leaving about a thousand times. If he wasn't going to go home, then I was. He couldn't just follow me out here and force me to face him after what we did. But I came to the conclusion that I did nothing wrong.

From the beginning, I didn't have a clue who he was. I mean, I won't lie, I kinda feel dumb for not recognizing his voice. Then again, I haven't seen him in years, and when we were in the club, he spoke deeper than his normal voice, raspier. Or maybe that was the alcohol and raging hormones inside me that made me think that. Either way, I was not the one in the wrong here, that's on him, and I'm not going to run away scared from *my* vacation with *my* family. If he wants to stay, I guess he can, at the price of fending off my mother's advances. Then again, maybe he won't fend them off. Maybe he didn't come here for me, maybe he wants to try again with her.

That's not the way it seemed last night when he essentially cornered you and told you that he was here for you.

Dismissing the obnoxious voice in my head, I slip out of my room and creep down the stairs in search of food because, in the mornings especially, I'm a hangry fucking bitch. I did end up actually falling asleep pretty early, so it's no surprise that I'm up well before everyone. At least, I thought I was.

My steps falter as I enter the kitchen and see Logan sitting at the island, cup of coffee in hand as he scrolls on his phone with the other. The instant his eyes come to me, I feel it. From the top of my head to the tips of my toes, I feel his stare like a hot, heady blanket suffocating me. Instantly, I regret not getting dressed before I came down here. Granted, I'm not wearing anything risqué, just a pair of sleep shorts and an oversized Iron Maiden shirt that I've had for years. Still, I might as well be naked with the way he's staring at me, watching me. I try like hell to hate it but come up short.

Pushing that thought to the side, I straighten my posture and move through the kitchen like I don't even notice him, digging through the fridge for something to eat. Wow, Aunt Marissa really went hard with the grocery shopping. Since I skipped out on dinner, I get started on breakfast for everyone. I see everything I need to make some eggs, hashbrowns, and pancakes.

Pulling out all the ingredients and a few bowls, I start with the pancake mix when Logan speaks.

"Want some help?"

"No," I answer simply.

I can see his reflection in the microwave, and I don't miss

his disappointed expression as he busies himself with his phone once more. Honestly, what the fuck does he expect?

A knock comes from the door, and I turn to see Logan stand to answer it. I frown, glancing at the clock. It's just after eight in the morning. Not sure who would be showing up, let alone at this time. A delivery, maybe?

Logan answers the door, his posture going stiff as he speaks to the person on the other side.

"What do you want?"

I peek around the corner to see Ty, Logan's younger brother. His golden wavy hair is a stark contrast from Logan's short black hair. Where Logan has deep brown eyes, Ty has these bright green ones that constantly shine with mirth. He has that effortlessly hot surfer thing going on. I, without shame, had a crush on him for years because, look at him, how could you not? Obviously, he was way too old for me, and I wasn't even on his radar, but that didn't stop me from admiring.

I smile when his eyes meet mine, a matching grin spreading across his face.

"Holy fuck! Is that little Ari?" He laughs, shoving past his big brother as he moves inside.

I set down the spatula, walking over to the doorway as he drops his bag and lifts me into his arms. I squeal in surprise as he spins me in a circle before letting me slide down to my feet. I don't miss the way he takes his time releasing me, every hard ridge of him pressed against me as we pull apart and smile at each other.

"Fuck, girly. You got...wait, how old are you now?" he asks.

I laugh at that. "Twenty-one."

"No shit? Okay then, sexy, you got sexy. Let me look at you," he says, taking my hand and lifting it above my head as he forces me into a spin.

I chuckle as I comply, and the wolf whistle he lets out has me waggling my eyebrows at him.

"Well, thanks for the ego boost. You're not looking too ugly yourself," I tease.

"You don't have to beat around the bush, Ari. I'm hot, it's okay to admit," he says with a lift of his eyebrows and a wink.

I snort, shoving his chest as I laugh.

"What are you doing here?" I ask.

"Well, my brother forgot to invite me," Ty says with a sour look to his brother before returning his smile to me. "Sorry I'm late."

Shaking my head, I smile.

"Just in time. I'm working on breakfast."

"Need a hand?" he asks.

"Sure," I can't help but see the frown that crosses Logan's face as Ty moves into the kitchen with me.

"I didn't forget to invite you. You weren't invited, Tyson," Logan says as he crosses his arms over his chest.

"Tomato, gelato." He shrugs.

Logan's frown deepens as I laugh at Ty, pointing towards the hashbrowns.

"Potatoes are your responsibility, don't let me down."

He mock salutes me with a smile.

"Wouldn't dream of it."

As Ty and I focus on breakfast, Logan grumbles something under his breath before storming out of the room and up the stairs. Ty looks to where he disappeared, scrunching his eyebrows together in confusion.

"What crawled up his ass?"

I shrug as he bumps his hip with mine.

"It's good to see you, Ari. It's been a while."

"A while since my slutty mom broke your brother's heart?" I question.

Ty lets out a surprised laugh as he shakes his head.

"I mean, breaking his heart is a stretch. I'm not sure he even has one if I'm honest. The slutty mom point, you nailed, no offense."

"Can't be offended if it's true." I shrug.

Speak of the devil.

Heels clack against the floor, a summer dress wrapped around her body as my mother's perfectly made-up face smiles.

"Tyson?"

I watch the amusement leave his face before he screws on a plastic smile.

"Kelly, good to see you."

"You too!" she grins. "What are you doing here?"

"I heard you all were staying here, and I had to come join in on the fun, if that's okay?" he asks.

She waves him off and smiles. "Of course. All the bedrooms are taken, but I'm sure we can find a spot for you."

"What do you say, Ari, up for a bunkmate?" Ty asks with a wink.

"Only if you're a cuddler." I shrug.

Excitement fills his eyes. "Oh, I'm an excellent cuddler."

"Are you trying to seduce my daughter, Tyson?" my mom tuts as she moves past us, filling up a cup of coffee.

"Only with her consent, Kelly."

"Good answer," she praises, lifting the cup to her mouth as she perches herself on the kitchen island.

I frown as I flip the last pancake. That's a good answer? Usually, when a mother comes downstairs and finds a man seven years older talking about climbing into bed with her daughter, they'd take issue with it. Not my mom, of course.

Logan emerges a few minutes later, his hair still wet like he just got out of the shower. He's wearing a black t-shirt and a pair of jeans that hug his muscles far better than they should.

It's funny. I've probably only seen him in jeans a few times. A shame considering how good his ass looks in—

Nope. Not even going to finish that thought.

My mom swings around to face him, giving him a megawatt grin as she tilts her head to the side.

"Morning, handsome. Did you sleep well?"

He nods. "You?"

"It was alright. I was a little cold, though. I hope tonight will be a little warmer," she husks in a way that has Ty and I rolling our eyes together.

Logan glances at my mom before pulling out his phone.

"I'm sure we can find you an extra blanket."

A strangled laugh escapes Ty before he quickly swallows it, plating the hashbrowns just as my Aunt Marissa and Uncle Tom come down the stairs. The twins follow shortly behind them, and we all sit down to have breakfast. Ty tells us story after story about his escapades as a bartender in downtown Seattle. I almost pee myself three times from laughing so hard, and everyone seems to be having a great morning, except for Logan. He's kept his eyes on his untouched plate the entire time, only offering irritated glances at his brother. I know it's been years, but I swear they were closer than this. Sure, Ty was always the 'obnoxious little brother,' but Logan never had a problem with him. At least not that I realized.

After breakfast, my mom and aunt decide to sunbathe while the rest of us go out on the lake. Uncle Tom brought his boat and some inner tubes, so everyone heads upstairs to get changed into their bathing suits. What we really need are wet suits, because Washington lakes in April are still cold as fuck. The sun shining this bright is deceiving, though, so maybe we won't actually be that cold, right?

I'm coming down the stairs in my blue bikini when a hand grabs my elbow, pulling me around the corner.

"Hey, what the fuc—"

My words die on my tongue when I see Logan staring down at me.

Clearing my throat, I pull my arm away from him as I frown.

"What do you want?"

"I'm sorry," he says. "I'm sorry for how I acted last night. I'm sorry I didn't tell you the minute I figured everything out. I'm just...I'm sorry."

He winces like the apology is painful, like he's never had to apologize for anything a day in his life. My guess is he hasn't. Not when you have his kind of money and power.

"It's fine." I shrug.

"It's not," he insists, taking a step towards me. When I take half of a step back, he frowns before retreating a bit, giving me the space I desperately need.

He looks down like he's struggling with his words for a moment before he speaks.

"I don't want you to feel uncomfortable around me, like I groomed you or something. I want you to know that what happened between us...if I'd have known...it wouldn't."

Why does a pang of hurt twist my stomach at his words? It makes no sense. They are literally my words from last night regurgitated. Yet somehow, in the light of day, I don't like them at all. They make me feel...too much. Way too much. So, of course, the only logical thing to do is to shove all of that way the fuck down where it belongs.

"Look, I'm sorry too. I flipped out on you yesterday, said stuff I didn't even mean. I just, it was all...surprising. I didn't know how to process it, and then you showing up like this—"

"I know," he agrees. "It's not fair."

"It's only not fair if I'm the only reason you're here. Tell me that's not true, and we can move past this, pretend it never happened."

He frowns, his hesitance speaking volumes.

"I don't know why I came. I just...ended up here, I guess."

I tilt my head to the side but nod.

"Okay. Well, we're fine, Logan. You're here, I'm here. Let's just move forward, have a good week, okay?"

He hmphs under his breath, a half smile breaking through the frown.

"Are we sure you're the young one here?"

I shrug nonchalantly. "What can I say? I'm wise beyond my years."

Logan smirks at that, his pink lips pulling up in a way that has me hyper fixating on them. Such soft, full lips that...fuck. Nope. Not going there.

Turning away from Logan, I call out to him over my shoulder as I head for the back door.

"Come on, Uncle Tom will one hundred percent leave without us."

Chapter Ten

Logan

I follow after Arianna, just a few steps behind her, and goddamnit, it takes everything in me not to stare at her ass. In my defense, her bikini barely covers her ass cheeks. In her defense, that shouldn't be an excuse, it's the only one I've got at the moment, though.

I wasn't planning on tubing. I've never been big on all that stuff. But when I see Arianna jump into Tyson's arms so easily, him taking the opportunity to cup her ass as he carries her to the boat, my plan changes.

My manwhore little brother should be kept as far away as possible from Arianna. Not only is she over seven years younger than him and Kelly's daughter, she's too good for him. She's the kind of woman that you'd want to settle down with, and Tyson is only interested in women for a night or two at a time. He'll hurt her if she lets him close enough, that's a guarantee. Something in me just can't let that happen.

Walking down the grassy hill that leads to the private dock, a hand reaches out, snagging mine. I look down to see Kelly in a black thong bikini, her tits literally spilling out of the top as she smiles up at me. Jesus, she really has no shame.

"Where are you going?"

"I was gonna join Tom," I say, tilting my head towards the boat, watching Arianna and Tyson climb into the boat as the twins lay on their stomachs on the tube.

Kelly pouts. "But if you go, who is going to rub sunscreen on my back?" she asks, turning around to wiggle her ass at me.

I don't even feel tempted to look at her as I pluck the bottle of sunscreen from her hands, passing it to Marissa.

"I'm sure Marissa will help you."

I walk away before she can stop me again, and I hear her sigh in irritation as my feet hit the dock. I know I can only push Kelly away for so long before she'll explode. She'll demand to know why I came if it wasn't to at least hook up with her, and I really don't have a good answer for that one. I should probably start coming up with something, and fast.

Tom gives me a head nod as I step on the boat. I return the greeting before my eyes lock on Tyson and Arianna, both sitting on the side bench, looking far too cozy for my liking.

"Are you ready?" he teases, tickling her sides.

She squirms in her seat, doing her best to hold in her laugh.

"Fuck! Stop! You know I'm ticklish," she says with a smile that's ready to explode into full-blown laughter.

Tyson grins at her and does it more.

"Oh, are you? Must have slipped my mind," he says before full on attacking her.

Arianna squeals and squirms as she laughs at the hands of my baby brother. Bull fucking shit, he forgot. He used to chase her around and torture her when she was younger. He'd make her laugh until she was crying and made it his entire mission to make her laugh as many times as he could when he was around.

I take a seat across from them, frowning. I was always so

preoccupied with Kelly that I never really noticed what Arianna was up to, especially with Tyson. I didn't realize how close they were or are. I don't know.

Tom slowly pulls away from the dock, and Tyson and Arianna settle down, watching the twins as they slowly start gliding across the water. I take the opportunity to watch Arianna. Her blue bathing suit looks amazing against her skin, hugging her perfectly. Or maybe she's just perfect.

I take in the graceful slope of her neck, involuntary memories flooding me from our time at the club. The way it felt in my hand, how smooth her skin was. Feeling her pulse thunder in my palm, knowing this beautiful stranger trusted me so implicitly from the start. It released something carnal, powerful. Now that I know that it was Arianna the whole time…I still have those feelings, those cravings. Now that I know what she's capable of, what we are, I…

A splash catches my attention, and I turn to see Brady has launched from the inner tube, the loss of balance sending Melanie into the water as well. Tom quickly slows down, making a wide loop as we swing by to grab the kids. They both climb into the boat, teeth chattering as they wrap towels around themselves. Just because it's sunny doesn't mean the lake is warm. It's only April in Western Washington, and the water is unbearably cold until July, but if you live here, you adapt, otherwise, you'd never have any fun.

"Let's go, Ari," Tyson says as he stands up, reaching out for Arianna's hand. She takes it happily, lacing her fingers through his. It takes not only me by surprise as Tyson looks down at her, grinning before squeezing it lightly and leading her to the inner tube.

Carefully, they both climb on, and when they're ready, Tom takes off again. Leaning forward, I rest my forearms on my thighs as I watch them. They laugh and smile at each other as they hold on for a surprisingly long time.

Tom begins swaying from side to side, forcing them to catch the wake from the boat. They start to gain a little air with each wake until they launch. Arianna screams as Tyson laughs before they land with a hard slap against the water that sends Arianna skimming across the surface.

I feel my chest clench as I watch her slip underwater. Leaning over the side of the boat, I frantically look for her in the water before she resurfaces just to the side. Relief fills me until I see her swimming awkwardly.

Forcing half my body out of the boat, I reach a hand out for her. She looks like she's going to refuse me, so I grab her, hauling her up and into the boat. She lands in my lap, and when she tries to get up, I wrap an arm around her, keeping her in place as I look her over. Her right hand is cupping her left wrist as she winces.

"What hurts?" I ask as my eyes run over her in concern.

She shakes her head before looking away. "I'm fine."

Frowning, I pinch her chin, forcing her to look me in the eye and say that.

"What. Hurts," I repeat.

Her blue eyes snap to mine, a million different emotions playing within them.

"I tried to hold onto the handle too long. Probably just hyperextended it. I'm fine."

She squirms in my lap, and it takes everything in me not to enjoy it.

Releasing her chin and unwinding my arm from around her, she stands as Tyson climbs into the boat.

"You good?" he asks, looking her over with worry.

I frown, watching my brother carefully. I'm not sure what he's up to, but whatever it is, I can tell you I'm not a fan.

She smiles up at him the way I wanted her to smile at me when I asked her what hurt.

"My wrist got a little twisted on my epic fail of a departure."

Tyson laughs at that, examining her wrist carefully.

"I swear to god, you were by my side one second, then in the clouds the next."

She chuckles softly, rolling her eyes as he gently touches it. She winces when he moves it, and I have to physically restrain myself from biting his head off and telling him to be more fucking careful.

"We can wrap it with some bandages when we get back to the house for support."

Arianna nods, a shiver running through her as the breeze rolls in. I grab a towel almost instantly, handing it to her. She takes it with a quick smile before Tyson snatches it from her and wraps her up tightly. They both sit down as the twins climb onto the tube again.

When we take off, Tyson wraps his arm around Arianna's back. It's a casual move, but I can see right through my brother. He's fucking into her. She looks up at him, and I wait for her to seem uncomfortable or offended, something that will give me permission to knock his front fucking teeth in. She doesn't, though. Instead, she smiles and leans into him, causing my stomach to sour as I roughly look away.

After a day on the water, we decide to have a bonfire and barbeque. I helped Tom do some baby back ribs, baked potatoes, and a salad, while Marissa and Kelly set up the backyard. There is already a picnic table, but it's not big enough for everyone, so they set up a few extra chairs around the firepit.

The sun is beginning to dip down behind the tree line when I decide to make a fire. Tom hands me several pre-cut logs from the woodshed to the side, and it's not long until we have a roaring fire that everyone is gathered around.

I'm currently sitting at the picnic table when Kelly comes over, dropping into my lap. I fight the instinct to immediately push her off as she wiggles her jean shorts clad ass against me.

"Well, hi, stranger." She giggles before a hiccup slips out of her.

I lift an eyebrow as I stare at her. Kelly and Marissa have been getting into margaritas all day, and it looks like they finally caught up to her.

"Hey, Kel," I say, casually moving my arms as far away from her as possible.

"I'm so glad you came, like, I genuinely didn't believe you'd show up. Thought you were screwing with me or something."

I shrug, not sure what to say. My eyes move around the firepit to see Melissa roasting a s'more while Brady taps away on his phone. Tom and Marissa are snuggling, and Tyson and Arianna are standing around the fire, deep in conversation. I hear her laughter, the sound echoing around the backyard, and I wonder if anyone else can feel her stealing the oxygen from the air around us or if it's just me.

Goddamnit, I can't keep doing this.

"What's wrong?" Kelly frowns.

I look at her, shaking my head.

"I think Tyson is into Arianna. I'll talk to him about it, though. Don't worry."

She scoffs, laughing softly.

"Why would I care? She's a grown woman, she can handle herself, and Ty is a sweetie."

Now, it's my turn to laugh, albeit considerably less humorously. "Tyson is a playboy, and we both know it."

Kelly shrugs. "Ari could use a little fun. She hasn't had a boyfriend in years."

"And you think Tyson is boyfriend material?" I ask dubiously.

"I don't know, maybe. Who really cares?" she shrugs as she lifts a cup of what smells like straight vodka to her mouth.

Who cares? You should. You're her fucking mother. How could you not care about your daughter?

Of course I say none of that, but fuck, I feel blindsided. I can't believe I missed the true nature of Kelly and Arianna's relationship for years. I always thought Kelly was a good mom, a little self-centered for sure, but what I've seen just over the last forty hours or so has me really reevaluating how checked out I was in our marriage. Or maybe how blinded I was by Kelly to notice the blatant disrespect she delivers to her daughter.

I should have paid better attention, intervened more. Arianna didn't deserve to grow up being treated like that, and she sure doesn't now.

My eyes naturally come to her, like I can't stop them from doing so, as I watch Tyson lean down, whispering something into her ear that makes her grin up at him. He smiles down at her, and I suddenly can't fucking stand it out here. Roughly, I push to my feet, cupping Kelly's hips so she doesn't fall, but once she's on her feet, I'm gone.

I can feel my footsteps thundering against the grass until I reach the back of the house. I slip inside the kitchen, heading for the fridge, before grabbing a beer. I don't know if I can do this. Maybe I should just pack up and go home.

"There more?" Tyson asks as he steps inside the house, shutting the back door behind him.

I pause for a moment, pointing my bottle towards the fridge, before taking a much needed swig. He slips by me, grabbing two beers. I don't have to ask who the second one is for.

"She's not old enough to drink," I snap far more aggressively than intended.

"Uh, yeah, she is," Tyson laughs.

I frown. Fuck, I guess she is. Otherwise, how would she have gotten into the club?

"I guess you're right. Time flies."

Tyson nods, an awkward silence settling over the room.

"What's going on with you?" Tyson asks.

I realize I've been staring at a blank wall, and I blink quickly, shaking my head.

"Nothing, why?"

He laughs bitterly.

"You've been a grumpy ass all day. You seriously pissed that I showed up? Bro, I came to talk you out of whatever weird reunification thing you and Kelly are trying. She hurt you, and she doesn't fucking deserve you. I'm sorry, but it's true," he says, lifting his hands in defense.

I don't dispute anything he says as he continues.

"But imagine my surprise when I show up and notice that you spend more time looking at your ex-stepdaughter than your ex-wife."

I feel my heart rate spike as I try to maintain my unaffected demeanor.

"What are you talking about?"

Tyson just stares at me, like he's waiting for me to come clean. Fat fucking chance.

He shrugs. "You just don't seem to be spending much time with Kelly, that's all. I thought you wanted to get back with her?"

"When have I ever said that?"

"I don't know, why are you here then?"

Shit. He's got me there.

"It's complicated," I say cryptically.

Tyson narrows his eyes.

"Uncomplicate it."

I shake my head.

"C'mon, dude. I'm your brother," he says.

Still, I stay silent. Tyson waits a few more seconds before shaking his head with a disappointed sigh. He makes his way out of the kitchen and to the backdoor, beers in hand. Running a frustrated hand through my hair, I huff in irritation before tipping back my bottle and draining the last of my beer.

Chapter Eleven

Arianna

Ty hands me a beer, and I smile in gratitude. I'm telling him about my classes and my ass of a professor when I see Logan emerge from the house. We all noticed him stomp off away from my mom. I felt bad for her. The way she was watching him, like the love of her life was walking away forever. It also made me feel a thousand percent more guilty, because if she knew that her daughter fucked her ex-husband... twice...forget disowning, she'd straight up kill me.

When Logan sits down, I don't miss how he intentionally sits beside my mom, so close their legs touch. She looks up at him, newfound hope in her eyes, and surprisingly, he smiles down at her. It's not a wide, breathtaking smile, but those rarely cross his face.

Something inside me, no matter how small it is, squirms at that. Something just...doesn't like his attention on her, his focus. Which is so fucking stupid because it should be on her. That's why he was invited, why he showed up...right?

My mom nuzzles into Logan's side, and the two begin talking intimately. Forcing my eyes off them, I try to focus on

Ty or my Aunt Marissa. Whoever is talking that isn't my mother or Logan. The twins end up heading inside to watch a movie, and Marissa and Tom follow suit. Me? I'm still sneaking glances at Logan and my mom, waiting for the inevitable kiss to come and waiting with bated breath to see if it will upset me, even though I have no right for it to. It's a special kind of torture that I'm truly hating every second of.

A shoulder bumps into me, breaking my stare as Ty smiles down at me.

"You good?"

I do my best to muster up a smile of my own as I nod.

"Yeah, I'm great."

He looks at me like he doesn't believe me when his eyes catch on the old treehouse. It's been there ever since we started coming here. It looks to be in decent shape, which is surprising. I used to play with the twins up there all the time when they were little. Sometimes, Ty would come up and join in too.

"What do you say we have a campout for old time's sake?"

I lift a brow at him.

"Are you just looking for a place to sleep because there are no free beds?"

He grins, tucking a piece of hair behind my face as he cups my jaw. The way his fingers dance over my skin sends goosebumps running down my back as he grins.

"You and I both know your bed is open, you already offered," he taunts.

I wave him off with a laugh. "I was joking."

"I wasn't," he says almost immediately, causing my stomach to dip.

Before I can respond, he continues.

"You grab the blankets. I'll grab anything else we might need. Meet back in five?"

I pretend to think it over before I grin at him.

Ty shoots me a quick wink as we both head back to the house. I go into my room and scrounge up a few blankets and pillows. Gathering them up into my arms, I make my way back outside towards the treehouse.

I do my best not to make eye contact with Logan or my mom, but before I can fully pass them, my mom calls out to me.

"Where are you going?"

Turning, I face them. My mom is currently perched in Logan's lap, her arm around his neck as his hand rests on her hip. My stomach turns as I look at them, but I do a good job of keeping my face neutral.

"Ty and I are going to do a campout in the treehouse."

She wrinkles her nose up like that idea couldn't be any less appealing.

"You're gonna sleep outside? Willingly?"

"Yeah," I say tightly.

She shrugs her shoulders. "Just make sure he doesn't knock you up."

My mouth parts in shock at the same time Logan's face scrunches up. She laughs, waving me off. Oh, I guess she thought that was a joke. I feel his deep brown eyes move to mine, but I strategically look away just before they can meet.

"Have a good night," I call out over my shoulder as I continue heading to the treehouse.

"You too," my mom says.

Climbing up the ladder with all the blankets and pillows proves to be a little more challenging than I anticipated, but soon, I'm inside the old wooden box, a comforter taking up almost the entire floor and pillows and two extra blankets scattered around.

Ty pops his head up through the entry hole in the next minute, grinning when he looks around.

"It looks awesome!"

"How can you even tell? I can hardly see my hand in front of my face." I laugh.

He lifts up a battery powered lantern that illuminates the entire treehouse. After that, he lifts up a six pack of beer and a bag of snacks he seems to have raided from the cabinets before hoisting himself up, closing the hatch behind him.

"Hi," he smiles.

I laugh. "Hi, looks like you brought everything but the kitchen sink."

He begins unpacking chips, cookies, and an endless amount of junk food. The last thing he pulls out is a pack of Uno. I laugh as he begins dealing the cards, and wordlessly, the game begins.

We play for a little while before I serve him with a draw four and a color I know he can't have because I swear to god, I'm holding all of them in my hand. He pulls card after card, quickly adding to his stack as he speaks.

"So, what's going on with you and my brother?"

My easy smile drops in an instant as Ty looks up from under his lashes at me.

"What do you mean?" I ask carefully, unsure of what he knows.

He cocks his head to the side but doesn't say anything. I swallow roughly, hoping he will drop it. Some piece of me wants to get it off my chest, though. I want to tell someone, vent, spiral. I don't know, but before I can properly think this through, I'm word vomiting.

"We hooked up, twice. I went to a sex club for my friend's birthday, and it's masked, so no one knows anyone's identity. We went into a room together, not knowing who we were, and had sex. Then he invited me back, and we fucked again, and that's when I figured out that I had just fucked my ex-stepdad, and I've been low-key freaking out about it, and I don't know what the fuck to do."

My erratic rambling comes to a quick pause as I glance at him, trying to gauge his reaction. His eyebrows are practically in his hairline, his mouth slightly parted, and eyes round with surprise. Maybe he didn't expect me to give him that much information. Or maybe he's just shocked and disgusted about the act itself.

"Where did you two leave things?" he asks carefully.

I frown at his question. "What do you mean?"

"I mean, are you two, like, together now or—"

"No! God, no. It was a mistake. A really weird, fucked up mistake."

"Then why did he come on this family trip that he hasn't attended since he and your mom split three years ago?" he challenges.

I throw my hands out at my side in disbelief.

"I don't know. When I found out it was him, I walked away. I never expected to see him again. Then he just...showed up here. He agrees that it was a mistake, and we are both trying to forget it ever happened, but things are just...awkward now, I guess."

Ty cocks his head curiously at me. "So, you're not into him?"

Though the answer feels so much bigger than that, I keep it simple.

"No, why?"

He scratches the back of his jaw, a small smirk lifting the corner of his mouth.

"Because it would suck having to compete with my brother for your attention."

I raise an eyebrow. "Compete for my attention?"

Setting down his cards, he scoots a little closer to me.

"Have I been subtle since I got here?"

"No," I say, mashing my lips together to hide a smile.

He reaches out, brushing a piece of hair behind my ear as he leans in a little closer.

"You've always been a pretty girl, but fuck...you're gorgeous, Ari."

"And no longer jailbait?" I tease.

Ty grins at that, leaning in until our noses are just barely touching.

"Exactly."

The air feels heavy as he slowly leans in, brushing his lips against mine. A light feeling flutters through me as his hand cups the back of my head gently, keeping me in place as his tongue tangles with mine. Holy shit, I can't believe I'm making out with Tyson. My teenage self would be jumping for joy right now.

He drags me into his lap, pressing us against each other as close as possible as he lays down. I pull my hair to the side, my hands running down his chest as his cup my ass, grinding me against him. We fall apart in a mess of hands and mouths.

One piece of clothing at a time is thrown across the room before we're lying there, skin to skin. My lips trail up and down his neck as I let out a soft laugh.

"What?" Ty smiles.

"Sixteen-year-old me would never believe this."

His lips meet mine, spreading into a smile as he teases me.

"Did you have a little crush on me, Ari?"

Biting his lower lip, I roll my hips against him in response, and he moans.

"If it's any consolation, twenty-eight-year-old me can't believe this."

Lifting up on my knees, I line myself up to Ty before pausing.

"Condom?"

He lets out a rough sigh and thunks his head against the floor.

"I wasn't exactly planning on fucking Kelly's little girl when I came out here."

Frowning, I look down at him.

"Are you clean? You'd tell me if you weren't, right?"

"Of course, but I don't want you to be uncomfortable, Ari. I can—"

Before he can speak, I sink down onto him, hissing as he stretches me. Ty's grip on my ass tightens as he groans in pleasure.

"Fuckkk."

My pussy aches for a moment but slowly subsides once I'm fully seated on him. His bright eyes collide with mine, and something about it has my pussy pulsing. He groans again, kneading my ass with his hand.

"Goddamnit, baby."

"Feel good?" I question, a soft whimper ripping through me as I lift myself up and back down again.

"Feel good?" he echoes before cupping my cheek. "You feel like a goddamn virgin. If I didn't know you've fucked my brother, I'd guess you were one."

I scrunch up my face at the reminder.

"Ah come on, just fucking around."

Shaking my head, I rest my hands on his chest for better leverage.

"Stop fucking around and fuck me instead."

His eyes darken at that as I begin riding him, and he meets me with every thrust. His cock isn't as big as Logan's. Fuck, I feel bad even thinking that. It's true, though. Still, Ty has a nice cock, and goddamn he knows how to use it, even when I'm on top.

The head of his cock rubs against my g-spot over and over, and I find myself fucking him harder and faster, moan after moan spilling out of me as I chase down this feeling.

"Fuck, fuck, fuck," I moan, my pussy spasming as my orgasm creeps in so close I can nearly taste it.

"Shit, I need you to come, or I'm gonna embarrass myself."

I laugh at that, grinding my clit against him. I do my best to focus on coming, but involuntary flashes of the last time I had sex come to the forefront of my mind. It was so different, so carnal. It was pure aggression and power and domination. It gave me a feeling that lit every single nerve of my body on fire. This is great too. It's just not that. It's not...

No. No. FUCK no. I'm literally on top of Tyson Cunningham. We are raw fucking in the treehouse that we used to hang out in when I was a teenager dreaming of him kissing me. It can't get better than this. This is as good as it gets. Right? Right.

Forcing myself to banish all other thoughts, I lean down, pressing my lips against Ty's. He meets me eagerly as his cock twitches and he gasps. My orgasm slams into me out of nowhere, but I only enjoy it for a moment or two before he's shoving me off him, turning on his side and stroking his cock as he comes all over my stomach.

"FUCK!" he moans. "Shit, that was a close one." He laughs, shaking his head. "I didn't know if you were on birth control. We didn't get that far in the conversation."

"I am," I say with a smile as I look up to him.

He rolls his eyes playfully. "Now you tell me."

Reaching over into the bag, he pulls out some paper towels he brought, quickly cleaning us both up before dragging me to him. I slip my leg through his, my head resting on his chest with his arms around me as he pulls a blanket over us.

Pressing a kiss to my head, we sit there in silence for a few moments before he speaks.

"You're something else, Arianna."

I smile, looking up at him.

"You too, Tyson."

His eyes bounce back and forth between mine like he has something on his mind, and I'm almost positive I know what it is.

"You don't have to worry about me. I'm not expecting anything out of this. We fucked, and it was great, and if you want to do it again before we leave, then I'm more than willing." I laugh lightly. "But no expectations. A little spring break fling sounds kinda perfect."

He takes a moment before nodding, smiling softly as his arms squeeze me tighter.

"Cool, yeah, I'll definitely be taking you up on that offer." He smirks before sliding out from under me, crawling between my legs, and throwing them over his shoulders.

The instant his mouth wraps around my clit, a needy moan that was entirely too loud echoes throughout the treehouse as I dig my fingers into his hair. Fuck, this is exactly what I need.

Chapter Twelve

Logan

My blurry eyes blink away sleep as I stare up at the plain white ceiling. I only had a few beers, but I feel gross, heavy. I think that had more to do with allowing Kelly to grind herself all over my lap than the alcohol, though.

I don't know what it is. I used to think she was the most attractive woman on the planet, but the rose colored glasses were ripped away when I found her with another man's cock inside her. Funny how that works.

Pushing myself to stand, I open the door and walk across the hall to the upstairs bathroom. Soon, I'm climbing into the hot water, scrubbing every inch of her off my body. I don't know why I let her close to me. Maybe it was because I felt I had to, or maybe it was to distract me from Arianna going into that treehouse with my little fucking brother.

For a while, I just sat there, my gaze burning a hole into the side of the thing like if I stared hard enough, I'd be able to see what was going on inside. Then the moaning began, and I lost my shit. I damn near threw Kelly off my lap before taking two large steps towards the treehouse until I stopped. What was I going to do? Barge in and beat the piss out of my brother for something that, as irritating as it was, is consensual?

Fuming, I stormed back to the house, Kelly quickly following behind, asking what was wrong. I told her that I was tired, which she didn't believe. Then I made some bullshit about having a hard time forgetting what happened between us. That shut her up quickly, a look of shame passing across her face as I stomped inside the house and to my room.

Surprisingly, Kelly didn't try to come in to talk or anything else, and I was grateful because, for the hundredth time, I'm wondering what the fuck I'm even doing here. Lusting after a woman who is twenty-five years younger than me, a woman who has made it abundantly clear she wants nothing to do with me. So, why the fuck am I still here?

Because what we shared in that club was something special, rare, and I'll torture myself for years if that's what it takes to convince her of it.

After my shower, I quickly get dressed and head downstairs to get some coffee. I'm taking my first sip when I look out the large bay window and see Tyson climbing out of the treehouse, pulling a shirt on over his head. Son of a fucking bitch.

I slam my mug against the countertop as I stand in place, watching as my brother swaggers up to the house wearing the biggest shit eating grin. When he steps inside, I'm on him instantly, yanking him all the way through the door and pinning him against the wall with my forearm to his throat.

His eyes bug out at me in surprise as he rasps.

"What are you doing?"

"What are *you* doing?" I snap, lowering my voice as my forehead presses against his. "What the hell do you think you're doing with Arianna?"

Tyson's eyes narrow before he lifts an eyebrow.

"I'm not sure how that's any of your business."

"Goddamnit, Tyson. If you're playing with her feelings, I swear to fuck I'll—"

"You'll what? What are you gonna do, Logan? You haven't seen this girl in years. Why does she get all of your loyalty so easily, and I'm just the bad guy?" he asks.

I waver at his comment for a moment.

"I know you. You leave a trail of broken hearts everywhere you go. You do whatever it takes to get women into bed and then—"

"Seems like that runs in the family, bro," Tyson says, leveling me with a hard look.

My eyes widen in surprise as I slowly lower my forearm from his throat, making sure to keep my tone quiet.

"She told you," I say.

He nods. "She told me."

"And?" I grit out, waiting for whatever comes next.

To my surprise, Tyson just shrugs.

"And nothing. She just wants to forget the night ever happened."

"I can't," I admit, breaking our eye contact as I look at the far wall.

"Well, you should. She's not interested in you, that much was abundantly clear to me last night."

Rage ignites my entire body, and I look back to see that shit eating grin from before firmly in place.

"You're gonna stay away from her," I threaten.

"Fat fucking chance."

I narrow my eyes. "Why?"

"Because I like her. She's fun and beautiful. We have a good time together. Why would I throw that away because you accidentally fucked your stepdaughter."

"Ex-stepdaughter," I correct.

Tyson looks at me with intrigue as he tilts his head to the side.

"Maybe not an accident then," he guesses.

"It was!"

The first time.

The second time, I don't know what the fuck I was doing. It was like I had been possessed, like a carnal beast had taken over my body and was acting out of lust and desire instead of logic and reason.

"Uh huh, well, I think that it's best if you forget it ever happened, move on. With Kelly or someone else, whatever. Just leave her alone."

I'm rendered speechless as my little brother stalks off towards the bathroom. How the fuck did this go from me warning him away to him warning me away? As if I need it? As if I'm no good for her, like I could hurt her or—

The back door swings open, and a sleep-tousled Arianna steps through. She's wearing the same clothes from last night, though they look rumpled and her eyes sleep deprived. I tighten my jaw, attempting not to speak when she notices me.

"Morning," she says.

"Morning," I grit through clenched teeth.

She looks at me for a moment, like she's not sure what to say. I'm doing everything I can to keep my mouth shut because I'm about two seconds away from losing my shit on her. I don't give a fuck who she is related to, who we are, or more importantly, were to each other, and I don't give a goddamn shit about our age difference. She feels like mine, and I don't share what's mine, ever. I'm trying to ignore the fact that someone who feels so undoubtedly mine just got fucked by my little brother in a treehouse not two hundred feet from me...

Yeah, I'm on the verge of losing my fucking shit.

Those bright blue eyes meet mine, sending my heart racing

despite the boiling of my blood before she gives me a tight, awkward smile and heads upstairs to her room. I don't realize I'm still standing at the bottom of the stairs, staring at where she disappeared, until Tyson comes back into the room, his hair wet from the shower and somehow in a new set of clothes.

I look him over with a scrunched look, and he shrugs as he pours himself a cup of coffee.

"I left my duffel down here," he explains.

I don't say anything as I just stare at him. What is there to say?

I've been told I'm an intimidating man. In business, in my personal life. I'm not overly warm or funny. I take my job seriously, and I take my life pretty seriously as well. I don't give a shit about everyone liking me, and I never take no for an answer. The exact opposite of Tyson. So, when I stare at him like I want him to be incinerated right here and now, and he doesn't even bat an eye, it takes me by surprise. And not in a good way. In fact, he matches my stare with a lifted eyebrow, like he's baiting me.

Little fucking shit.

Breaking up the intense moment, Marissa and Tom wander down sleepily, greeting us with a good morning before Kelly quickly follows. Her eyes land on me instantly, though she isn't throwing herself at me like she has been. Instead, she approaches me meekly, quietly.

"Morning," she says softly.

"Morning."

She rolls her lips together as she glances around the room.

"Do you think we could talk?"

More than anything, I want to say no, but I also need to be away from my brother for now, so I agree.

Inclining my head, I gesture for her to lead the way to the living room. It's not too far away, but it's enough to talk privately. Folding my arms over my chest, I look down at her before waiting for her to begin.

She looks as if she's trying to search for her words before she blows out a heavy breath.

"I'm sorry," she says, catching me off guard.

I don't let my reaction show, instead, keeping my gaze impassive as I let her continue.

Her brown eyes look up at me, filled with watery tears as her lip wobbles.

"I made such a mess of things. I ruined everything. I was so in love with you...I still am. I was stupid and lonely, and I hurt you. I'll never forgive myself."

Her apology seems genuine, but it's missing some depth. She knew who I was when she met me. I'm a workaholic, but I tried to make things work. We took trips together, I tried to make it home as many nights as humanly possible, no matter how late it would be. So, as heartfelt as her apology seems, it falls on deaf ears.

Still, her regret does make her a little more bearable. Though I've long gotten over her, groveling is something I'll never turn down. Doesn't mean they'll get shit in return. Does that make me a cold son of a bitch? Maybe.

Her glossy eyes stare up at me like she's desperate for me to forgive her, like she needs more than anything for me to say... something. I don't really have anything to say, though. Instead, I'm entranced as I stare at her, but not for the reason you'd assume. I'm absolutely baffled how two women could look virtually identical, with the exception of their age and eye color, yet also look so different. Arianna and Kelly have the same jet-black hair, the same pert nose, and full lips. They are almost carbon copies of each other, and yet...the feeling is completely different. There is a purity to Arianna, a warmth. She can be standoffish at times, but I also know that her heart is huge. She cares about others and always seems to be self-sacri-ficing. These are traits that make it easy for others to walk over her in life but also make her so goddamn admirable and desir-able. Kelly is selfish, greedy, and forever self-serving. Her pretty packaging is tainted by what I've seen on the inside, both from what happened between us and how she treats those around her. It's amazing what inner beauty, or lack thereof, can do to outer beauty.

"I appreciate that," I say, knowing that I have to acknowl-edge her apology in some way, shape, or form.

"Would you ever...could we ever try starting over? Fresh?" she asks with a wavering voice.

My impassive mask doesn't slip as I look down at her.

"I'm not sure. Maybe."

Hope fills her eyes as she blinks quickly in surprise.

I dip my chin, effectively ending this conversation as I turn and head back to the kitchen. Did I just give her false hope so she wouldn't ask why I came? Sure did. Would I have been willing to admit that I drove all the way out to the mountains just to spend a few days with her daughter instead of her? If she pushed enough, potentially.

Speaking of the devil, Arianna comes down the stairs wearing a tight pair of jeans and a pretty white top that somehow magnifies her blue eyes. Those sparkling gems meet everyone's gaze except mine before coming to Tyson. She smiles as he reaches out an arm, dragging her towards him before blowing a raspberry into her neck. She giggles, squirming in his arms before he places a quick kiss against her nose, stealing another from her lips.

The kitchen goes silent as Marissa stares open mouthed.

"When did this happen?"

"Last night." Kelly laughs like it's hilarious. "You should have heard them moaning like teenagers in the treehouse."

I frown at her as Arianna does the same.

"Mom, stop."

"What? I'm just saying, if you wanted privacy for your little vacation romance, you chose the wrong place to do it."

"No way this is just a vacation romance. There is no getting me away from her now," Tyson cuts in with a smile to Kelly and a challenging side eye to me.

"That's nice. Ari, are you sure that's the shirt you want to wear? It looks a little tight in the stomach. Those college pounds really caught up to you," Kelly says, her eyes raking over Arianna coldly.

My eyebrows raise as Arianna seems to shrivel up on the spot, every set of eyes on her. I'm ready to lose my fucking shit on her when Tyson beats me to it.

"Are we looking at the same woman? She's fucking perfect."

"There is no such thing as perfect, Ty," she says with a roll of her eyes.

He shakes his head, smiling at Arianna as he cups her face the way I want to. The way I'm meant to.

"She comes as close as possible."

Arianna seemingly melts into his touch, and I can physically feel my blood begin to boil as she does. Kelly makes an irritated noise under her breath before Tyson pulls Arianna against him, pressing her back against his chest. His hand comes down to her hip, resting against it possessively in a way that has me seeing red. I don't know if he's just trying to rile me up at this point or if he's really into her.

Either way, I'm going to kick his front fucking teeth in.

I decide to sit outside for a little while and catch up on some work. Mainly to escape Kelly trying to grope my fucking cock under the table. I know I used to find her sexual confidence appealing at one point, but now, Jesus Christ, I need her to leave me the fuck alone. Even if I am trying to use her as a distraction of sorts. That sentence sounds gross when I think about it, but I'm not deluded. I know very well she misses my wealth and my cock, nothing else. I used to be fine with that, but after getting just the barest glimpse of a relationship with more...it just feels bland, unappetizing,

I'm slowly working through my inbox, which is a fucking nightmare since I never take time off. I also never allow anyone into my inbox to manage it while I'm gone...because I'm never gone. Goddamnit, this trip is going to set me behind weeks, and for what?

As if my mind somehow conjured the torturous beauty herself, Arianna comes wandering into the backyard before moving to the dock. Her camera is held up as she sits there for a while, snapping pictures. I find myself watching her more than the screen in front of me.

When she turns around to face the house, I quickly make myself busy, tapping out next month's scheduled meetings for the firm. I hear her walk towards the fire pit I'm sitting at, expecting her to continue past me. Instead, she takes a seat on the grass four feet away from me.

I watch her out of the corner of my eye as she lies on her back and begins snapping pictures of the tree that's slightly shading her.

"Why are you taking pictures looking up?" I ask, unable to help myself.

She doesn't stop what she's doing, adjusting the focus of the camera lens as she speaks.

"If you don't change your perspective from time to time, you could risk missing the most beautiful parts."

Her words are deep and prophetic, and yet again, I'm amazed by this woman. I want to say more, but I know I shouldn't. I'm putting up a wall between us, and it's working. Kind of. I'm trying. She made her desires clear, and I have to respect them, even if being this near to her, unable to touch her, makes my skin crawl.

A soft breeze blows by us, pushing some of her hair into her face. She doesn't immediately move it out of the way, and I feel my fingers twitch with the ache to run them through her silky strands just once more.

Arianna tilts her head to me, moving her camera out of the way so her eyes meet mine.

"What are you doing out here?"

"Just catching up on some work."

She nods, her eyes moving back to her camera as she continues.

"Do you like what you do?"

I think about that for a moment, setting my phone down as I ponder her question.

"Yes and no."

"Why's that?" she asks.

"The money is good, the work is steady, and once you've defended one sleazy businessman, you've defended them all."

"And the bad?" Arianna asks as she looks away from her camera.

For just one moment, I hold her attention, those piercing blue eyes on me. It sends my heart racing and my palms sweating like a goddamn teenager. I'm not a nervous man, and I'm not nervous now. More like...off kilter. She throws me off. I'm not able to speak freely, act freely. If I did, she'd be pinned to the ground, naked beneath me, and we'd never come up for air. Unfortunately, that reality isn't possible. She's drawn a boundary, and no matter how much I hate it, I'd never break her trust or disrespect her in that way.

"The bad," I say, attempting to refocus my mind because, fuck me, what were we even talking about again? "Defending sleazy businessmen."

Her lips tip up in the corners, the motion barely noticeable if I wasn't paying such close attention to her mouth. She's amused, even if she doesn't want to be. Something in me likes that I can do that to her, for her. A lot.

"Couldn't one argue that you're also a sleazy business-man?" she asks.

My brows furrow at that.

"How do you figure?"

She shrugs. "You make a shit ton of money, you run a huge business, I'm sure you're the type to do whatever it takes to get your way."

Her playful expression falls away when she looks at me, and I can't help but lean forward, resting my forearms on my knees as I look at her.

"You're correct. I will undoubtedly do whatever it takes."

Her eyes widen slightly, and I swear to god, I see her physically gulp. I hold her eye contact for several more seconds before easing back into my seat, fixing my eyes back on my phone screen as I deliver my next words effortlessly.

"Can you say the same, Arianna?"

I see her frown out of the corner of my eye as if she were truly thinking over my words. I expect her to get up, done with...whatever this encounter is. To my surprise, she doesn't. In fact, she stands, moving to take the seat beside mine. I don't outwardly react, but I can't help but get eager with her this close to me.

We don't say anything to one another. Instead, we both

begin our tasks once more, enjoying the comfortable silence between the two of us for the next hour or so. Once I've answered my fifth repetitive email, I'm completely fried and decide to pocket my phone.

Looking over Arianna's shoulder, I find her scrolling through the pictures she took, deleting ones and saving others. She must feel my eyes on her because she quickly turns the camera away, frowning at me as she does.

"Do you mind?"

"Not at all," I answer.

She rolls her eyes at me in mock annoyance.

"You don't let others see your pictures?"

"No, not really."

"Why?"

Arianna shrugs.

"Are you afraid of someone else being too critical, or are you being too critical of yourself?"

Her uncertain blue eyes meet mine as she pauses. She blinks a few times before slowly turning the camera to face me. I keep my gaze on hers for several seconds, showing her that I appreciate the risk she's taking in opening herself up, and I don't take it lightly. Trust is the most precious thing one person can give another, and that is something I'll never take for granted.

When my eyes do move to the screen, I'm stunned. I just thought she was taking pictures of the underside of a tree, but that's not what she captured. The branches are swaying with a gentle breeze that is caught in perfect time. The colors are vivid and striking while still maintaining their authenticity. Like how she put it, her perspective has taken an ordinary vantage point and transformed it into something...

"Extraordinary," I say lowly.

She looks up at me.

"You like it?"

I hear the uncertainty in her tone, and it gnaws at something in my chest. This brilliant woman has not been given near the amount of praise and recognition that she deserves. In fact, it seems she's been given less than anyone deserves. That stops today.

My eyes meet hers as I nod sincerely, meaning every word.

"It's fantastic. May I see more?"

She doesn't say anything, but I notice her posture perk up slightly as she begins scrolling through the images she took, each just as unique and beautiful as the last. I'm no art major by any means, but I can admire a beautiful picture and understand the skill and raw talent it must take to see what others can't and then capture it, delivering it on a silver platter for those less inclined.

When she's gone through them all, she lowers her camera to look up at me with insecurity that doesn't belong in those clear blue eyes.

"You're extremely talented, Arianna."

"Thanks," she says, her eyes dropping to the floor like she isn't truly accepting the compliment.

Before I can think better of it, I catch her chin with my fingers, tilting her head up to meet my gaze.

"I mean it," I emphasize. "Talent like yours...it's a gift. You need to believe that."

She swallows roughly as an earnest look touches her face. I don't realize that my thumb is gently stroking her chin until she blinks hard, looking away and ripping us back to reality.

"I'm gonna head inside," she says as she climbs to her feet, tucking her camera protectively in her grasp as she makes her way towards the house.

Without an ounce of shame or remorse, I watch her go, memorizing every single step until a solid wooden door cuts off my view.

Chapter Thirteen

Arianna

I walk inside as quickly as I can manage while still appearing like I'm cool, calm, and collected. Even if I'm anything but. That was more...intense than it should have been. Right? That wasn't just me? Wasn't all in my head? The way he spoke to me, the way he looked at me. It stirred up things inside me that I had no right or no way to feel, let alone process. So, like the little chicken shit I am, I ran.

When I step inside the house, a messy golden head of hair pops out from the hallway, grinning ear to ear.

"There you are! Get in here! We're gonna play beer pong!" Ty says happily.

I arch one eyebrow but let out a laugh as I follow him towards the rec room.

"It's like eleven in the morning, Ty."

He shrugs. "It's a game, and we're on vacation. Societal expectations for drinking are null and void."

He has a point, I guess.

Looking around the room, I see that Ty has covered the pool table with some cardboard boxes so the beer doesn't spill on the felt. All the cups are arranged on either side, and he's topping off the last few before coming up to me. He practically bounces on his feet as he drops a kiss to my nose that has me giggling.

"You're way too amped for this."

"I'm the king of beer pong, I suggest you be on my team."

"Oh yeah?"

He raises his eyebrows playfully as he turns to the room where Uncle Tom, Aunt Marissa, and my mother are hanging out on the couch.

"Who wants to play us?" Ty challenges.

Marissa and Tom look at him before shaking their heads.

"It's too early for that shit." Marissa laughs as Ty rolls his eyes.

"Lame."

My mom turns up her nose at Ty as she busies herself with her phone once more.

"We're adults, Tyson. We don't want to play college drinking games."

The sound of the back door opening and shutting echoes through the house, and all eyes turn to the new figure emerging through the doorway. Logan steps into the room, his eyes assessing the table before he speaks.

"Really, Tyson?"

Ty shrugs. "Just because you're shit at it doesn't mean that you have to ruin the game for others," he goads.

Logan rolls his eyes. "Please, I was the one that taught you how to play, remember?"

"Yeah, when you were what? Thirty?"

Ty's tone is playful, while Logan's is nothing but irritated. He's so uptight and so serious all the time. It's incredible that these two are brothers because they couldn't be more different.

I don't know what makes me jump in on the hazing, but I do before I can think better of it.

"Come on, Ty, leave him alone. Senior citizens wouldn't be able to hang anyways. We'll just have to play one on one."

Ty cackles maniacally as Logan slowly turns to me, his eyes narrowed and stare lethal.

"Who do you think you're talking to, little girl?"

His voice is deep and rumbles like thunder. I try to hide the way it sends a shiver down my spine before I strengthen my resolve.

"I'm just saying, you clearly couldn't keep up with us. Best not to get the old folks smashed before noon."

Logan's glare intensifies, if that were even possible.

"You're going to regret those words," Logan says before rounding the table, taking up the position on the opposite side of us.

I hope I do.

Shit, no. Bad Arianna.

"Fuck yes! Kelly, want to come join your man?"

I don't like the way Ty says that. Even if I can't have Logan, I mean, I don't want him, my mother is awful. She hurt him, cheated on him. She doesn't deserve to be in the same room with him, let alone on his team. Then again, I could be completely overanalyzing a simple drinking game.

She looks to Logan, and he shrugs like he could take her or leave her. Clearly, that's enough for her because she leaps to her feet, sprinting over to his side. My mom attempts to pull him down for a kiss, but when he turns his head, her lips only land on his cheek.

I don't miss the irritated look that Logan cuts Ty or the challenging one that Ty throws back at him. What's up with that?

When my mom finally pries herself off Logan, Ty holds the

ping pong ball up, tossing it in the air and sinking it easily into a cup in front of Logan.

"Let the games begin."

Logan glares at his brother before lifting the cup to his mouth, draining the liquid in one go. I attempt not to watch, but I can't look away from his throat working the liquid down so effortlessly.

Once he's finished, Logan takes the ball and tosses it into a cup in front of me. I reach for it when Ty grabs it, swallowing it down for me.

"My hero," I sigh dramatically, causing Ty to wink at me.

I laugh as my eyes snag on an irritated Logan. Ty gives me the ball, and I line myself up before tossing it and hoping that it'll make it in. Unfortunately, it hits the rim, bouncing out of the cup and across the table.

Logan leans forward, that cocky tone I hate rolling through me.

"What were you saying again, little girl?"

Annoyance flickers inside me as my mom takes the ball, also trying and failing. She stomps in irritation like a goddamn toddler, causing both Logan and I to share an eye roll before taking it from her. From there, it's pretty much Logan and Ty playing against each other, both getting progressively more buzzed, although Ty definitely shows it more. I eventually took over and started drinking Ty's cups because he was swaying way too much. However, the beer brings out my competitiveness.

When I toss the ball, and it sinks into a cup right in front of Logan, I holler, galloping around the room as I point to Logan.

"Take that, grandpa!"

"Grandpa?" Logan mimics, a hint of malice lacing his tone.

"Yeah, you're way too old to be daddy," I snort, my foggy brain catching on too late to what I just said.

My mom looks bored, Ty looks shocked, and, to my surprise, Logan seems amused.

He doesn't say anything as he takes the ball and sinks it into one of our last remaining cups.

"I believe that's one point, grandpa," he rumbles, a knowing smirk playing on his lips.

"There are no points," I say with a roll of my eyes, though I'm not nearly as irritated as I'm pretending to be.

Logan grins at me, and no matter how much I will my body to ignore it, my heart thumps out of rhythm. This is a side of him I haven't seen before. A teasing, playful one. It might be my favorite yet. Besides the one where he dominates me in bed, pins me by the throat, and spanks my ass.

Did. I mean, the one that *did* do all of those things. Because it's in the past. It'll never happen again.

Look how convincing I am.

Tom and Marissa ended up wandering outside when the twins came in and said they were setting up the waterslide. After my mom's third missed ball, she gave up and went out in search of a 'stronger drink than this piss water.'

We each have one cup left. Ty goes to throw it but loses his balance at the last moment, swaying hard to the side. Before he drops the ball, I quickly grab it, tossing it in the air with extreme precision, obviously. When it makes that beautiful *plink*, I leap into the air.

Ty and I begin hooting and hollering like we just won the Super Bowl before I run up to Logan and begin my victory dance. He watches me with an amused look, but when I spin to face him, I don't realize how close he is. My chest brushes against his, forcing all the air from my lungs to be sucked out as my eyes meet his.

He's staring down at me steadily. Suddenly, Ty's cheers become muffled, and all I can think, all I can see, are those deep brown eyes. In the next moment, I'm ripped away from Logan and tossed over Ty's shoulder as he celebrates obnoxiously.

"Weeee are the champions, my brotherrrrr, and we kept on fightingggg until we beat youuuuu motherfuckerrrrr," Ty slurs.

I laugh as he begins carrying us through the house and out the back door. I can barely see the slip and slide through the curtain of my hair, but I do see Ty pick up speed, his bare feet running through the grass before he's leaping with me over his shoulder onto the plastic slide.

I tense instantly as I feel our balance shift, only making it a few feet before Ty loses his footing, and we both go flying. He wipes out onto the slide and continues gliding all the way down, whereas I hit the ground with a hard thud and skid off into the grass. My arm stings from what is no doubt grass burn, and my hip throbs in pain.

I groan as I curl up onto my other side while Ty's laughter can be heard in the distance.

"Are you okay?" Melanie asks.

I open my mouth to speak when I feel a presence drop beside me, voice low and full of concern.

"Sparrow," he whispers gently before correcting himself. "Arianna, are you okay?"

I blink up at him, my vision blurry with tears. God, I hate what a wimp I am when it comes to pain.

I feel Logan's hand cup my face gently, a look of pure heartbreak in his eyes.

"Where does it hurt?" he asks.

"My arm and my hip," I grit out.

He looks me over before his eyes come to mine once more.

"Do you think anything is broken?"

I shake my head. "I'm fine, it just hurts."

"Come on, let's get you inside," he says as he goes to pick me up.

"For Christ's sake, she can walk, Logan. She's just being dramatic for attention," my mom dismisses with an eye roll as she knocks back whatever was in her martini glass.

Logan doesn't even give her a second look before I nod.

"I can walk."

He frowns like he doesn't like the idea before helping me to my feet. I hobble for a moment, my right hip incredibly sore as I limp. Logan immediately slips beneath my arm, forcing me to hold onto him as he helps me hop towards the house.

"Ari? Are you okay?" Ty calls out like he just now realized I wasn't beside him.

"No, she's fucking not!" Logan snarls protectively at his brother.

I turn to see Ty staring at us with a drunk but concerned look as he pushes himself up from the ground.

"It wasn't his fault. It was an accident," I say softly as we continue moving towards the house.

"A reckless one. He had no business putting you in danger like that."

"It's not like he knew we were going to fall. He's buzzed, Logan."

We make our way inside the house, and when the door shuts, he looks down at me.

"Buzzed or not, it's no excuse. I would have never put you into that kind of situation. Ever."

He's being a little intense, it was just an accident. It could have happened to anyone. Somehow, I believe him, though. I believe that he is the type of man who doesn't take risks, and my safety would never be in jeopardy with him. Maybe that's me being naïve, though.

Logan helps me over to the couch before laying me down. He then quickly moves to the kitchen, grabbing a few ice packs and bringing them over for my hip and arm.

"You're not bleeding, just a grass burn and a quickly developing bruise. Keep these on for at least ten minutes."

I nod as he grabs a blanket, laying it out over me before tucking me in tightly, like he doesn't want an inch of my skin exposed. It's a sweet gesture, and I can't help but watch him as he does each task with a furrowed brow, like he's deeply upset by this incident.

Ty comes barreling in soon after, spilling apologies all over the place. I try to placate him, but he isn't having it, curling up on the floor beside me like a dog as he hands me the remote and tells me he's not going anywhere. I smile at him as I look up to see Logan watching us with that same frown. Shaking his head, he leaves the room and heads up the stairs.

I stare off in that direction for longer than I realize before Ty begins gently rubbing my uninjured leg. I give him a tight smile as I curl myself deeper into the blanket and disassociate into the screen in front of us.

Chapter Fourteen

Arianna

The next day, Mom, Aunt Marissa, and Melanie decide to drive a few towns over and go to the nail salon. They did invite me, but I decided to pass. I'm still a little sore and used that as my excuse, but mainly, I just didn't want to be trapped in a car with my mom and then at a nail salon for god knows how long. Sounds like hell itself, really.

I don't even know why I came this week. We don't get along, we haven't for a long time, and now that I'm an adult, there are no concrete obligations to one another. Aunt Marissa is more of a mom to me than anything anyways.

Uncle Tom and Ty decided to head out onto the lake and do some fishing, so that just left Logan and me.

I'm sitting on the couch catching up on my latest read when a large figure steps in front of me. Glancing up from my book, I set it down to see Logan staring down at me with a frown.

"What?" I ask.

He's quiet for a moment before his deep voice rumbles.

"You can't be with him."

I lift an eyebrow at him.

"Ty?"

"No, the Easter bunny, yes, fucking Tyson."

I slip my bookmark into my page, standing to my feet as I go toe to toe with him. He may be taller, stronger, and all-around more intimidating than me, but I've had enough of his disrespect.

"I don't know who you think you're talking to, Logan, but I don't respond well to commands."

"That's not what I remember, Sparrow."

A bolt of electricity zips through my body, and I feel myself flush out of anger or arousal, does it really matter? Doing my best to navigate the conversation back, I release a heavy exhale.

"You have been so disrespectful to me since we got here. About everything. I'm not your property. I'm not your child. You don't get to bark orders and make demands of me."

He tightens his lips like he's holding himself back from speaking before he shakes his head.

"I apologize. I'm not trying to be disrespectful. I just..." He blows out a ragged breath, closing his eyes for a moment before reopening them.

That chocolate color is rich, swirling with a million emotions as his voice pierces into my soul.

"I'm worried about him with you. He's not the type to settle down, and he's so goddamn irresponsible. Look what happened yesterday! He's not known to take care of anyone but himself."

"I don't need anyone to take care of me," I say.

He pauses for a moment before carefully lifting his hand to cup my face. At first, I'm ready to shove him away, but when I feel his palm against my cheek, I can't help but enjoy the feeling, too much, probably.

"You deserve it, though. You deserve a man that will care for you as much inside the bedroom as out. You deserve someone who will let you be free but take control when you need it, someone who can keep you safe and protected while also bringing you to heights you couldn't have even dreamed were possible."

His words are like a drug, laced with the strongest dose of arousal, all-encompassing, addicting, and leaving me desperate for each new syllable. I feel myself staring up at him, silently begging for all of that. Goddamnit, what is it about him about... this? He makes everything seem so simple, so intoxicating. This is what first drew me in at the club, it's what made letting go of the idea of him so challenging, and it's what makes this moment so fucking hard.

"What makes you think Ty can't offer me all of that?" I ask, my voice sounding far too breathy for how unaffected I *should* be right now.

The soft look in his eyes hardens as his jaw clenches. I feel his hand tighten against my cheek as his growl reverberates through my body.

"Trust me, he doesn't have what it takes. Not for someone like you."

"Someone like me?" I counter. "What's that supposed to mean?"

He stares at me for so long, I think he's going to ignore me completely.

"He's not what you need, Arianna. He's going to hurt you."

I shrug, hyper focused on the way Logan's thumb is slowly rubbing against my cheek.

"I'm not exactly looking for my one true love at this point in my life, as you know."

He frowns at that. "Meaning?"

Shaking my head, I manage a sarcastic smile.

"Come on, Logan, I was in that club for the same reason you were. No strings attached hookup."

"Yeah? Is that what you were looking for when you came back the second time?"

My mouth parts, and my next response dies on my tongue.

"I know you feel like this is wrong, and morally speaking, it is, but you can't tell me you don't feel this."

Of course I do. But nothing can come of it, so what's the point in admitting it? Torturing us both with some forbidden taboo tryst we both want but can never have?

"I feel like there is another woman in this house who is desperate for your attention. I have my vacation fling set up, maybe you should do the same."

His face hardens as his hand drops from my face. He quickly takes several steps away from me as his posture goes rigid.

"You know what, maybe I will," he says before storming off.

The instant the words slipped out, I regretted them. I recognize that it's stupid that I'm lusting after him, hence why I keep pushing him away. But pushing him towards my mom? The very thought of it makes me sick.

Seconds later, a bright, warm smile pops into the room, grinning at me as he runs a hand through his wet hair.

"There you are! I thought you were gonna go into town with the girls?"

I smile at Ty as he drops a kiss on my cheek.

"Didn't feel like it."

"Well fuck, if I'd have known I had a choice between knee boarding or taking you to bed, we'd be naked right now," he teases.

A grin spreads across my face as I shrug.

"No time like the present."

Excitement lights up his eyes, and before I know it, I'm up and over his shoulder as he takes the steps two at a time. When we make it to my room, Ty opens the door quickly, kicking it shut before dropping me onto the bed. I land with a bounce, and by the time I push my hair out of my face, he's already half naked.

I laugh at his efficiency before he reaches for my pants, unzipping them as he pulls them down my legs. Piece by piece, he strips me down until I'm completely naked. Climbing between my legs, he runs his tongue through me before circling my clit.

"Fuck! Ty!" I moan, louder than I probably should but not giving a fuck.

"Feel good?" he murmurs against me.

I dig my hand into his hair as I grind against his face.

"Uh huh," I gasp as he begins sucking on my clit.

I feel my orgasm begin to creep up on me when he pulls away. I whimper in protest as he lines himself up to me, his head pushing inside.

"Shit. Don't think I'll ever get used to you," he hisses as he pulls out and pushes back in.

"Fuck!" I groan. "Fuck me, Ty. Fuck me hard."

"You got it, baby."

Ty begins a steady rhythm that hits just the right spot for me. It feels amazing, and he definitely knows what he's doing, but I can't help but fight the feeling of missing...something. I couldn't tell you what it is because this feels incredible, and I know I'm seconds from coming. It just feels...routine, standard. Gross, that sounds awful to even think.

It's true, though.

There are no butterflies, no rush of excitement at pushing boundaries and exploring limits. It feels as good as any other sex I've had with boyfriends and hookups at the bar. It's great, but it's not...epic.

Closing my eyes, I do my best to get out of my head and be in the moment. I feel Ty lean down to kiss me, and I do my best to return it with as much passion as he is pouring into me. I don't know what my problem is. I've had a thing for Ty for years, and on top of him being fucking gorgeous, he's the nicest guy. I'm being stupid.

I feel his hand circle my clit as his tongue wraps around mine, a moan escaping me as I arch into his touch.

"More," I beg.

He responds perfectly, applying just the right amount of pressure as he quickly moves his hand, pressing into me just hard enough to send me shattering apart. I let my orgasm crash over me, my moans echoing through the room despite Ty's mouth covering mine.

I feel him follow right behind me, his cock pulsing inside me as he fills me with his cum. The moment is hot and perfect as he slumps down over me, attempting to catch his breath before he rolls off of me and moves to the bathroom. He comes back seconds later with a warm washcloth, gently wiping the leaking cum from between my thighs before laying down next to me.

He lifts his arm in invitation, and I curl into him, resting my head on his chest. We lay there in silence for several seconds before he speaks.

"What's going on in that pretty little head?"

I turn to look at him, trying to sink into this moment.

"Nothing. I'm good."

He's quiet for a moment, his eyes tracing over me like he's trying to memorize me before he speaks.

"You know this isn't just sex for me, right? We're friends. I care about you, which means I care about what's bothering you."

See what I mean? Seriously, the nicest.

Unlike his asshat of a brother.

"Logan pissed me off earlier, it's nothing."

I try to look away when Ty catches my face, his hand slipping beneath my chin to bring my eyes to him. He's frowning with concern as he looks down at me.

"What did he do?"

"Nothing, it was what he said. He just...he said that we shouldn't be hooking up. That you'd hurt me."

Among other things.

His expression tightens, what looks like hurt splashing across his features before he holds me tighter.

"You know that's not true, right? I've been a fucker in my past, I won't deny it. You're not just anyone, though. You're Ari, you're...more, you know?"

I smile softly at his sincerity.

"And we're just having fun. We agreed to a casual fun thing."

"Yeah, exactly," he says, his smile slipping slightly, his tone coming across more hollow than before.

"He's just jealous," he says, rebounding before I can respond.

I shrug. "Don't really care what he is, as long as he stays away from me."

"Yeah. You one hundred percent sure there isn't some lingering tension or desire or something?" he asks.

No.

"Yeah. I still can't believe he even came. I mean, what the fuck did he think was gonna happen?"

Ty shrugs his shoulders. "He's impulsive. Always has been. He sees something, he wants it, he takes it. Nothing else to it. He's always been that way, hence why he's so successful. He's a goddamn shark."

"Well, hopefully, he's gotten the hint that I don't want him," I shrug.

"As long as you're sure it's what you want," Ty says carefully.

Glancing up at him, I can see he's watching me carefully, almost like he's testing me. I give him my most convincing smile as I press a soft kiss to his lips.

"Trust me, right here is the only place I want to be."

A genuine smile spreads across his face as he leans down, capturing my lips with his and holding me there for so long, I begin to forget why I was irritated in the first place.

Chapter Fifteen

Logan

I went to the den after I walked away from Arianna. I needed some space, and it seemed as far away as possible at the moment. And there was beer, a lot of beer. One turned into three, and when Tom came in from the lake, he started cracking them open as well. One twelve pack later, we're attempting to shoot pool as we talk about...fuck, I don't even know what he's rambling on about right now.

"Her pussy is the best I ever had, man, swear to gods," he slurs.

Oh, right. Marissa.

"She's a beautiful woman, you're a lucky man." I nod, attempting to focus on only one of the three Tom's currently standing in front of me.

"Yeah, I know," he says with a sigh as he lines up behind a ball and misses completely.

How long has it even been since we've been here? Hours? Days? Fuck, I don't know. Long enough for me to struggle to stay standing upright.

The door swings open, Marissa and Kelly smiling widely at

us. Marissa's smile falls quickly, though, as she takes in her husband. Her eyes roll into the back of her head as she walks towards him.

"Did you guys drink yourselves under the table or what?" she tsks, looking around at all of the empty beer bottles.

"I'm stillz s-standing," Tom defends.

Marissa sighs as she takes the pool stick from him and begins gently pushing him towards the door.

"Hey, can I put it in your ass tonight? Pleaseee?" he says as his voice disappears down the hallway.

I laugh under my breath, shaking my head as Kelly comes closer.

"You as drunk as him?"

I blink hard, looking up at her. There is only one Kelly currently, which, thank fuck for that, because I can't imagine a world with three. I think it would actually implode on itself. Still, everything feels fuzzy and hazy, like my entire body is sluggish compared to what my brain wants it to do.

"I'm fine. How was town?"

She lifts one shoulder and takes another step towards me, the back of my legs bumping against the pool table as she closes in on me. Her hand reaches out, swirling light patterns against my chest as she wiggles her fingers.

"I got them done red, your favorite."

Looking down at her hand, I nod. I do love red nails on a woman. Something about it is just so classically sexy. And have you seen a red manicured hand wrapped around your cock? Doesn't get much better than that.

As if Kelly can read my mind, she reaches for my belt, slipping it off before I grab her hands with one of mine, stopping her from reaching the button of my jeans.

She looks up at me with pleading eyes, like she wants this more than anything in the world. A million memories smash into me when I look down at her like this. Arianna keeps saying she wants to forget that we ever happened, that I should spend my energy chasing her mom or at least succumbing to her. Maybe she's right.

Slowly, I let go of her hands, dropping my own to my side. Surprise fills her eyes as she carefully unbuttons my jeans, pulling them and my boxers down to my ankles. Looking down, I watch as she wraps her hand around my cock. Instinctually, I close my eyes and hum out a soft groan. Her buttery smooth hand strokes me up and down, twisting on the way up as she does. It feels fucking good.

"You're so hard for me." Kelly smiles.

I open my eyes, my vision slightly blurry as her hand continues stroking me. I don't say anything, I just stare and watch her while her eyes stay firmly on me. Lifting my hand to her face, I cup it softly, and she nuzzles into my touch like she's desperate for it. This is what I'm used to, giving a woman an ounce of attention and having her relish in it. This is why Arianna is so goddamn infuriating. She doesn't listen to me, doesn't give in. She fights me at every step and turn, and it pisses me the fuck off.

Especially when I know what a good Sub she can be for me. How beautifully she gives in to me. She's capable of so much, *we* are capable of so much. She doesn't want it, though, so I have to try to move past her.

If that's even possible.

My hand skates across Kelly's face before settling up to the top of her head. I push down slightly, and she automatically knows what I'm asking of her. She drops to her knees so fast, I'll bet anything she dented the floor. Her hand releases my cock, and the next moment, her mouth is wrapped around it.

"Fuckkk," I grit through clenched teeth.

She bobs down a little before gagging, pulling back, and

sucking me down once more. Her tongue rubs against the head of my cock as she continues this rhythm. My hands move to either side of her head, weaving my fingers through her silky black hair.

Her eyes meet mine, her mouth stuffed full of my cock. It has me twitching in her mouth as she pushes me down further. Her eyes drop, and her hair falls over her face as she begins sucking the life out of my cock.

I feel my balance waver, and I don't know if it's from the alcohol or the blowjob. One moment blends into another and then another before I'm looking down at that long black hair, and I swear to god, I must be hallucinating because, suddenly, it's not Kelly sucking my cock, it's Arianna. Her pretty face is hidden, but in my mind, it's hers. The perfume isn't right, and the blowjob is a little sloppier than Arianna gives, but my cock throbs when I imagine the woman before me is her. So, I lean into it.

"Fuck," I pant, thrusting my hips into her.

She gags again, trying to take me as I begin using her face to suck me. I feel her hand lift up, playing with my balls. Fuck, that's good shit. Arianna keeps pushing me down her throat, and it feels so good to feel her again that I'm ready to fucking lose it any second.

"I want you to come down my throat." Kelly smiles, pulling away from my cock to look up at me.

Irritation flickers through me as I force my cock back down her throat and hold her in place. She gags and gasps, but I'm not giving her room to speak again. She's fucking ruining this fantasy for me. Holding her head in place so all I see is her long hair, I begin violently face fucking her, replaying all of Arianna's soft little moans, the way her body responded to my touch. How she was so goddamn obedient for me. The perfect little Sub. My Sub.

One mental image of her smiling up at me like I hung the moon, and I lose it. My cock throbs as I feel myself come hard. The mouth wrapped around me tries to swallow it all but struggles and pulls away. I grab my cock, stroking myself to get every last bit of orgasm out of this. The delusion is gone. Arianna wouldn't have wasted a drop. She would have stayed on her knees and asked me for more.

Instead, Kelly lifts up her skirt, revealing a pair of crotchless panties as she sits up on the edge of the pool table and spreads her legs. Her pussy opens up, and I look down at it for a moment. She is literally serving herself up to me on a silver platter.

My hand reaches out, tracing a finger down her slit before pausing at her cunt. She's leaking all over the felt of the pool table, and her breathy moans fill the room even though I'm barely touching her. Slowly, I push inside her wet cunt. She moans like a porn star as I pull out, adding another finger.

"Fuck! Logan!"

Her voice irritates me. It's not the sound I want to hear, but I do my best to block it out, my cock hardening again as I close my eyes and imagine it's Arianna I'm playing with, that it's her who wants me so desperately. Pulling my fingers out of her, she reaches down, spreading herself open. Running my hand over my cock, I keep my eyes closed, that beautiful face still firmly in my mind before I open them.

Fucking Kelly isn't exactly a hardship. She broke my trust, broke our marriage, and I'd never be willing to take her back. But at this moment, none of that matters. Right now, I just want to stop thinking about her daughter for two goddamn minutes. So, I push inside.

Kelly moans as I thrust my cock into her, holding her in place as she squirms. Gripping her hips tightly, I begin slowly fucking her. She shouts and groans her pleasure to the point of annoyance.

"Quiet," I snap.

"I don't want to," she whines as she begins rubbing her clit.

That's the problem with Kelly. She was never a good Sub, never much of a Sub at all. She was and still is a brat, through and through. Outside of the occasional moments, I've never cared too much for brats. Which is still confusing to me how I ended up with her for so long, let alone married to her. I'm going to chalk it up to a midlife crisis. Or maybe this infatuation with my ex-wife's daughter is my midlife crisis. Either way.

Fuck. Is it seriously so impossible to get her off my mind? Even when I'm literally inside her mother? Goddamnit, that statement itself is disgusting. I'm disgusting, this whole situation is fucked. Yet, here I am, fucking my ex as memories of her daughter's bare pussy flash in my mind.

I'm not just gonna burn in hell, I'll be incinerated on day one.

And I deserve it.

Slumping over her, I bury my face into her hair so I don't have to look at her as I snap my hips violently. Her body begins to convulse beneath me, and I keep her body pressed as close as possible as her pussy spasms around me.

"Oh god! Oh fuck! Logan!" Kelly screams.

It hinders my orgasm for a moment, but I'm able to get it back as I fall over the edge. Pleasure washes over me as I do, tipping my head back as I enjoy the last few moments of pleasure before I lift my head. When my eyes open, though, I freeze. The door wasn't shut all the way when Tom and Marissa left, and there, standing in the open sliver of the doorway, is a wide-eyed Arianna. Her mouth is parted, her face near gaunt as she stares at me.

Guilt rips through me as I attempt to shield us and make

myself decent. How decent can I be when she just caught me raw fucking her mom against a pool table and filling her with my cum? My cock is still inside her for Christ's sake.

By the time I manage to get my pants up and cock tucked away, Arianna's gone. I thought it would feel good to fuck someone else, maybe set me free from this weird hold she seems to have on me. Now, I'm just left here feeling guilty for something I shouldn't and ashamed when I should feel anything but.

Right?

Regardless if I'm right or wrong, I feel like a cold bucket of water has been dumped over me, and suddenly, my buzz is gone, and I'm left feeling stone cold sober.

"That was amazing." Kelly smiles as she leans up. "Grab me a napkin?" she says as she points to the stack of napkins on the wet bar.

I grab a stack of them, allowing her to clean herself before she winds her arm around my neck, dragging me to her. Her lips are on mine before I can stop her. Why should I, though? I'm a grown man. I'm single. I can fuck and kiss whoever I want. God knows Arianna is. With my little fucking brother of all people. If I want to make out with my ex-wife, that's my business.

Kelly's lips attempt to pull me in, and I hesitate for a moment before allowing it. She drags her body against me as our tongues tangle together, and I take control of the kiss. She melts into my touch as I lift her up into my arms, pinning her against the wall. Throwing her head back, I feel her pussy attempting to grind against me through my jeans as she moans.

"I've missed you so much, Logan," she whimpers against me.

I pull my lips from hers, peppering her neck with kisses as I attempt to fully invest in this moment. When I pull back, I look at her, truly look at her. There was a part of me that thought I loved her, that might always care for her. I can't tell her that I've missed her too, though. So, instead, I kiss her.

She's the one to pull away this time, her voice softening as she speaks.

"I know I have a lot to make up for, and I'm going to do it if you'll let me. No expectations, and after this week is over, if you never want to see me again, I'll accept it. Just don't shut me out until then, okay? I need more of this, more of you."

Her hold on me is ironclad, like she can keep me if she holds on tightly enough. I mull over her words, wondering if there is a downside. I chose to put myself in this position, not knowing I'd have to spend a week watching from the sidelines as my little brother mauls my newest obsession. I knew I'd have to fend off Kelly and even expected it to continue long after we leave. She's giving me an out here, though. A week of casual, no strings attached fun and a hefty distraction from the one thing I want and can't have, with no promise to continue if I don't want it to.

If there is a downside, I'm not seeing it.

"Alright," I rasp as I slowly let her stand.

She looks up at me with hope and relief shimmering in her eyes.

"Really?"

Leaning down, I press a kiss to her cheek.

"Come on," I say as I wrap my arm around her and walk her out through the hall.

Chapter Sixteen

Arianna

I'm standing in the mirror, staring at myself because I truly think I'm in shock. There is no way in fuck I just walked in on what I thought I did, right?

I know I did, though. I heard my mother's moans all the way from outside. When I came in, I heard her shout Logan's name, and my stomach dropped. I couldn't stop myself, my feet carried me there on their own accord. When I got there, it was like witnessing a car accident. No matter how badly I wanted to, I couldn't look away.

The instant Logan looked at me like a dazed deer in the headlights, I wanted to run. Unfortunately, yet again, my feet wouldn't cooperate. Instead, I just stood there, staring at him and him at me. I felt the sting of betrayal running through my veins, but why? He owes me nothing, I'm nothing to him, he's nothing to me. Hell, I literally told him that he should stop hyper focusing on me and redirect that attention to someone who wants it, specifically my mother. And he did.

I just didn't realize how soon or well he would take directions. Usually, a man like him doesn't take directions from anyone. Guess there's a first for everything.

Blowing out a heavy breath, I choose to brush off whatever feelings I'm currently experiencing because, frankly, they are unwarranted and not welcome. Well, I try to at least. The souring in my stomach refuses to pass, and a whole host of thoughts begin running through my mind.

Why does this upset me so much? I literally told him to do just this. I should be happy his attention is off of me once and for all. This is a good thing. Right?

You'd think so.

Swallowing back the bile attempting to rise in my throat, I open the bathroom door. Ty is there with a patient smile, like he's been waiting for me. I smile, a little bit of my agitation settling as his eyes light up when he sees me. Pushing off the wall, he closes the distance between us, his hands gripping my hips to steady me.

"Hey, you okay?"

"Yeah," I answer too quickly. "Why do you ask?"

He frowns slightly. "Well, I came inside and saw you sprint to the bathroom. You looked upset."

Before I can respond, two figures emerge from down the hallway. Ty and I both turn to see my mother wearing the most sated smile I think I've ever seen while Logan has his arm wrapped around her shoulders. Ty's jaw nearly hits the ground as they saunter past us, my mother throwing me a Cheshire grin over her shoulder.

"Make sure you knock next time, Ari. I taught you better than that."

A sting flares inside my chest at that. Maybe it's the reminder of what I just saw or the reminder that she was such a shit parent and still manages to be condescending.

They disappear out the back door, joining my Aunt

Marissa and the twins. When the door shuts, Ty whips around to face me, outrage splashed across his face.

"He didn't."

I let out a bitter laugh. "Oh, trust me. He did. I walked in at the end and...yeah. They most definitely did."

The mental image of Logan inside my mother...is something that will haunt me for the rest of my life, no doubt. Okay, maybe not haunt, but disgust, absolutely. Ty curses under his breath, rolling his eyes before looking at me tenderly.

"Are you okay?"

I dismiss him with a wave and smile. "Why wouldn't I be?"

He continues watching me with concern, and I feel my smile slowly fall before I shrug.

"I have no right to be jealous or upset or whatever. I literally told him to give his attention elsewhere—"

"But now you miss it on you?" he guesses.

"No!" I argue. "I just...my mother is the worst."

"That she is. You know you can talk to me, right? We're friends."

His hand reaches up to cup my face, and I sink into it, smiling up at him.

"I know. In a few short days, you've become one of my favorite people in the whole world."

He grins at that.

"It's because I'm so excellent at sex, huh?"

I let out a laugh and shake my head.

"I mean, yes, that helps, but it's you. I adore *you*."

Something in his eyes soften at my words, but he doesn't speak, and I realize I might have made him uncomfortable.

"You know what I mean. I adore you in the sense that I care and appreciate you. I'm really glad we agreed to no strings or expectations because I'd hate to jeopardize a friendship like this!" I add on.

His smile becomes tight, and I instantly feel like I've already made this awkward. Mr. Playboy doesn't do relationships or big feelings. We agreed to be light and carefree, but now I'm sitting here telling him how much I adore him.

Blowing out a heavy breath because I'm just killing it tonight, I wrap my arms around his waist so he won't pull away from me.

"I'm being stupid and rambling. Ignore me, please."

His tongue runs over his lower lip like he's contemplating something before he smiles, bending down to press his lips against mine. I welcome it happily as his hold on my face deepens.

"Coming up for air anytime soon?" my mother snarks.

Ty and I break apart, my irritation bubbling back up as I turn to her.

"What happened to knocking, Mother?"

"In the hallway?" she asks with an eyebrow raise. "Besides, now we're even. We all decided to head up to Leavenworth for the night tomorrow. You guys in?"

Leavenworth is a cute little Bavarian themed village in the middle of the Cascade Mountains. It's a little over two hours from the lake house, so it's great for a day trip but even better for an overnight stay. It's a total tourist trap, but really fun to go to once in a while.

"Sure, we're in," Ty answers as he looks down at me to check.

I nod my head, and my mom actually smiles at that.

"Great, I'll let Logan know," she says as she saunters out of the room.

"More like she'll let his credit card know."

Ty snorts before letting out a sigh. I nuzzle into him as he holds me tighter and places a kiss to the top of my head.

My Aunt Marissa and Uncle Tom took their car with the twins while Ty, my mom, Logan, and I all piled into his car. Though Ty and I tried to get out of it, Logan insisted, which felt like a special brand of torture. The whole ride, my mother was practically in his lap as he was driving, kissing his hand, his neck, and I'm pretty sure at one point rubbing his cock before he politely stopped her. What happened? I thought he loved a good voyeur moment.

Ty and I just minded our business, and in true Ty fashion, he wouldn't stop cracking jokes the entire ride up. He was definitely the much needed comic relief for the car.

When we finally drive past the "Welcome to Leavenworth" sign, relief washes through me. Despite not really being able to get away from them, we can at least get some space. Logan booked us all rooms at one of the hotels right in town, or should I say, my mom booked it with his credit card.

We check in, grabbing our room keys as we go to drop off our stuff. The plan is to shop around town a little and then get dinner later. Ty and I drop off our bags, and I go to head back out the door so we can meet everyone when Ty playfully tackles me, pinning me to the bed as he begins peppering my face with kisses.

I giggle and squirm under him as he continues, his large body effectively rendering me helpless.

"Ty! Stop, Stop!" I laugh as he smirks and pulls away.

His hand comes up, brushing away some hair from my face as he smiles down at me. It's a heavy smile, like there is way more beneath it than you can tell from the surface. I tilt my head curiously as I reach out to cup his cheek.

"You okay?"

"Yeah, I just wish we could stay in bed all day together."

I lift my eyebrows in suggestion and wink.

"I mean, technically, we could."

He groans, burying his head into my neck.

"Don't tempt me, Ari."

Lifting his head up again, I smile at him as he stares into my eyes.

"What?" I ask.

"I just always want to remember you like this."

I give him a funny look as I tilt my head.

"You act like we're on borrowed time or something."

He shrugs. "Feels like it sometimes."

"We still have a few days before we all head back to the city," I remind him.

"Yeah." He nods, rolling his lips together as he seemingly mulls over something. "Maybe when we get back, we could go to a Crusaders game."

"Didn't know you were into football?" I smile.

"Lots you don't know about me, Ari."

"I guess so," I tilt my face towards his. "I'd love to."

He smiles at that, a wide, blinding white, dopey smile.

"It's a date."

With that, he presses a quick kiss to my nose and stands up, grabbing my hands and hauling me to my feet before lacing our fingers together and heading down to the lobby to meet everyone.

Chapter Seventeen

Logan

We are all standing in the hotel lobby waiting on Arianna and Tyson. The twins are doing something on their phones, Marissa and Tom are whispering to each other, and Kelly currently has herself wrapped around me. It doesn't bother me like I thought it would. Maybe because we had some great sex last night and again this morning. I tell myself that the post-orgasm guilt is unnecessary and will fade soon, but I'm still waiting on that part.

The elevator doors open, and Arianna and Tyson walk out hand in hand. A sharp stab of jealousy rips through me no matter how hard I try to fight it. Looking away from them, I focus anywhere they aren't as Kelly speaks.

"About time! You guys ready?"

"Yeah, sorry. Lead the way," Tyson says as we all walk out of the hotel.

Since the place we chose is right on the main strip, we are all filing in and out of shops in no time. There are a lot of antique and gift shops around here, some things gimmicky and others more practical boutique items. It's a cute family friendly town that our parents used to bring Tyson and I to as kids, especially in the winter.

Arianna has her camera around her neck and is snapping pictures every few minutes. Some are of all of us; some are just of the town itself. She smiles so widely with each snap taken. I don't know how I didn't notice that before, all those years ago.

I suppose it's good that I didn't. If I had, then I would have been watching her far too closely. More than appropriate, that is. Then again, is it appropriate now? Definitely not. I can't stop myself, though, no matter how hard I try.

"Oh my god, Rissa, do you see that bag? Come on!" Kelly says as she grabs her sister's hand, rushing into the store in front of us.

She only pauses for a moment, lifting up onto her toes and pressing a kiss against my lips before giggling as she runs off. I feel several sets of eyes on me as Tom, Tyson, and Arianna stare at me with confusion. Tom follows after his wife, his kids in tow, and slowly, Arianna does the same. I move to step inside the store when Tyson blocks the way, turning to face me with his arms folded across his chest.

"What are you doing?" he asks.

My brows furrow as I look at him.

"Shouldn't I be asking you that?" I question as I attempt to sidestep him.

He blocks me again, his tone cool and stern.

"What the fuck are you doing with Kelly?"

I give my little brother a blank look.

"I don't see how my love life is any of your concern."

A disgruntled scoff escapes him as he shakes his head.

"Spare me whatever bullshit lie you've convinced yourself. You don't love her. You fell out of love with her the moment you found out she'd been getting more cock than days in the week."

I grit my teeth together. "It was one time."

"Yeah, another bullshit lie I don't believe for a goddamn second. What are you doing, man? Her? You're really starting shit up with her?"

"I'm a grown man, Tyson. If I want to hook up with my ex-wife while we're on vacation together, then I will. I don't answer to you."

I try to sidestep him, but yet again, he blocks my path, lowering his voice as he speaks.

"A vacation you're only on because you're obsessed with her daughter."

My eyes snap to his, irritation radiating from me in waves.

"Drop it," I say steadily.

"No! You know what, fuck you. First, you come out here, torturing her, not allowing her a goddamn second to breathe, and then the next, you're fucking her mom? What kind of plan is that? If you think you're gonna win her over with that kind of behavior, you've lost your goddamn mind."

"I'm not trying to win her over!" I snap. "She wants to forget it ever happened. It's for the best. We've moved on. I'm moving on. She moved on, with you of all people!"

"She doesn't want me, dude. Not like she wants you."

I narrow my eyes, curious as to what he means by that. Has she said something? What does he know?

"I'm just saying, if you want her, you're gonna have to stop being an ass. Stop trying to force her to want you and then pushing her away in the next breath. You're not god. You don't get to control and handle every single thing and every single person, Logan."

My jaw tightens as I drop my gaze. Losing control isn't

exactly a strong suit of mine. My eyes come back up to him as I turn my head curiously.

"Why exactly are you telling me all of this? I thought you were having fun with her?"

"Oh, I am. She's amazing and beautiful and the sex is—"

A feral growl tears through my chest before he can finish that sentence. Like I have any room to talk. Still.

"But...I don't know. I can tell she's not over whatever happened with you. Something is unresolved or whatever. She can't see me because she's too busy looking over her shoulder for you."

Involuntarily, my eyes move to the shop to see Arianna staring at me through the shop window. Her eyes are so bright, even from this far away, and I can feel them pulling me towards her. Like an invisible tether beckoning me to come closer.

When her eyes move to Tyson, the tether snaps, and I blink hard before focusing on him again.

"If you want her, you better knock off this charade with Kelly, and soon."

"Why soon?" I question as he takes half a step back towards the shop.

"Because I'm wearing her down, and if she falls for me, I won't be letting her go."

With that, he slips into the shop while I'm left frowning on the sidewalk. A million thoughts run through my mind, and I have absolutely zero time to process any of them before everyone begins spilling out of the shop. Kelly and Marissa have cream and black shopping bags from the store in hand, smiling like their purchases are a victory of sorts.

Kelly slips her arm through mine, and we begin walking down the sidewalk for a little before a gasp comes from behind us. We turn to see Arianna's eyes full of excitement as she nearly drags Tyson's arm out of its socket towards the store in front of them. Kelly makes a disgruntled noise under her breath because if she's not interested, no one should be, right?

Goddamnit, she's a spoiled brat. I can't believe it took me years to actually notice.

Looking up at the sign as we step inside the shop, I notice that it's the Christmas store. All year long, this store is up and has people flocking to it. Inside sits trees, ornaments, décor, and the largest Christmas town display you've ever seen. Or at least that I've ever seen.

Everyone fans out, all heading in different directions. Kelly heads to the right as I keep moving further and further into the store. I've never been a fan of Christmas. Maybe because our parents passed away on Christmas Eve. Tends to spoil the mood.

Arianna, though. She loves it. I remember her constantly baking, singing Christmas carols through the house, and binging Christmas movies for days at a time. It's funny, all these little details that I've catalogued over the years but never really realized that I did. All these little quirks and facts about her that some part of my brain decided were worth tucking away, keeping safe.

I stop a few feet short as her and Tyson are looking at the snow globes. He smiles, pointing at one before his attention is drawn to something across the store. He leaves her side, but she hasn't even noticed, too enraptured with the item in her hands. I can't help but take a few steps closer, the curiosity of what could hold her interest so intensely too overwhelming to ignore.

When I'm only a step or two behind her, I'm able to look over her shoulder and see what she's holding. It's a silver-plated base with a little cabin, trees, and a family out front. As she tilts the snow globe, the snow falls, dusting the entire scene. The white glitter swirls, and I don't need to see Arianna's eyes to know that she's transfixed.

"Beautiful," I murmur.

She nearly jumps out of her skin, gasping as the snow globe goes flying. I reach out, grabbing it easily before it shatters. Her breathing is ragged, eyes wide as I offer the snow globe back to her.

"I didn't hear you," she says, her eyes glued to mine.

"Sorry, I didn't mean to startle you."

"You didn't, I just...you're fine."

I nod, attempting to offer it to her once more. She grabs it from me, looking at it once more before placing it back on the shelf. Frowning, I glance at her.

"You're not going to get it?"

"Why would I?" she asks.

"You like it."

Arianna shrugs. "I like a lot of things, doesn't mean I need it."

"But you want it," I point out.

She doesn't argue. Instead, her eyes move from the snow globe to me, a heaviness dimming her bright blue orbs.

"Just because you want something doesn't mean it's good for you. A want and a need are two very different things."

Her double meaning strikes a nerve, and before I can speak, she's making her way back to the front of the store. I'm left standing there for several seconds, unsure how to process her words, when the sound of the door chime catches my attention. Looking across the store, I see everyone beginning to file out. I take a step in their direction before I pause, looking over my shoulder at the snow globe.

Fuck it.

I snatch it off the shelf, bring it up to the counter, and pay for it before I'm back out on the sidewalk where everyone seems to be waiting. Murmurings of eating echo through the group, and everyone decides to head back to the hotel to drop off their purchases before meeting up for dinner.

Kelly glances down at the bag in my hand with an excited gleam.

"What do you have there?" she asks with an expectant smile, like I'm about to surprise her with something.

"Nothing," I say, as I tighten my hold on the bag.

She pouts but lets it go easily as we make our way inside the hotel lobby. Everyone begins heading in their own direction when I reach for Arianna, pulling her to the side. Her brows furrow as she looks at me before I hand the bag to her.

Tilting her head to the side curiously, I speak.

"Just because you don't need it, doesn't mean you don't deserve it."

Understanding crosses her face, but I turn and move towards the elevators, sliding inside before she can say anything or attempt to refuse my gift.

Ten minutes later, we are all heading to a restaurant just down the road. Dinner goes by very uneventfully. Kelly fills most of the conversation, per usual, and everyone pretends to listen. Except for Arianna and Tyson. He keeps whispering in her ear, making her giggle, and it's distracting as fuck.

I don't even realize I've got a death grip on my steak knife until the waiter comes over to collect our plates. Releasing my weapon, I notice Tyson watching me with an amused expression. I narrow my eyes at him because I truly don't understand what he's playing at.

After our early dinner, the twins beg us to go to the ice cream shop, where everyone but Kelly gets something. She watches us all with distaste as she begins scrolling on her phone. My eyes move around the group to notice one person is noticeably missing. Panic fills me momentarily before Tyson catches my eyes, pointing in the direction of the gazebo. I follow his direction, and a swell of relief fills me as I see Arianna snapping pictures while somehow holding her ice cream cone.

"The kids and I are gonna head in for the night," Marissa says as she begins hugging everyone.

"Night is still young, anyone up for grabbing some beers?"

"Make it a vodka soda and I'm in," Kelly says as she glances up from her phone.

"Of course, can't have you consuming more than three calories, princess," Tom mocks.

She shoots him a narrowed look and shoves his shoulder before continuing to type on her phone.

Slowly, Tom and Kelly begin moving towards the closest pub as Tyson and I pause, glancing towards Arianna. Tyson attempts to wave her over, but she doesn't see him, too infatuated with the woodwork of the gazebo at the moment.

"I've got her," I say as I begin crossing the street.

"I'm sure you do," Tyson mutters behind me.

I don't pay him any attention, though. I'm only a few feet away from her when she turns to the side. I just stand there and watch her for a moment, enthralled, the way I seem to always be when I'm near her.

I watch as her mouth wraps around the top of the ice cream cone, a small amount coating her lips. In the next moment, she sees me beside her. Slowly, she lowers her camera, turning to face me fully as I close the distance between us.

As if I were possessed, as if I had no control over my body whatsoever, I keep moving until our bodies brush against one another. She looks up at me, her tongue darting out to wipe away the vanilla ice cream coating her lips. Missing a little, it begins to drip down her lower lip, and I reach out, brushing it away with my thumb. It's meant to be a quick move, but it feels like I take minutes to do so.

I can hear her breathing hitch, her pupils dilating as I slowly pull away, lifting the tip of my thumb to my lips and licking it clean. Almost like if I try hard enough, I can taste her, not just sugared frozen cream.

"We're heading to a pub," I rasp. "Let's go."

Surprisingly, she doesn't argue or ask questions. Instead, she nods, throwing the rest of her ice cream away in a trash can and following after me.

Chapter Eighteen

Arianna

When I step into the pub, I can feel that my cheeks are still flushing from outside. No, it definitely isn't from the tepid spring temperature. It's from Logan staring down at me like I was on the menu, like I was his dessert. Then, when he reached out and wiped ice cream off my lip before sucking it off his finger? Fuck, I'm surprised I stayed standing. In my head, I passed out then and there. I don't think I've ever seen anything so simple yet so erotic in my entire life.

My eyes land on Ty instantly, who is already at the bar with two drinks. He hands me a shot as he lifts one for himself.

"What is this?" I ask.

"Tequila," he shouts over the music.

"Oh god, what are you trying to do to me?"

"Hopefully get you drunk enough to fall into bed with me," Ty teases.

Throwing my head back, I laugh at that before taking the shot. I set the glass down against the bar top as I cock an eyebrow at him.

"Definitely don't need tequila for that to happen."

He waggles his brows, pulling me towards him and pressing his lips to mine. I don't even know why I put any stock into my interaction with Logan. Especially when I have Ty right here in front of me. He's sweet, funny, and gorgeous. He hasn't fucked my mom, nor is he currently fucking my mom. He's closer to my age. He isn't controlling or broody. He's kinda perfect.

Breaking apart, he presses a quick kiss to my nose before ordering two more shots. Clinking our glasses together, we toss them back, and I wince. How is the second one harsher than the first? Shouldn't it be the other way around?

Looking around the room, I notice karaoke going on in the corner with a ton of people dancing in the middle of the pub. Kind of surprising how many people are out and about in the middle of the week in April.

My eyes stop on my mom who is tossing back vodka sodas like it's her job. Pulling the neckline of her top down, she begins shaking her tits into Logan's face as she starts singing along to the song. She is so fucking embarrassing.

Logan looks down at her with disinterest, though his hand rests on her hip in a possessive hold. I'm not sure if it's there because he wants it to be or because he knows that if he lets her go, she'll wander off to god knows where with god knows who. Uncle Tom looks at her, shaking his head as he lifts his beer to take a sip.

Like they always seem to be, Logan's eyes slowly gravitate to me. A fluttering erupts in my stomach, and no matter how hard I try to fight it, it refuses to give way. It may be the tequila beginning to fog my head, but I'm beginning to forget why I have to fight so hard, why it would be so terrible to give in. I mean, if memory serves me right, both times were easily the best sex of my life. Could that be because they were moments drenched in lust, kink, and passion? Possibly. Does more than a large part of me think that it was really just Logan, that he was the cause behind that feeling of release and freedom?

Absolutely.

"What's going on in that pretty head?" Ty asks with a smile, forcing me to face him.

I feel myself give him a dopey smile as I lean into his touch. Yep, tequila is officially in control here. I blame Ty. Reaching across the bar, I grab Uncle Tom's beer, taking three large gulps as Ty takes it from my hand.

"Easy slugger. You want me to have to carry you home?"

"Sure," I say with a shrug. "It's not like you'd mind."

"Having my hands all over your perfect body? No, I wouldn't mind at all."

"Her mother can hear you two," Logan gnashes over the loud music.

Ty and I look from him to my mother, who couldn't be less interested in what we're discussing. In fact, she's already swaying on her feet, spacing off as she orders another drink.

I know what you're thinking. We don't really mess around when it comes to alcohol. We've been here a whopping ten minutes, and we're all on our way to being utterly trashed. Well, maybe just my mom and me, but still.

"I don't care about that shit," my mom says with a wince from sipping her drink. "She's a grown woman. She should get dicked down."

"Mom!"

"Kelly!"

Logan and I both chastise her at once, causing her to roll her eyes and shrug. Her and Uncle Tom begin chatting about something, and I hear the DJ calling out for any karaoke volunteers. I'm not really sure what got into me, mainly because I've never sang in public before, and honestly, I'm not all that great. What the hell, though, right? I'll never see any of these other people again.

Grabbing Ty's hand, I lift my other in the sky, waving wildly as we rush to the stage.

"What the hell are you doing?" Ty laughs like he's not against it.

I smile at him over my shoulder as I wink. When we get to the stage, I only stumble a step, which isn't bad considering I feel like my entire body is floating. The DJ sets two microphone stands up as he walks over to us.

"What do you guys want to do?"

Before Ty can respond, I blurt out the first duet song I can think of.

"'You're the one I want' by Olivia Newton-John and John Travolta."

The DJ blinks like that's an odd choice, but I don't care. He walks over to his set up as Ty looks at me wide-eyed.

"I don't know that song!"

"Oh, come on, you've never seen *Grease?* Seriously?" I ask in disbelief.

He pauses, and I smile. "You have!"

"I had a John Travolta phase as a kid, yeah, but I haven't sung that song in years."

"Oh my god, this is perfect! Okay, we're gonna do the whole scene, dance and all!" I laugh, clapping my hands excitedly.

He looks out at the room and shakes his head. I think he's about to tell me I'm nuts or something, but instead, he drags me in for a kiss, holding me until the crowd starts to holler. When he pulls away, he gives me a panty melting look.

"Fuck it, let's do this."

I smile excitedly as the beginning music starts. I grab my microphone as Ty does the same before I frantically look around. The DJ has an unlit cigarette behind his ear, and I snatch it quickly.

"Hey! What the fuck!"

"Sorry!" I snicker as I face Ty, holding it between my fingers as I channel Olivia Newton-John.

"Tell me about it, stud."

Ty pauses for a moment, and I think he's going to back out. Then, it's as if I'm watching a rendition of the movie. His performance completely comes alive. He drops to the floor on the word 'electrifying,' and I toss the cigarette on the floor, stepping on it before pushing my shoe onto his chest.

From there, we put on a musical show, and the crowd is eating it up. Everyone is dancing and singing along. Well, everyone except one. Logan is standing with his arms crossed at the bar. Uncle Tom and my mom are dancing, and Logan is just...standing there, staring. It unnerved me at first, but I'm having too much fun to care. So, I play into it.

Pointing at him, Ty and I belt the words.

"You're the one that I want!"

The crowd echoes us before we all sing.

"Oooh oooh oooooh!"

"The one I need! Oh yes, indeed!" I sing into the microphone, my finger still pointing towards Logan.

Once the song is over, the pub erupts into cheers, and Ty picks me up, spinning me around the stage before kissing me. He holds my face tenderly, and I smile into him before we break apart. When we do, my eyes skim over the crowd, pausing on Logan's glare. It feels more aimed at Ty than me, and when I look up to Ty, I see him staring back at Logan.

The DJ ushers us off the stage and we walk back to our

place at the bar, receiving nonstop arm pats and praise from others. Ty wraps his arm around my waist, pressing me into his side as Logan moves to stand beside me.

"Did you have fun?"

"I did." I smile. "I've never done anything like that before."

"You were a natural, you lit up the entire room," he says, his words of praise making that fluttering feeling fire up once more.

"What about me?" Ty intervenes. "I lit up the room too, right, bro?"

Logan cuts an irritated look to Ty but doesn't get a chance to speak when my mother comes barreling into me, literally. She almost falls to the ground as we collectively try to hold her up.

"That's waz amazing! Yourz my daughter. Shez my daughtersss!" she shouts.

"Alright, I think it's time you went to bed," Logan says.

"No!" she says with a wrinkled up frown. "I wants to stay and have more drinks! Bartenderrrr!" she shouts before falling apart into a fit of giggles.

The bartender looks at her, not impressed at all.

"She's gotta go."

Logan nods when Uncle Tom steps in, bending down before tossing my mom over his shoulder.

"I got her. Marissa has been texting me anyways. See you guys in the morning."

"Put me downz you buffalo! I'll beat your asses if you don't," she shouts at Uncle Tom as they slip through the doorway and head towards the hotel.

"What do you guys say? A few more drinks?" Ty asks.

I shrug as I look up at Logan. I hope I don't look as desperate for him to agree as I feel. I don't know why, maybe it's just my lowered ambitions. Maybe it's the way he hasn't taken his eyes off of me for longer than a moment since...well, all day. I don't know how to explain or justify it. All I know is right now, the last thing I want is for him to go home.

Logan looks down at me like he's asking if I want him there, like he'll go if I ask him to. Quick, how do you properly beg someone to stay without saying a word? Puppy dog eyes? Puppy dog eyes. That's what I'm going with.

I might be wrong, but it almost seems like Logan melts right before my eyes. Okay, that may be an exaggeration, but he does soften as he turns to the bartender.

"Three tequilas. Can you make them doubles?" Logan asks.

"Add it to your tab?"

Logan nods as the bartender quickly pours our drinks. We thank him before clinking our glasses together and knocking them back. The sharp burn of the liquor slithers down my throat before settling into my stomach. If I was buzzed before, I know this is about to send me into full-fledged drunk territory. Here's hoping I'm not as sloppy as my mother.

Someone starts singing, and I sway to the music happily. Ty and Logan are chatting about something, but I really can't find it in me to pay attention. Instead, I'm watching the woman on stage absolutely dominate. She's radiating confidence, and her voice is incredible. Oh, the kick she probably got out of our little show. I start snickering to myself, earning the attention of both men.

"What's so funny, giggles?" Ty teases.

"Just thinking about how funny we were up there." I grin.

"Oh, we were the funniest and the best," he agrees.

"What a modest pair," Logan taunts.

"What a stick in the mud you are." Ty rolls his eyes before slipping his hand into mine. "Come on, Ari. Let's show the old man what it looks like to have fun."

I let Ty drag me out to the dance floor, spinning me in circles, bringing me into him before twirling me away again. As if my head wasn't already spinning, I don't know what's moving faster, the world or my head.

Very ungracefully, I slam into his chest, laughing as he holds me upright. I blink up at him lazily as he smiles down at me. I don't even realize the music has changed until something slower plays. It's one of those sexy, fast, slow songs, you know? The kind you'd grind to at a club or something. So, of course, that's exactly what Ty and I do.

He spins me once more so my ass is against his cock before he settles his hands on my hips. I wiggle myself against him, swaying to the music as he grinds against me. I feel him getting harder and harder as my head turns, looking up and locking eyes with Logan. Just like when we were on stage, he has a murderous glare covering his otherwise handsome face. Except, this time, his glare is directly pointed at me.

"You're torturing him, baby." Ty chuckles into my ear.

I break my eye contact with Logan to look up at him.

"I'm not doing anything."

He lifts a brow like he doesn't believe me, dragging me against him harder to prove his point.

"Dry humping his brother right in front of him. So close he can almost taste you but never have you."

I shrug. "That's his own fault."

"How so?"

"Because he knows where to find me."

The words slip out of my mouth before I can stop them. Nervously, I glance up to see that Ty isn't mad, he doesn't even look surprised. Instead, he gives me a small smile and an understanding nod.

"You turn down a man enough, a good one stops trying. Logan is a good man, Ari."

I shrug, trying to focus on the music. Ty doesn't let me,

though. Instead, he cups my jaw, forcing me to look at him over my shoulder.

"If you want him to come over here, all you have to do is tell him."

I frown at that. "What about you?"

"My brother can try to steal you from me. I like my odds." He winks, causing me to laugh.

Ty releases his hold on me, and my eyes instantly snap to Logan's. He's holding onto a new glass of tequila like it's the only thing tethering him to this world. I don't know what to do, what to say to convince him to come over here. I don't even know if I want him to come over here.

Okay, that's a lie.

Without overthinking it, I keep my eyes on him as I softly whisper, "Please."

I'm not sure how he was able to read my lips from across the room. Maybe he wasn't and just instinctively knows what I need. Whatever the reasoning, he tosses back the tequila in one gulp, setting the empty glass against the bartop as he begins moving across the room towards me.

My heart is hammering in my chest, my hands shaking with each step he takes until he is inches from my face. He pauses just short of our chests brushing against each other as he looks down at me while speaking to Ty.

"You giving up?"

"Fuck no, just giving you a chance to get in the race," Ty taunts. "Besides, it's what Ari wants, and I want what makes her happy."

Slowly, Logan lifts a hand to cup my cheek.

"Is that right, Ari? Are you tired of fighting me? Do I make you happy?"

My chest is heaving with ragged breaths, and my head feels lightheaded as I try to process my emotions.

"I don't know."

Logan frowns, his hand slipping to the back of my head, wrapping his fingers around my hair and yanking stiffly.

"Maybe you need some time to think about it."

In the next moment, the song changes, and Logan and Ty both begin grinding against me, one from the front, one from the back. Logan's knee slides in between my thighs, and suddenly, I'm riding his leg while his brother's cock is grinding against my ass.

I could overthink and overanalyze this. Question every single second of it until we all decide it's better that whatever is happening starts and ends here.

But what would be the fun in that?

The brothers sandwich me between them as we all move to the music. One of Logan's hands is still buried in the back of my hair, and the other is resting on my hip, pulling me closer to him. Ty sneaks a hand around the front of my throat, forcing my face to tip backwards and look at him. A sweet smile spreads across his face as he grins.

"Hi."

I smile at him.

"Hi."

He closes the distance between us, our lips brushing together as we sway to the music. Ty's tongue twirls against mine as he deepens the kiss, his hold on my throat true and steady before he breaks away. My head is dizzy, and my eyes are barely open before he's forcing me to face forward. To face Logan.

Logan is staring down at me with a deep hunger in his eyes as Ty continues holding my throat, offering me up like some type of meal for his brother. I feel Ty's lips begin skating against the back of my neck as he murmurs.

"Better take what you want before I change my mind, brother."

Apparently, that's all it takes for Logan. In the next moment, he cups my face on either side, cradling me like I'm something special, like I'm his most prized possession. He tilts my head slightly, staring down at the sparrow tattoo behind my ear before he whispers against my lips.

"Sparrow."

My heart clenches in my chest at that nickname again, and before I can even attempt to control the dizziness I feel from this moment, his lips are on mine. My pulse thunders, my stomach flips, and as corny as it sounds, I swear to god I see fireworks. Pure euphoria rushes through me with just a simple kiss. I forgot what it was like to be in his orbit, to have his attention. He doesn't rush the kiss like Ty always seems to; instead, he savors it, his lips commanding and dominating while still taking his time.

When he pulls away, his chest is heaving, and his eyes are dilated. It's clear that he's just as affected by this...thing as I am. Maybe even more. Before he can say or do anything, the pressure on my neck intensifies as Ty drags me back to him once more.

As he begins kissing me once more, I feel a second pair of lips on me. The feeling of having both of their attention at the same time is unexplainable. Back and forth, I move between Logan and Ty, both more than happy to pepper my neck and chest with kisses until they steal me back.

The tequila in my system is still giving me a lightheaded and floaty feeling. Maybe that's why I can't remember how we got from the pub to the hotel lobby. Did we really just make out the whole way down the road, me staying pressed between these two gorgeous men?

We stumble into the elevator, and Ty drags me inside,

Logan pressing the close button as he follows after, hitting a button before his attention is on me. Ty's tongue is currently down my throat as his hands come to my front, pulling my shirt down, exposing my breasts. He cups one as Logan covers the other. He pulls my nipple into his mouth, his teeth grazing against it as I cry out in pleasure.

The elevator doors open, and we tumble out together. What the fuck are we even doing? What if there was someone waiting for the elevator? We are in the same hotel as my entire family. We could be seen, we could be caught.

Why does that turn me on even more?

I don't realize that we're at the door to our room until Ty hands Logan the keycard. He swipes it and pushes the door open as we move into the room, slamming the door shut. From there, we dissolve into a heap of limbs. I don't know whose mouth is whose, what hand belongs to what man. All I know is that I have two mouths, four hands, and two rock hard cocks on me.

Ty manages to lay on his back while Logan has me pinned to the bed. His hands slip underneath my top, tossing it to the side of the room before he works on my pants next. One by one, each piece of clothing is tossed until Ty reaches for me, dragging me up to him.

"Open," he says as he strokes his bare cock in his fist.

I look up at him as I open my mouth, slowly taking him down my throat. Ty throws his head back in pleasure as I push him all the way down before I come back again, repeating the motion as I wrap my tongue around him.

"Fuck, yes. That's it, Ari," he grits as he reaches down to cup either side of my face, guiding my movements.

I'm now left completely naked as I hear the sound of a belt jingling before I feel the warmth of Logan's head pressing against my pussy. I gasp at the feeling. It's not enough to cross the line, but it's just the right amount of pressure to have me aching for more.

My head turns to the side to look at him. My buzz seems to have faded with the knowledge of what we're about to do. I know what I'm agreeing to. I know that we are about to cross a line we will never be able to come back from. Last time, we didn't know, or at least I didn't. This time, though, I have zero hesitation or regret, which says a lot about my character, I guess.

Wiggling my hips, I encourage Logan, and he doesn't pause for another second. Just like in the club, he violently pushes into me with one thrust. I'm starting to think he can't help it. When he gets that close, he just has to shove into me, like he'll combust if he doesn't.

His piercing rubs against me in a way that has my toes curling as he snarls.

"Fuck."

I pull my mouth off Ty as I speak.

"What's wrong?"

A rough chuckle escapes Logan as his hands tighten on my hips.

"Absolutely nothing, Sparrow. I just forgot what heaven was like."

I smile as I turn to face Ty, who is staring at me with so much heat in his eyes.

"Feel good, Ari?"

Logan's thrusts come in steady and rough, like the carnal raw fucking I've come to know him for.

"Yes!" I moan.

"Good." Ty smiles. "Now, be a good girl and choke on my cock while my brother fucks you senseless."

My pussy pulses at his words before his hand moves behind my head, shoving me down onto him. We all find a sloppy yet steady rhythm, each trying to wring as much pleasure out of this as possible.

Ty is the first one to fall apart. I feel his cock twitch in my mouth, my eyes reveling in the sight as his head falls back and he moans. His cum coats my tongue as I quicken my movements, taking him deeper and deeper, allowing his cum to run down my throat.

When he's finished, Ty looks down and smiles at me sweetly, cradling my jaw as he rubs his thumb against my cheek. Logan doesn't let the moment last for long. In the next moment, he has me flipped on my back and is covering my body with his as he thrusts inside me once more.

I whimper at the intensity of his movements.

"Shh, it's okay. I've got you. I've got you," he promises as he begins peppering my neck with kisses.

My whines soften as I sink into his touch. When he pulls back, he wraps his hand around my throat, squeezing the sides. I can still breathe, but my blood flow is beginning to slow, causing my already dizzy head to feel like it's floating away. I hear the dull sound of a door opening and closing, but I'm too wrapped up in this moment to focus on it.

My eyes lock with Logan's, such intensity in those deep brown eyes. A million different things run through my head. It looks like they are running through his too. We both stay silent outside of our moans, fully sinking into this moment together.

"Logan!" I whimper.

"It's Sir," he grunts.

"Huh?"

"In bed, you'll call me Sir. Or Dom, I liked that."

I can't help but feel a little embarrassed as he reaches a hand up, pinching my cheeks together to hold me in place as he fucks me harder.

"What do you say, Sparrow?"

"Yes," I pant, focusing all of my energy on the pleasure overtaking my body.

His hand holding my cheek pulls back for a moment, lightly smacking me in a way that has my eyes bulging.

"Yes, what?" he asks sternly.

A rush runs through me as I lock eyes with him.

"Yes, Sir."

Another light smack comes to my cheek, and for some fucked up reason, my pussy pulses at that.

"That's my good girl."

I feel my orgasm come out of nowhere. One moment, I'm looking into his eyes, and the next, my back is bowing, my pussy spasming, and my voice screaming. Logan covers my mouth with his other hand as he fucks me through my orgasm. I feel his cock pulse and twitch inside me before he's following me right over the edge.

He slumps against me, his chest heaving as he attempts to catch his breath. When he does, carefully, he rolls us so that he's on his back, and I'm straddling him. I try to pull off him when his hands come to my hips, forcing me to stay.

"You're still in me," I point out with a small smile, the post-orgasm glow still in full effect.

"Good," he growls lowly. "I'm gonna stay inside you all night. Now, just relax and sleep, Sparrow."

Something in his words sends my heart stuttering, and I lay back down, settling myself onto his chest as he stays inside me. My pussy is full of his cum, his cock preventing it from spilling out. Thank god for birth control, or this man would have undeniably just fucked a baby into me.

I notice as I look around that Ty is gone. I frown at that. He didn't have to leave. Where could he have gone, and why didn't I notice earlier? I feel another soft kiss from Logan press against the top of my head, sending a flurry of butterflies rushing through me. That. That's why. Because anytime Logan and I are within a two-foot radius of each other, the rest of the world seems to fade away. I know I'm supposed to feel guilty for that, and in the morning, I no doubt will, but right now, I'm...happy.

I don't know how long we lie there for. Long enough for me to almost say, and then decide against it, a million things. This moment is too perfect. I want to leave it untouched. Preserve it forever. Even if we only have tonight. It's good enough for me.

Chapter Nineteen

Arianna

My eyes flutter open, and the first thing I notice is sunlight streaming into the room. The second is that I'm lying on top of a rock hard body. I look down to see a sleeping Logan beneath me. Holy fuck. For half a second, I forgot what happened last night. Now that it's all coming back to me, though, I can feel Logan's cock still inside me. That has to be some record cock warming, right?

Turning to look the other way, I notice that Ty is lying on the other bed in the room, and he's awake. I give him a small smile, and he returns it, though it doesn't quite reach his eyes.

Carefully, I peel myself away from Logan, sliding out of bed as I move towards Ty. Instantly, I feel Logan's cum run down my leg, but I do my best to hold it in as I crawl in next to Ty.

He lifts up his arm for me, and I hesitate for a moment before deciding to snuggle into him. He presses a kiss to the top of my head and holds me tight for a moment before sighing.

"Where did you go last night?" I whisper.

"What do you mean?"

"You didn't stay in the room after we..." I say, trailing off.

He looks down at me as he lifts an eyebrow.

"Be honest, did you really notice I was gone?"

No, and I feel like shit for that. I was so wrapped up in Logan and...Ty was the last place my mind was.

I stay silent, and he nods, a look akin to hurt passing across his face, but he doesn't let it sink in too deep.

"Felt like I was intruding if I stuck around."

"You weren't!" I insist.

"Hey, Ari, it's okay," he says calmly. "You and I, we were... you said it yourself, casual. But the way you and Logan fucked, there was nothing casual about that."

I frown at his words, even if deep down I know it's true. I can feel the hurt seeping out of him no matter how hard he's trying to fight it. We were casual, we agreed, and I'd be a liar if I said I didn't notice Ty had started developing deeper feelings, though. Maybe I did too. I don't know. Things are just...complicated now.

When I don't speak, Ty continues.

"You and Logan...it's messy, but you guys will figure it out. You're both in it too deep not to."

"I'm not in too deep," I defend.

A sad smile passes his face.

"Whatever you need to tell yourself, Ari."

We're both quiet for a few moments before I look at him again.

"So...are we okay?"

That same sad smile is on his face as he cups my cheek tenderly, similar to last night. He holds me for minutes as he stares, like he's committing my face to memory, before he bends down, pressing his lips to mine. It's a featherlight kiss, tentative and sweet. It also feels bitter, like it's a goodbye, a farewell. I can't lie, it hurts my heart a little.

"We're okay. You and I will always be okay," he says, his lips dragging against mine like he's seeking one last touch.

I smile against his mouth, allowing him to be the one to pull away. When he does, he looks at me once more before releasing a heavy breath. Then, he's pulling his arm out from under me and standing up, moving to the bathroom before the sound of the shower turns on.

Turning to look over, I see Logan is awake and staring at me. I slide out of the bed and move over to join him.

"Are you alright?" he asks.

"Yeah, I just...I think I hurt Ty," I say with a frown.

Logan runs his fingers through my hair in a soothing way as he speaks.

"He'll be okay."

I lift a brow. "You're not very sympathetic towards your brother."

"If I'm honest, I'm still trying to find a way not to be pissed that he touched what's mine. That he..." He trails off.

"I wasn't yours when Ty and I were together. I mean, even now, I'm not—"

"Arianna Marie Fulton, you better choose your next words carefully. If you were about to insinuate that you haven't been mine since I touched you for the first time in that club and that you're not mine now, we are going to have a fucking problem."

"Fuck, you went all full name on me," I tease, though my smile drops when he doesn't smile.

I swallow roughly, shrugging.

"I don't know what to call...this. Just because we want each other doesn't mean it's okay. Doesn't mean we should."

"I don't give a fuck what we should or shouldn't do. All I care about is what you think here," he says, touching his finger to my temple. "And what you feel here," he says, moving his hand to cover my heart.

My heart beats out of rhythm at his words.

"What about my mom? Aren't you two like back together?" I say, the words tasting like acid on my tongue.

"No. You are all I want, Arianna."

I shake my head, wanting to believe him so desperately but terrified in the same breath.

"You two have history, though. I mean, she's your ex-wife and—"

"None of that matters."

My eyebrows lift as he continues.

"What she was to me is irrelevant. She was my past, but you're my future. I know that sounds fucked up. It probably is fucked up, but life is too goddam short to play it safe. I let you slip through my fingers before. I won't let that happen again."

I mull over his words slowly.

"So, what you're saying is that, basically, I have no choice?"

His mouth quirks up on one side, his thumb rubbing against my skin as he speaks.

"You always have a choice, but it won't stop me from locking us in this room and fucking you hard and raw until you agree to be mine."

A smile twitches at the corner of my mouth, but I try to remain composed.

"That sounds an awful lot like coercion, Mr. Cunningham."

"Absolutely. I won't be playing by the rules when it comes to winning you."

"Clearly." I smile at him as he gives me one in return before rolling on top of me effectively pinning me beneath him.

His mouth crashes down on mine, and a relief I didn't know I was seeking, that I was craving, washes over me. His lips move against mine in a way that has my heart thundering in my chest. His hands move across my naked body before one of his hands slips between my thighs. He pushes a finger inside before pausing.

"Are you still full of my cum, Sparrow?"

I shrug. "You stayed inside me all night. I haven't had a chance to clean up."

A low growl rumbles through his chest as he pushes his finger inside me again, slowly pushing in and out.

"That's my good girl."

Pleasure sparks through me, and I feel his cock begin to harden against me when the bathroom door opens.

We startle as Ty comes out wearing just a towel around his waist. His eyes take us in, but his face gives nothing away.

"If you guys are going for a morning fuck, better make it quick. Kelly has been blowing up my phone this morning trying to figure out where you are," he says to Logan.

"Christ," he mutters under his breath, resting his face into my neck before placing a soft kiss to my skin.

He pulls his finger out of me, pushing himself to stand before taking me with him.

"Stall, give us a few."

Ty shrugs as he drops his towel and begins getting dressed, not an ounce of shame as he does. Why should he feel any, though? It's nothing everyone in this room hasn't seen. I still can't believe I did that. I had a threesome with two brothers. My ex-stepdad and ex-step uncle, I guess? Ew, I don't like the sound of that.

Logan and I jump into the shower, and he gently cleans me from head to toe like I'm his deity he'll forever worship. It's such a powerful feeling to have a man like him on his knees for me. He doesn't submit, that's apparent. He is always in control, always in power. A true Dom through and through, so to have him doting on me like this is the absolute best form of aftercare.

Chapter Twenty

Logan

After we showered, I split off and headed back to my room. Mine and Kelly's room if I'm being technical. Relief washes through me when I crack the door open and find the room empty. Good, I'm not ready to deal with her just yet, mainly because I don't know how to explain where I was all night.

I mean, I guess I don't have to lie. It was late. I stayed in my brother's room since there were two beds. I don't have to include the whole sleeping with her daughter thing because that statement alone sounds too cheap, too meaningless for what happened last night.

What was mine finally came back to me, and now that I have her in my grasp, I'm not letting anything get in the way of that. Including her mother.

I can't really describe what I feel when I'm with Arianna, all I know is that it's unlike anything I've ever experienced in my life. She quiets the world around us, calms the storm inside me. With just a look or a simple touch, she has my steel-coated exterior deteriorating, ready to lay bare and vulnerable before her. Two things I've never had any interest in doing with any of my Subs before.

She's not just a Sub, though. She's...everything. *My* everything. I don't give a fuck how fast or rushed or fucking crazy that sounds, I'm keeping her for good.

Quickly, I gather up my things, noticing all of Kelly's is already gone before heading out of the room and to the elevators. When I make it down to the lobby, I see that the restaurant adjacent to the check-in desk is bustling with activity, and a very hungover looking Kelly spots me from inside.

She comes out, moving as fast as she probably can without puking all over the floor. Her huge designer sunglasses cover half her face, and she's wearing a men's dress shirt over a tank top. Wait, what the fuck? That's my shirt.

"What happened to you last night? I woke up this morning, and you weren't there," she says, pulling me in for a hug.

I stiffen at the embrace as I see Marissa watch me curiously as her and her family leave the restaurant, Arianna and Tyson right behind them. Arianna's eyes cut to me immediately, and just one glimpse of her disappointment has me practically shoving Kelly away.

She stumbles a step or two before righting herself. It looks like she's going to ask me what's wrong, but then she's grabbing her head, wincing as she rasps.

"Can we head back to the cabin? My head is killing me."

"Sure," I say. "Let me get us checked out."

"Already did it," Marissa says with a smile.

I give her a grateful dip of my head as we all head to the parking lot and get into our respective cars. This time, instead of the front seat, Kelly makes a beeline for the back, taking up the whole seat as she lays down. Arianna and Ty stare at each other for a moment before I make eye contact with her, silently telling her to get in the front.

She nods, taking the front seat, and Ty silently pouts, his shoulders dramatically dropping before he's shaking his head, sliding into the other side of the back and roughly patting Kelly's head.

"Move over."

She grumbles but shuffles over. However, as soon as Ty sits down, her head is back in his lap. He squirms in discomfort but eventually settles into his seat. Arianna reaches for her seatbelt, but I'm faster, leaning over the center console as I buckle her in. She gives me a funny look as she lowers her voice.

"I'm perfectly capable of doing my own seatbelt, Logan."

I know that she's capable of it. She's more than capable of so much. She's smart, creative, and talented. She is the most capable woman I've ever met. That doesn't mean she should have to be all the time, though. There are people who play the Dom/Sub role only in the bedroom for the kink of it all. Don't get me wrong, it's hot, but when you have a true relationship that extends outside the bedroom, it makes everything that much better.

She is a strong, independent woman, but being her Dom means that she doesn't have to be. To the world, she can conquer anything, and then she can come home and curl up in my lap, knowing she is safe, loved, and cherished. Her being my Sub doesn't mean that she is less than me, that she must obey my every command. It's about a shared trust that I will always act in the best interest of us both, that I will always prioritize her needs above everything else, and whatever she needs, I'll move heaven and earth to provide for her.

I give her a small smile and nod, reaching over and patting her leg. I want more than anything to leave it there but with her mother's face inches away, I decide it's best if I don't.

Forcing my hands onto the steering wheel, I grip it tightly as I begin maneuvering us out of this little town. I always thought it was like magic as a kid, but now that it's the place I've secured Arianna as mine, it's heaven on earth.

We begin cruising down Highway 2, weaving in and out of the mountain lined road. Waterfalls, hills, rivers, and awe-inspiring cliffs surround us every mile we go. It's one of the most beautiful drives in the world.

After a few minutes, I hear Kelly's soft snoring, and after waiting another two minutes, I casually slide my hand over to Arianna, resting it on her thigh. She looks at me cautiously, and I squeeze her thigh, begging her not to deny me this. I can't possibly be expected to go two full hours without touching her. Just my hand against her jean clad thigh sends a calming buzz that envelopes me from my head to my toes.

My thumb begins rubbing mindless circles on her thigh before she smiles at me, gently slipping her hand under my own. Moving my eyes back and forth between her and the road, I lace our fingers together, satisfaction rolling through me because of it.

I glance up to the rearview mirror, catching a look of hurt that passes across Ty's face before he looks out the window. I hate that my brother has to be hurt because of this. I hate that he had the opportunity to fall for her in the first place. I should have worked harder, been more convincing, more compelling. I should have done a better job at proving to Arianna that what we have isn't some weird fetishized fantasy. This isn't just a fling or even the start of a relationship, this is forever. And I'm sorry if it makes me a shit brother, but I won't let anything stand in the way of our forever, even if that means hurting Tyson in the process.

His eyes meet mine, and there is a heaviness there. I sense a bit of acceptance, but I know it's not enough. We have to have a conversation and soon. Clear the air. Hell, maybe he needs to get a hit or two in. I'm happy to cater to whatever he needs because as much as I love my brother, I have no doubt that Arianna will rule my entire goddamn world.

After an hour or so, Arianna reaches down to her purse and pulls out her camera. She makes some adjustments before she begins snapping some pictures out the window. I find myself spending more time watching her watch the world than I do with my eyes on the road. Can you blame me, though? At first glance, she is stunning, but when she has a camera in her hand, when she is seeing the world through her own lens, she completely transforms into an ethereal being. It's a sight all men should witness...from afar.

A murmured noise from the back has me regrettably ready to move my hand when I look back to see Kelly turn her head towards the back of the car, right into Tyson's crotch. She makes another mewling sound as she begins rubbing her face against him. Tyson's nose is wrinkled, and his mouth is pulled into a grimace as he attempts to push her away. Whether she is asleep or somewhere in between, she doesn't stop rubbing her face against Tyson, and eventually, he fully shoves her, sending her tumbling to the floorboard.

"Jesus Christ!" she grouches as I casually pull my hand away from Arianna to adjust the radio volume before resting my hand on the center console.

"You were basically trying to suck me off," Tyson says with a roll of his eyes.

Kelly lets out a derisive snort as she forces herself to sit properly for once, grabbing her seatbelt and pulling it over herself.

"You wish. Sorry, not interested in my daughter's sloppy seconds."

A disbelieving sound escapes me as Arianna sets down her camera and turns to face her mom.

"What the fuck, Mom? What kind of mother talks like that? Could you not be a piece of shit for five minutes?"

She lets out a shrill condescending laugh as she glares daggers at her daughter.

"You're lucky I'm hungover, or I'd smack the fuck out of that mouth."

"Enough," I bark, taking the car by surprise as I keep my eyes on the road.

Kelly backs down, too desperate for my attention and approval to go against me, but I can tell by the way she pouts and folds her arms like a goddamn toddler she's not happy. Arianna huffs, shaking her head as I send her a warning look to drop it. Mainly because if things get out of hand and Kelly puts hands on her, I don't know what I'll do. Arianna is mine to protect now from everyone in this world, including her mother.

We make the rest of the drive in silence, thankfully, and when we get back to the house, Kelly rushes inside before disappearing to take a nap.

Chapter Twenty-One

Arianna

When we get back to the house, everyone goes off and does their own thing. My mom takes a hangover nap, Tyson and Uncle Tom turn on some kind of sporting event, the twins watch a movie in the rec room, and my Aunt Marissa and I begin making lunch. Logan lingered in the kitchen, making small talk with Marissa before he finally joined the guys. I did my best to hide my smile when he'd look my way, but I'm not sure I did a very good job.

My god. I'm insane, right? I've lost my mind. I must have if I'm seriously considering pursuing an affair with my mom's ex. Okay, is it technically an affair, though, if neither of us is in a relationship? That's just called dating, right? Maybe there is some hidden rule of thumb when the age gap is well over twenty years, though.

Jesus.

There is no debate. I am. Fucking insane.

Unfortunately, I don't seem to care. There is so much Logan and I have to figure out. I mean, we don't even know each other that well. It's a strange limbo because we do and we don't. He knows what foods I like, and I know that he prefers to wake up early in the morning rather than stay up late at night. He takes a deep interest in my photography, and I've always been fascinated hearing about his work.

We know each other at surface level, friend level, I guess. We don't know the deep stuff, but then again, I guess we don't have to. There is no rush, in fact, there shouldn't be a rush. We need to take it slow, one step at a time and just...wing it, I guess. I've pushed him away long enough out of some warped moral code that society has created. Age gaps, especially of a forbidden nature, are seen as disgusting, but I couldn't give a flying fuck.

I like him, and he seems to like me. I enjoy who I am with him. I feel safe, free. Like I could push the boundaries in all facets of life, and he would be there ready and willing to catch me within a moment's notice. That kind of trust, that kind of bond, you don't throw it away because things get messy.

People will get hurt when this finally comes out. Ty is already hurting despite how hard he's trying to cover it up. I regret starting anything with him while consciously knowing I was holding...something for Logan. I thought I could push past it, but clearly, I was wrong. Though I know Ty will bounce back quickly, my mother will be another story. She's going to lose her goddamn mind, might even try to kill us all. So, I definitely think Logan and I should wait as long as possible before letting her know about...us.

Once we get back to the city, back to reality, Logan and I can give this a try, and if it doesn't work out, no harm done. If it does and it gets to the point where family has to know...well, we can cross that bridge when we come to it.

"So, things seem to be going well." Marissa smiles.

I look up from the lettuce I'm chopping for the burgers and tilt my head.

"With?"

"You and Ty. He seems really into you," she says as her eyes move to the living room.

As if his ears were ringing, Ty looks over the couch, smiling at the both of us before facing the TV. It's a warm smile, the most genuine one I've seen since last night.

"He's pretty wonderful," I say with a nod and a small smile.

"Are you kidding?" she whisper shouts to me. "That's all I get? Come on. Mel is like a vault, she never wants to talk boys with me! Let an auntie thrive. I'm begging."

I laugh at that, setting down my knife before closing the distance between us. I pull her in for a hug, and she chuckles as she hugs me back.

"Thank you."

"For what, sweetie?" she asks as we pull apart.

"For proving that there are good mothers out there, good female role models to look up to."

A sad look passes over her face as she sighs heavily.

"Your mother loves you, she just—"

"Loves herself more?" I snark.

Marissa winces before running a hand through her hair.

"I wish I could tell you what goes on in that woman's head, Ari. She's just...Kelly," she says with a sad shrug.

"Guess so," I say as I turn back to the toppings for the burgers, arranging everything on a tray before Marissa calls for Tom.

"Tom, burgers are ready to go on the grill."

"Two minutes," he says, staring at the TV as he does.

She shakes her head with a smile and leans against the counter as she whispers.

"So, come on, spill. Is he amazing in bed? I can't lie, when he started coming around, I was sorry I was already married."

My mouth parts, and I admonish her with a laugh.

"Marissa!"

"What?" She laughs. "These women out here are living up their best cougar life. I'm kinda jealous. I'd love to have some hot, spontaneous, forbidden sex."

I'd agree with her, but I can't relate to the wanting. I mean, I had a threesome not fifteen hours ago with two men in this very room. That's pretty hot and spontaneous, and with their ages and the nature of our relationships, extremely forbidden.

"Ty is great all around. In bed, out of bed, and he doesn't skip a meal, if you know what I mean," I say, teasing her with a wink.

She howls out a laugh, attempting to stifle it.

"Oh my god, that's amazing. Tom and I never have time together anymore. Since we had kids, things sort of declined, and now I'm lucky if I get laid once a week. We haven't been together this entire trip," she says, a sadness to her tone as she stares off at her husband.

I frown at that. What the hell is up with that? Marissa is beautiful, not just a pretty face and great hair, but an amazing body. If she was single, she would have a line out the door. Why do so many people, of all genders, give up when they get married? If I got married, I'd want to constantly date my partner. I'd want to fall in love with them every day because life is too short not to, right?

Easier said than done, though, I suppose. I don't know what it's like to balance life and kids and a marriage. Maybe I'm talking out of my ass, but I think she deserves better.

"Maybe you should fire up the hot tub tonight? Even if it's raining, fuck it. Warm, bubbly water and a skimpy bikini sounds like an aphrodisiac to me," I say with a waggle of my eyebrows.

She thinks on that for a second before she nods. "You know what, you're right. I think I will."

"Good." I smile. "Just to clarify, I said fuck it, not fuck in it, because you know we're still here for three more days."

Marissa lets out a laugh that has the guys all turning to investigate what is so funny. Their confused faces only make the both of us laugh harder as Tom stands up, giving her that same look before taking the burgers out to the grill.

We eat kind of a late lunch, so we decide to skip dinner and just snack. We played an impromptu game of pool, which was hard for me since the last time I came in this room, I found Logan and my mom...yeah. That image will probably be burned in my head for all eternity, unfortunately.

My mom didn't surface until around seven at night, looking a hell of a lot more refreshed than she did before. Of course, to fight off her wicked hangover, why would she eat food filled with calories when she can just start drinking straight vodka? I swear to god, her relationship with food is so unhealthy, especially paired with her borderline alcoholism. It's no wonder she's so thin.

After pool, Melanie, Marissa, and I played a few rounds of Uno, which was fun until Mel got a phone call. She hid the phone quickly and ran up to her room, but not before I saw the name Brianna with a red heart beside it. Maybe that's why she doesn't want to gush about boys with Marissa. I'm just glad that she has such an amazing mom that if she ever does want to tell her, she will undoubtedly support her. And probably make Brianna a permanent member of the family within five minutes of meeting her.

I'm sitting in the living room cleaning up the Uno cards when Marissa leans over to Tom seductively.

"So, I was thinking you and I could take a little dip in the hot tub, relax a little?"

He shrugs, barely glancing at her as he lifts his beer to his mouth.

"Kinda tired, babe."

Rejection flashes in her eyes, and her smile falls as she dips her head. She looks two seconds away from crying, and I want to simultaneously smack the shit out of Tom and hug Marissa.

"I'll jump in the hot tub with you," I say softly.

She looks like she's going to decline when Ty cuts in.

"Hot tub? Fuck yes, I'm in."

My mother pulls the vodka bottle away from her mouth as she slurs.

"Oooo, me too!"

She pulls her shirt over her head, dropping it to the floor, revealing her pink lace bra to the room. My eyes pop open in shock as Brady looks around uncomfortably.

"Yeah, I'm gonna head to bed," he mutters, running for his life.

Trust me, Brady, if I could run away from her, I would too.

"I'm in," Logan says, his eyes coming to me despite my mother smiling up at him sloppily.

"Yay! Think I should takez off a fews a layersss," she continues slurring.

"I think you need to go get changed," he says. "Now."

His tone isn't harsh, but it's not warm either. It's just authoritative, and she listens, stumbling up the stairs to her bedroom.

"Come on, Tom. Now you have to join!" Ty says, clearly trying to sway him for Aunt Marissa's benefit.

He nods, finishing his beer before setting the bottle down.

"Sure. It'll be relaxing," he says.

Marissa gives him a smile, but the instant she turns away, I see the disappointment on her face. Why would it have been so hard for him to say yes to just the two of them? He had to be peer pressured into it.

"I'm gonna go help Kelly so she doesn't wear a shower curtain as a swimsuit."

We all chuckle at that as she heads up the stairs, the rest of us following to get changed into our own suits.

Ty and I walk into my room together, pausing when we look at each other. When we left for Leavenworth, we were obviously sharing this room. Now, things have changed.

"I'll take the couch tonight," he says like he can read my mind as he grabs his bag and moves to the bathroom.

"You don't have to do that. We're adults, we can share a bed, Ty."

He lifts his eyebrows in disbelief.

"It's like you've never even met my brother before, Ari. Trust me, he will insist upon it."

With that, he shuts the door. I pause only for a moment before rifling through my things to find a swimsuit. I brought a few, but I haven't worn this one yet. Mainly because it's my skimpiest one. It's black, my tits spill out the top, and the bottoms are considered cheeky, but let's be honest, it's a thong. It's a bold move wearing it in front of Logan, especially with everyone else around. There is something exciting to that idea, though, and I'm slipping it on before I can talk myself out of it.

I know I brought a swim wrap, I just need to find it. Bending down to my suitcase, I continue digging through it when the bathroom door opens. My head whips around to see Ty staring at me with wide eyes. I quickly stand up, grab a sundress, and call it good, sliding it over myself before looking at Ty.

"Fuck, Ari. Are you trying to kill me? I'm trying to be a

good guy but...goddamn, you're not something that's easy to let go."

"Sorry. I didn't mean to—"

"Of course you didn't. Unfortunately, now I'll be a while," he says as he adjusts himself in his swim trunks before heading back into the bathroom. The door shuts, and my jaw drops.

"Ty! Tyson! Don't you dare jerk off in my bathroom!" I say through the wood.

"It's this or you help me. Take your pick," he says back, his breathing becoming a little more labored.

Oh my god.

Shaking my head, I reach for the door to find Logan there, frowning.

"I heard shouting, everything okay?"

"Yeah, everything is fine." I nod.

"Where's Tyson?"

I point to the door.

"Jerking off."

"What?" Logan asks, his eyes narrowing with irritation.

I shrug as he slips past me, banging his fist against the door.

"Tyson!" he snarls. "You're sleeping in my room tonight."

"I figured," Ty calls out.

"Your room?" I ask. "Where are you going to sleep?"

"The only way I'm ever interested in resting from now until forever is with you on top or beneath me."

I blink up at him in surprise as he looks behind us at the open door. His hand lifts to gently cradle the back of my neck as he slowly backs us up away from the door until my back hits the wall. Logan lowers his face to mine, his lips ghosting over my own as he speaks.

"That okay with you, Sparrow?"

"Yes," I breathe out.

"Yes what?"

"Yes, Sir."

I'm panting desperately as his lips skate across my cheek, moving to the sensitive part of my neck as he whispers against my skin.

"Are you going to be a good girl for me tonight?"

"Every night," I correct.

Pausing, he pulls back enough to look at me. Those deep brown eyes have become almost black as he growls under his breath.

"Good answer."

In the next moment, his lips are on mine, his hold on my head tightening, smashing me against him as he dominates my mouth. I become putty in his hands as I soak up every second of his attention because having Logan Cunningham's attention is like sunbathing for the first time after a long winter.

When he tears his mouth away, Ty opens the door, looking plenty satisfied. Logan turns away from me to face Ty, lowering his voice as he speaks.

"Don't you fucking ever jerk off to the thought of my woman again."

"I will definitely be doing that, often. You're just gonna have to get over it, bro. You get the real thing, and I just get... memories," Ty says, his cocky attitude slipping as a wistfulness covers his features.

That seems to strike something in Logan. I know it does in me. He takes a step away from his brother, clearly not happy but...accepting, I guess? Which is such a strange thing to be accepting of, but I feel the same.

Logan brushes past me, pressing a soft kiss to my forehead before slipping out through the door. I look at Ty with a questioning look.

"Did you seriously jerk off?"

He barks out a laugh and shakes his head.

"Fuck no. I just like to rile him up."

A disbelieving chuckle escapes me as I head down the stairs to the hot tub. When Ty and I get out there, everyone else is already in. Marissa and Tom are cuddled up on one side, my mom to Tom's left, where she is basically dry humping Logan's leg. There is barely enough room for me and Ty, but we make it work.

Ty climbs in first, taking the spot beside Logan, which is probably for the best. Gripping the bottom of my sundress, I pull it up and over, dropping it to the floor before looking up. Uncle Tom looks away uncomfortably as Logan and Ty devour me with their eyes, or I guess more specifically, my bathing suit.

I step into the hot water and don't miss the opportunity to turn away from Logan slightly, allowing him a discreet view of my bikini bottoms before I lower myself into the water. When I turn back to face him, his jaw is tight, eyes drenched in lust. He blinks the look away quickly, though.

My eyes move to my mother, who miraculously has both of her eyes open despite how wasted she clearly is. Her face twists up with a sneer as she looks at me.

"Where the fucks did you get that suit? You look like a cheap whore."

"Heyyy," Ty warns, his tone not friendly or playful in the slightest.

He's glaring at my mother, who's completely oblivious as she continues.

"I mean, honestlys, no ones wants to see that! Lose twenty-five pounds, then maybe."

"Enough!" Logan snaps, looking at my mother like she's lost her fucking mind. "That is your daughter, Kelly. I don't give a fuck how drunk you are. You're so far out of line."

"Are you serious? You think you look better than Ari?" Ty scoffs as he reaches out for me, dragging me into his lap.

I don't push away, allowing him to play up whatever he's trying to do. I mean, for all they know, Ty and I are still together.

"Yeah, I do. I—"

"Jesus, Kelly. Just shut the fuck up!" Marissa snaps.

My mom frowns as she looks up at Tom with a pout.

"Your wife is being mean to meeee."

He looks down at her like he's not impressed before shaking his head and looking up at the sky, effectively tuning this conversation out. Logan takes the opportunity to scoot away from her, coming over until he's brushing against Ty. I look to my right to see that I'm basically in both their laps now. Thankfully, beneath the jets, you can't see what's happening under the water. I feel a hand slip between Ty's front and around my waist, yanking me off Ty's lap and into the seat. Logan moves to make room before resting his hand on my thigh.

Ty looks nonchalant as he pulls his arms out of the hot tub, resting them on the edge.

Logan's fingers begin teasing the edge of my bikini bottoms, slipping beneath them when Marissa tries to break the awkward silence.

"So, Logan, how is business going? Any exciting cases you're working on?"

"Nothing that wouldn't bore you to tears. Helping billionaires stay out of jail when they are caught embezzling, or god knows what else," he laughs derisively, his face completely impassive as one of his fingers pushes inside of me.

My breath catches softly, but thanks to the sound of the jets, I don't think anyone notices, aside from Ty, of course. He casts me a knowing look but turns his attention back to the conversation.

"You have to be lonely," my mom interrupts with a slow

flutter of her eyes. She's so trashed right now she's not even really making sense. She's just being obnoxious.

"Pardon?" Logan asks, continuing to pump his finger in and out of me.

"All work and no playyy." She giggles.

As if on cue, the whole hot tub rolls their eyes. I want to do the same, but it's taking everything in me not to fall apart right here in this hot tub. So, I keep my mouth shut and attempt to stay still.

"I have my hands plenty full right now," Logan says as he slips another finger inside me, cupping my pussy as he does.

Fuck.

I feel myself spasm around him as he increases the speed of his fingers. My heart is beating out of my chest as my eyes move around the hot tub. This is the most insane thing I think I've ever done. Forget the high from the exhibitionist room. This is just terrifying. If anyone besides Ty knew what was happening under this water, all hell would break loose. I'm sure of it. The very idea of us teetering on something so dangerous also gets my heart beating faster, my legs trembling in anticipation.

My mom moves in the water, coming closer to us before sitting just beside Logan. You'd think he would pull out of me or at least stop finger fucking me in front of everyone. Of course he doesn't. He just continues thrusting his fingers in and out of me, his thumb rubbing my clit as he turns to face my mom.

"What?" he asks.

She smiles at him, and despite his calm demeanor, I see his pulse thundering in his neck. He's getting a rush out of this just as much as I am. He's inches away from his ex-wife with his fingers inside her daughter. The feeling of getting caught is an exciting one that I'm not quite sure why I enjoy so much.

Marissa and Tom begin discussing something, and Logan casually speaks to me quietly.

"Go underwater when you're ready."

"What?" I gasp, my vision unsteady as my building pleasure begins to cloud everything.

"Now," he demands as he curls his fingers up, thrusting them against my g-spot.

At the last second, I slip under the water, wave after wave of my orgasm thrashing into me as I moan and whimper. Or at least I feel like I do. I'm not sure if any sound actually comes out.

Logan doesn't stop, moving his hand faster and faster until it feels like my body is going to break from so much pleasure. Then, as casually as he slipped inside, he pulls out just as I resurface.

When I do, I emerge away from Logan, closer to my Uncle Tom, as I wipe the water from my eyes. Everyone gives me a funny look, and I shrug.

"I was getting cold."

Everyone shrugs it off except for Marissa, who looks like she doesn't quite believe me.

Thankfully, Ty steers the conversation away from me as he begins talking about a time he got into a fight with a MC member at his bar. During the conversation, Logan grabs my gaze, casually rubbing the tip of one of his fingers over his lip and into his mouth. My pussy pulses as his dark brown eyes promise so many filthy times to come.

Chapter Twenty-Two

Logan

I ended up sneaking into Arianna's room last night after everyone went to bed. It was easy enough since Kelly had to be all but carried to bed before she was retching her life away in the bathroom. Marissa and Tom went to bed shortly after, and Tyson slept in my room.

When I was finally able to sneak into Arianna's room, I found her fast asleep. I planned to wake her up, to fuck her good and hard the way I was desperate to in that hot tub. She looked too peaceful, though. Too perfect.

I wanted nothing more than to be beside her. So, I slid into bed, and wrapped myself around her, covering her body with my own. She stirred for a moment but fell asleep again almost immediately, and I was out like a light in no time as well.

This morning, I slipped out of the room and went about my morning routine like I hadn't had the best sleep of my life over the last two nights. The rest of the day was a slow start. I answered some emails, took a few phone calls and watched as Arianna laid on a blanket in the yard and snapped pictures of the trees above her.

I did that for what felt like hours and enjoyed every second of it.

Kelly woke up sober for once and has been following me around like a lost puppy. I keep pretending to be on extra phone calls just to get some goddamn space from her. I make the mistake of sitting down on the loveseat in the living room and Kelly immediately drops herself into my lap. Ty and Arianna are on the couch watching a movie while Tom is in the recliner. Arianna's eyes come to mine, jealousy brewing in them.

I wish she realized she has nothing to be jealous of. Now that she's mine, I'll never waste an ounce of energy on anyone but her again. That's a fucking promise.

Marissa comes into the room, sitting on the arm of Tom's chair as she looks at me and Kelly.

"I thought we could get out for a little double date tonight? Maybe pop over to Woodinville and do dinner at one of the wineries?"

The word no is immediately on my tongue when Kelly nods excitedly.

"We'd love to," she says, attempting to wrap her arm around my neck. I easily dodge her reach as I gently push her off me completely.

"What about us?" Ty pouts, though I see right through it.

Marissa turns to him, an unusually sharp edge to her words.

"Oh, I figured you guys would want a break from hanging out with the old folks." She laughs.

Ty shrugs the very obvious brush-off away as he drags Arianna into his lap, smacking the side of her ass as he does.

"That's fine, I can spend more time with my girl."

Fire ignites in my veins at his words because she has never, and will never, be his girl.

"I have some more things to catch up on," I say, pulling the room's attention to me. "Next time."

"Oh, come on, Logan. You're on vacation. We only have a few more days," Marissa scolds.

There is a funny lilt to her words, a challenge in her eye. I watch her carefully as she tosses a sly look to Arianna, like she's tracking her reaction.

Shit.

Seems like someone is on to us. Schooling my face, I shrug as I look down at my phone.

"Alright, I can push it to tomorrow morning."

"Yay!" Kelly says as Marissa smiles. "Come on! Let's go," she says as she yanks Marissa's arm harshly, rushing upstairs like they are getting ready for the prom.

Tom sighs like he can't wait for this night to be over already. Same here.

"Wish you would have stuck to your guns. I don't want to go to a fucking winery," he grouches.

"I didn't hear you speaking up?" I say with a lifted brow.

He shrugs his shoulders. "Happy wife, happy life, yeah?"

"Not sure, clearly I didn't have a happy wife." I laugh bitterly.

Tom frowns, nodding like he understands, before facing me a little more.

"She's happy now. She's so in love with you dude. She's desperate for you to give her another chance and from where I'm sitting, you don't seem to feel the same."

My eyes move to Tyson and Arianna, not feeling like having this conversation at all, but especially with an audience.

"I'm just saying, if you don't want her, let her go. If you do, put the girl out of her misery."

If only it were that simple. He doesn't know how messy things have gotten. How bad things will be when the truth comes out, because it will, eventually. There is no way Arianna will go the rest of her life without seeing her family again, and there is no way I'm spending a single day without her by my side. So, something will have to give.

Arianna stands, moving through the living room and up the stairs. I know she's going to her room, and I wait long enough so no one will think anything of it before I stand.

"Guess I'm gonna go get changed."

"You wear whatever the fuck you want, I'm not changing," Tom grunts.

Shaking my head, I meet Tyson's gaze. He's watching me carefully, a blank look on his face. Eventually, he turns his attention back to the TV and I head up the stairs.

I step up to Arianna's room, slipping inside quickly to find her sitting on her bed reading a book. Closing the door behind me, I lock it before prowling towards her. She looks over the top of her book before focusing back on the pages. I reach over for the bookmark on her bedside table and save the page before snapping the book shut.

"Hey! I was reading th—"

I end her argument as I press my mouth to hers. She resists me for a moment before I pull back, keeping her in place as I speak.

"I think Marissa suspects something. She looked at us in a way I didn't like when she suggested the double date. When she turned down the idea of you and Tyson joining. Don't be pissed at me because I'm trying to not raise alarms, Sparrow. You want to tell everyone down there that we are together, I'll lead the way. If you don't, though, then this is what I have to do."

She frowns at that.

"She gave me a look last night too, in the hot tub after you made me come."

I nod. "If you think for a second I'd rather be anywhere but right here, you're insane."

"I just don't like the idea of her throwing herself at you all night," she says with a frown.

I let out a low laugh.

"How do you think I feel about leaving you here with my degenerate brother?"

She gives me a pointed look and shakes her head. "He's not a degenerate."

"The moment I step foot off the property he's going to try to worm his way back in."

"You really think that low of him?"

No, but I know he has feelings for her, and she's too precious to risk. He's a flight risk until I've determined otherwise.

"I'm going to be gone for the shortest amount of time possible, and when I get back, I'm going to spend the entire night making sure it's ingrained into your soul that you are mine, and I am yours."

She smiles softly but doesn't seem to be too convinced.

Alright, I guess we are doing this now.

Scooping her into my arms, she squeals for a moment as I carry her across the room, setting her down in front of the door before dragging her leggings down her legs, tossing them across the room along with her panties before picking her up again.

"Logan, what are you—"

"Shhh. Stay quiet for me. Don't make a sound until I tell you, is that understood?"

Arianna swallows roughly before nodding.

I press her against the door, managing to free a hand to undo my jeans before pulling my cock out.

"Words, Sparrow."

"Yes, Sir."

Gratification washes over me, the beast inside pounding his chest with pride at her obedience. Such a perfect girl for me.

I push into her with ease and when her jaw drops open, she follows my command beautifully and doesn't make a sound. My thrusts are slow and measured, making her feel every ounce of my affection for her as I push and stretch her. I angle my hips in a way I know pushes my piercing against her g-spot, and she immediately turns to putty in my arms. Arianna arches her neck, inviting me to latch my mouth to her skin, sucking and nipping at the delicate flesh, satisfied when I pull away to see her marked with my imprint.

My cock twitches inside her, and I fuck her with a new sense of urgency until I hear the worst sound of my goddamn life.

"Logan?" Kelly calls out for me.

Arianna's eyes spring open in fear when a knock comes from her door. The door I currently have her pinned against. She tries to wiggle away from me, but I keep her still, continuing to push in and out of her as Kelly speaks.

"Ari, have you seen Logan? I want his opinion on my dress."

She looks at me in a panic, and I lift my chin, giving her permission to speak.

"N-no. I haven't! I'm sure what you have on is great. H-he'll love it."

Kelly doesn't speak for several seconds as I slowly pump into Arianna. Her eyes roll into the back of her head before I grip her jaw, forcing her mouth to mine. I feel her pussy tremble around me, a soft whimper escaping her that I quickly punish her for. Sinking my teeth into her lip, her back bows off the door as Kelly speaks.

"Okayyy. Well, if you see him, send him my way."

"Yes!" Arianna shouts, a little too breathily to not raise

suspicions before she clears her throat, shaking her head as her orgasm begins to finish right as my own begins.

I bury my head into the base of her neck, muffling my groans as I begin sucking on the sensitive skin once more. My cock jerks and pulses as it empties inside her.

When we both come down from our highs, I pull away, leveling her with a steady look as I speak quietly.

"I have to go now. Not because I want to, but because it's what's best for now. I'll think of you every second that I'm gone, and when I get back, I'm sliding right back where I belong," I say, punctuating my words by forcing my cock deeper into her.

She gasps as I continue.

"In the meantime, I want you to be a good girl and keep all of this cum inside you, okay?"

"Logan," she whines. "That will be so uncomfortable. For hours?"

I push into her again, so far that she squirms.

"Be a good girl and you'll be rewarded. Disobey and you'll be punished."

"I gotta be honest, my curiosity is piqued with this punishment you speak of," she says, a mirth-filled smirk on her face.

I slowly set her down to her feet.

"Trust me, you don't want the punishment any more than I want to give it to you."

"How do you know?" she challenges as I slowly pull out of her, missing her tight cunt already.

Tipping her chin up, I stare down at her mesmerizing eyes.

If only she knew the fire she's playing with.

I know what she'll choose, though. She's too good not to. Too eager to please, anxious for the praise. She's my good little Sub, and I can't wait to reward her all night long.

Chapter Twenty-Three

Arianna

Brady and Ty are playing air hockey in the den while Melanie and I are in the living room watching a movie. As much as I love this movie, and because I'll never get tired of crying my eyes out to a sappy romance movie, I can't focus on it. Instead, I'm checking my phone every five minutes and looking out the side window for headlights every two.

I don't know why I'm so anxious. I know Logan has no interest in my mom, I know he was only with her on this trip because I essentially shoved him at her, and though he hasn't admitted it, I'll bet anything he was just trying to make me jealous.

It worked.

No, I know nothing will happen between them tonight. Doesn't mean it will be for a lack of trying from my mother. We have two more days until this vacation is over. What's stopping us from leaving now? I'm more than ready to be away from my mom, and maybe Logan and I can...I don't know. Spend time together away from all this and figure out what it means, if it means anything outside this place.

"Why do you keep checking your phone?" Melanie asks.

I look up from my screen, almost unaware that I was looking at it as I smile at her.

"Just texting my friends."

A bald-faced lie. We haven't really spoken much since I've been here. The house has terrible reception and going up and over the pass to Leavenworth wasn't any better. There have been a few check-in messages, but since Cassi's birthday, it's been quiet in the group chat, which is definitely not normal. When I get back, I have to call them and tell them how much my life has changed since that night in the club. I don't even think they'll believe it. Maybe that night has something to do with why they also have been radio silent.

Melanie gives me a disbelieving look that is so similar to one Marissa would give, it's frightening.

"You're not texting, though. You just keep checking it. Like you're watching the time or checking for a message. I thought your boyfriend was in the other room," she says, gesturing to Ty.

I shake my head. "He's not my boyfriend."

"You two are just hooking up then?"

My eyes widen as I blink at her several times.

"How do you even know what hooking up is?" I balk.

She rolls her eyes at me.

"I'm fourteen, not five, Ari. Besides, your mom pretty much talks shit about you and Ty hooking up whenever you're not in the room."

"Language," I admonish, to which I earn another eye roll.

God, my mom really is the worst.

"We're friends," I say as Ty and Brady walk into the room.

"Who's friends?" Ty asks.

"You and me," I say as I look up at him from the couch.

He smiles, his hands coming to rest on my shoulders before dropping a kiss to the top of my head.

"Oh yeah, the best of friends."

I smile at him when the front door opens, Uncle Tom and Aunt Marissa walking in followed by Logan who is carrying what looks to be my passed out mother. Seriously, this is just getting ridiculous. She's always been a partier, but if she regularly drinks the way she has on this trip, she needs help.

Logan's eyes come to mine immediately. I smile at him, but he doesn't return it; instead, his eyes laser in on my shoulders. I frown until I look to see that Ty is still holding onto me. As slyly as I can manage, I move away from Ty before looking to Aunt Marissa who is already watching me curiously.

"Did you guys have a good time?" I ask.

Marissa pauses for a moment, that tint of suspicion still in her eyes.

"We did."

"Until someone killed two bottles of wine herself," Uncle Tom mutters.

Looking towards my mom, I feel my shoulders droop in disappointment as Logan moves through the room.

"I'm going to put her to bed and wind down for the night. I had a good time until..." He pointedly looks down at my comatose mom in his arms.

Marissa and Tom nod their agreement as Logan carries her up the stairs and out of sight. Standing to my feet, I round the sofa, Ty in tow as I lower my voice to speak with Marissa.

"What happened?"

She sighs. "She got drunk, per usual. Started making a total ass out of herself. She was so rude to the waitstaff and then tried to give Logan a blow job in the middle of dinner."

"Jesus," Ty murmurs.

"It gets worse." Tom laughs humorlessly.

"When Logan pushed her away, she started screaming, pulled out her tits, and asked why he wouldn't want them. I mean, thank god there were no children there, but we were obviously asked to leave. It was fucking humiliating."

"I never see her anymore except for holidays and stuff like this. Is she always like this?" I ask.

Marissa shakes her head. "She's gotten worse over the last year or so. Since her and Logan split it's been a slow decline but this weekend? My god, she's consumed more liquor than I thought would be possible for someone of her size."

I exhale heavily before looking up at Ty.

"You ready for bed?"

"Sure. Night guys," he says to them, wrapping his arm around my shoulders.

I give him a look but don't say anything until we round the corner.

"Why did you put your arm around me?"

He shrugs. "Why'd you ask if I was ready for bed? As if we were going to bed together? Seemed like you were putting on an act and I was just playing along. Is it so terrible for me to hold you?" Ty asks as we move up the stairs.

"Yes, it is," Logan answers before I can.

He hauls me out of Ty's hold, wrapping a possessive hand around my hip as he stares at his brother.

"No need to sleep on the floor. You can take my bed tonight," he says, his voice low as he turns us towards my room.

I hear Ty mutter something under his breath, not catching what it is before Logan ushers us through the doorway, shutting and locking the door behind us.

"Did he try anything with you?" Logan asks immediately, like he couldn't hold them in any longer.

"No, of course not."

He blows out a breath and nods. "Good. It was all I could think about, I obsessed over it all night."

"Even if he did, you know I wouldn't have done anything, right? I mean, we haven't really labeled this...thing but—"

"I know," he hushes lightly, cupping the back of my neck as he presses our foreheads together. "You're just too special, too precious. I'm never going to not worry about losing you."

"Losing me? Are you sure you even have me?" I ask with a teasing smile.

His grip on my neck tightens as a possessive growl rumbles through his chest.

"Oh, I've got you, alright, and I'm never letting go. You get that, right, Sparrow?"

I swallow roughly, nodding as he closes his eyes.

"Good."

"What about you?" I ask. "Sounds like you had an interesting night."

He releases his hold on me, standing up straight as he runs a hand down his face.

"Fucking nightmare. Any chance you'd want to leave tomorrow? Maybe tonight even? I just want to be at home, with you."

I give him a half smile at that and exhale roughly. "Tempting, but I think you're right. Melissa definitely suspects something. My mother is very clearly a mess. I don't want there to be any more complications to this than there already is."

He purses his lips like he doesn't like that answer but agrees all the same.

"Fine. We're leaving first thing Friday, though."

"Deal."

"Now, on to more important matters," he says as his hands come to my hips.

His fingers wiggle beneath my waistband before slowly

peeling down my leggings. Logan's fingers move up my thigh, running over my thong before slipping beneath and pushing inside me. It was uncomfortable at first not to clean up after we fucked, and I'm sure I'll be getting a UTI in the future, but the pride that shines in his eyes when he realizes that I did as he asked makes it all worth it.

"That's my good girl," he rumbles as he pushes his fingers in and out of me, shoving his cum deeper and deeper.

A breathy moan slips out of me as he pulls his fingers away, gripping the material and ripping the fabric straight from my body. I gasp at the action as he lifts them in his hand, tucking them away in the pocket of his jeans.

"What are you doing?" I ask.

"These are mine now. In fact, I'm confiscating all of your panties, effective immediately," he says in mock seriousness.

A laugh bubbles out of me as his hands run over my body before he pulls me towards the bed, forcing me to lay on my stomach.

"Face down, ass up," he says sternly.

Something fucked up in me loves it when he bosses me around like this. When he's being an ass during day-to-day conversation, definitely not, but in the bedroom? Absolutely.

I feel his hands grab my leggings that are currently sitting around my ankles. He pulls them off, tossing them to the side before the zipping of his pants echoes in the room. I feel his hips line up to me as he slips an arm beneath my stomach and hauls me into the air.

"Get that ass up in the air, Sparrow. Let me see all of you."

Doing as he says, I arch my back as much as I can, forcing my ass up for him as he groans. His hand massages my ass cheek before coming down with a sharp crack. I yelp as the pain rips through me before his other hand digs into the back of my hair, yanking sharply as he lowers his mouth to my ear.

"Quiet, Sparrow. You're going to take all I have to give you as silently as possible. Make a sound, and I stop. Understood?"

A moan is right there, ready to be released, but I swallow it down as I nod my head quickly, earning myself another sharp slap. I flinch but don't make any noise, and his deep voice growls against my cheek.

"Good fucking girl."

Another slap. Then another. I feel my ass turning red and hot, but my pussy is beyond dripping. It's a strange pain/pleasure combo that has me dangling in some kind of lust limbo.

"Touch yourself," he says as he makes a rustling sound.

I do as he says, my fingers swirling around my clit when he smacks my ass.

"Not your clit, your cunt. Shove your fingers in your cunt. Finger fuck yourself for me."

Turning to look at him over my shoulder, I see him lean back to watch, his eyes darkening to black as I push two fingers inside myself. Slowly, I move them in and out, enjoying the way it feels.

My eyelids flutter but open wider when I see Logan pull out a bottle of lube. My brows furrow and my mouth opens to ask him when he brought that in when he lifts a finger to his lips, signaling me to stay quiet. I do as he says before he squirts a generous amount of lube onto his fingers, coming down and spreading it over my asshole.

The cold liquid catches me by surprise for a moment, and my body tenses before he whispers against my back.

"Easy, relax for me, Sparrow. Let me in."

Closing my eyes, I blow out a soft breath and loosen my muscles. Logan pushes a finger inside me, and I tense, the feeling of both my own fingers inside me and now his making me feel too full. It reminds me of the club when we used the plug, though I know I won't be just getting a plug in my ass tonight.

Slowly, he works me until I'm able to take more before he inserts another finger, then another. The stretch burns and I sink my teeth into my lip until it slowly subsides. I don't know how long we stay like that, me trying to muffle every whimper and moan while he takes his time stretching and working me until he's satisfied.

"Ready for me?" he asks.

My stomach flips at his question, nerves fluttering inside me as he presses the head of his cock to my asshole and slowly begins pushing in. Fuck. This is worse, this is much worse. I usually enjoy anal, especially with proper foreplay, which Logan achieved tenfold. Having my pussy filled at the same time, though, it feels like too much.

I pull my fingers out and Logan catches it instantly, speaking as he continues inching his way inside me.

"I don't remember telling you that you could pull your fingers out, Sparrow."

"Please," I whimper.

His movements pause and the temporary relief is welcome, until my body throbs, aching for more.

"You make a sound, I stop. That was the rule. Are you going to stay quiet for me?" he says lowly, keeping his voice just above a whisper.

I nod my head, swallowing roughly as his hand massages my ass cheek lovingly.

"Good, now be a good girl, and get that cunt nice and full like she belongs."

Taking a deep breath, I push two fingers back inside myself just as Logan fully seats himself in my ass. He lets out a low rumble as a gasping breath escapes me. It must not be too much noise because he doesn't stop. Then again, maybe he can't.

I turn around to look over my shoulder at him and find him in a daze. He's looking down at us, mesmerized as he watches his cock go in and out of my ass, my fingers pushing into me before I pull them back out and do it all over again.

"Goddamnit. You're so perfect. You take me so fucking well," he groans.

I want to tell him how perfect he is, how perfectly we fit together, but instead, I bury my face into the pillows, riding out every wave of pleasure that overtakes me.

Logan takes it slow at first, allowing me time to get used to him before he begins savagely thrusting inside me. My mouth drops open when he hits a spot that I love and I push my ass into him, begging for more.

His thrusts line up with the rhythm of my fingers perfectly and in the same breath, we fall apart together. I feel my pussy and ass spasm as my orgasm washes over me and Logan's muffled groans nearly shake the walls of this room. His cock pulses inside my ass as he fucks his cum deeper and deeper. Christ, at this point I'm going to be drowning in his cum.

Something tells me that's the idea.

We fall apart into a heap of limbs, gasping for breath as the high from our orgasm fills our heads. We lay there for a few more seconds before Logan slowly pulls out of me and stands to his feet. He pulls off his shirt and pushes his jeans all the way off before scooping me into his arms. I'm still wearing my shirt and bra, but he makes quick work of tossing those to the side before he's leading us into the bathroom.

With one hand, he starts the shower, walking us into it once it's warm enough. He presses me against the wall before resting his head into my neck. He doesn't say anything and neither do I. We just stay like that in perfect silence, my fingers slowly scratching his head. He sinks into my touch like he's never felt anything like it before pulling away from me and looking deep into my eyes.

"I hope you're ready for this, Arianna. I've been trying to hold myself back, slow this thing between us down, but I'm afraid I see no stopping now."

A soft smile passes across my face.

"This was you trying to hold yourself back?"

An amused sound escapes him as he presses his mouth to mine, his lips moving softly, our tongues tangling together languidly before he pulls away. A feeling of disappointment washes over me at the missed connection before he changes the water from shower to bath, plugging the drain and lowering us down. It's not a huge bath, so it's a tight squeeze, but I end up cradled in his lap which I can't deny is a pretty fantastic place to be.

As the water begins to rise, Logan reaches up for the body wash, squirting some into the water and creating a bubbly bath all around us. He begins cupping the soapy water over my body, massaging every inch of my skin. I sink into his gentle touch, such a sharp contrast from the firm and harsh touches that I just experienced. That's the beauty of it, though. It's a perfect balance. He's rough and doting. Stern and kind. He's a perfect storm, and no matter which version he is in that moment, I never doubt that I'm not the most important thing to him.

I don't remember closing my eyes or falling asleep. All I can feel is his hands on me, the hot soapy water filling up inch by inch and slowly, my eyes flutter closed.

Chapter Twenty-Four

Logan

It felt nearly impossible to leave Arianna alone in her bed after she fell asleep in my arms. I held her in that bath until the water ran cold, and then I got us out, drying us both off with a towel before tucking her into her sheets. I peppered her face with kisses and promised her things I don't think she's ready to hear consciously. Then, I went back to my room where I found Tyson hogging the entire bed. I smacked him in the head, and he woke up just enough to roll all the way to the wall. Good enough. At least I knew if he was sleeping in my room, he wouldn't sneak into Arianna's.

Goddamnit. I'm starting to feel like a piece of shit for thinking so low of him. I know he wouldn't do that, especially if Arianna has expressed disinterest in him. I was definitely not sleeping when they were talking at the hotel in Leavenworth. I need to give him the trust he has earned and deserves. It's just so much easier to operate under the guise that everyone is against you and out to get you. He isn't the prosecutor, though, he's not a judge. He's my little brother. We're all each other has in this world, and I need to step up and start acting like it.

I'm getting out of the shower the next morning, sliding on a pair of jeans when I feel something in my pocket. Pulling out the scraps of red lace, I smirk to myself. Almost forgot I took these as a memento last night. Tucking them back into my pocket, I pull on a black button down because jeans are about as casual as I can get.

Tyson steps into the room, towel around his waist from using the downstairs shower, and looks at me with a suspicious gaze.

"What are you smiling about?"

I school my expression before shaking my head.

"Nothing."

Tyson sighs, shaking his head before moving to his bag. I didn't realize he already brought it in here.

"She'll do that," he says as he begins getting dressed.

"Do what?"

"Make you smile for no goddamn reason. Give you a reason to smile for no reason. She just has this...light about her," he says with a ghost of a smile, though it falls when his eyes come to me.

"Ty..." I trail off, frowning as I look at my little brother.

He shrugs like he doesn't care when we both know that's a lie.

"No hard feelings, bro. I get it. You saw her first, she chose you. I'm good. We're all good."

I don't say anything, mainly because I don't know what to say. As a good brother, shouldn't I want to step aside? Let him be happy and have the girl? Because I don't and I won't. I'll give him whatever he wants in the whole world. Anything but her.

"It's just..." he starts as he pulls on a shirt, his eyes coming to mine. "Don't make her regret that choice."

My brows furrow as I cock my head to the side curiously.

"What do you mean?"

"I mean, be worthy of her attention, of her affection. Don't fuck this up. She deserves your absolute best and if you can't give that—"

"I can. I promise," I say as I hold out my hand for him.

He watches me for a moment like he's not sure if he believes me, but slowly nods in acceptance, taking my hand in his as he lowers his voice.

"You know I'll kick the shit out of you if you hurt her, right?"

I shove him away, shaking my head smugly.

"Little boy, I'd like to see you try."

He jumps at me, trying to wrap me up, but I easily twist out of his hold, keeping him in a headlock like I did when he was a kid. He struggles against me as we move around the room, but my hold on him never wavers. Eventually, he taps out and I release him. Tyson scrubs a hand through his hair, panting heavily.

"Damn, I was just joking. You didn't have to go all Hulk smash on me," he grunts like he wasn't trying.

I roll my eyes and pat his back, urging him forward as we make our way downstairs. Everyone's already eating breakfast, but my eyes seek out Arianna immediately and find her already looking at me. She smiles before covering it with a sip of orange juice, but I have no such tool. So, I just grin. I grin like a goddamn fool in love. Because I am, or at least it feels like love. I know that sounds psychotic, but I don't really give a shit. I've never felt this way about anyone in my life. It's the closest thing to love I'll ever feel. I love that girl right there, and one day, she'll love me too. I'll make sure of it.

Tyson and I take up the empty seats, one beside Arianna and another between Kelly and Tom. As much as I hate it, I know where we're expected to sit. So, I take my spot beside Kelly, ignoring her presence completely as I grab some eggs and bacon from the serving plates, looking at Marissa with a grateful smile.

"Thank you for breakfast."

She waves me away like it's nothing when Kelly speaks, effectively spoiling my good mood.

"Can we talk? In private?"

Her voice is just above a whisper, and I turn to look down at her. God, she looks awful. Her face is pale and gaunt, like she's been puking out what little weight she has left all night. Her hair is in a greasy bun, and she's wearing a baggy t-shirt and sleep shorts without an ounce of makeup on her face. I know something is seriously wrong because she'd sooner be on her death bed than be seen by anyone without being fully presentable. I was her husband, and I probably saw her without makeup less than a dozen times. That's how vain she was.

"I'm not sure there is anything to say, Kelly."

Tears begin welling in her eyes as she looks up at me pleadingly.

"Please, Logan. I need to apologize. Explain. I've just been under so much pressure at work, and I'm so lonely all the time. I miss you more than anything in the world. I just didn't want to screw that up and—"

"Drop it," I say lowly, my eyes moving around the table.

Everyone is pretending to mind their own business, but make no mistake, every last one of them is eavesdropping.

"I can't!" she says, reaching her hand out to my thigh. "Marissa told me what happened last night. I'm so embarrassed. So ashamed. Can you please forgive me?"

Fuck, this is exhausting. "You don't need my forgiveness, Kelly."

"I do, though!" she says, her hand moving to hold onto me tighter like that will stop anything. "I need you to forgive me so that we can—"

Her words stop abruptly, a strange look passing her face before she looks down. Slowly, she lifts up torn-up red lace panties.

Fuck.

She holds them high above the table, capturing everyone's attention. Her eyes stay on them for a long time, like her brain is carefully analyzing them in an attempt to figure out what they were doing in my pocket. My eyes move across the table to see Arianna wide-eyed with terror, Tyson's mouth hanging open and Melissa and Brady watching with confused expressions.

Marissa quietly leans over to them, whispering something before they quickly get up and move upstairs. That seems to set Kelly off.

"What the FUCK!" she snaps, shoving her chair back so violently it rocks the table.

She's on her feet instantly, her eyes wild and furious as she screams.

"Why the fuck do you have ripped panties in your pocket, Logan?!"

I don't say anything because I have nothing to feel guilty for. Okay, maybe that's not entirely true, but it's not like I'm going to apologize to her for it. I won't lie or backpedal. So, I just let her rage.

"Are you serious right now? You're so fucking serious? You come all the way out here to try to reconcile with me, and what? Accidently slip into her?"

My face remains impassive, and she lets out a humorless chuckle that sounds downright diabolical before turning to the table. I watch Tyson place a protective arm across Arianna, like he's ready to push her away at any second. Instead, Kelly's eyes come to Marissa.

"You fucking skank!" she screams.

Marissa looks taken aback as she stares at her sister.

"What are you talking about?"

"You! You fucked him! You took the one man I've ever loved and fucked him right when I was just getting him back!"

What?

Marissa jumps to her feet, brows pinched in confusion.

"I don't know what you're on about but—"

"Did you tell her, Tom? Is that what this is? Some disgusting revenge plot?" Kelly snarls.

Tom turns as white as a ghost as Marissa's brows knit together. She looks down at her husband before back to her sister.

"Tell me what, Tom?"

He stares straight ahead, not moving a muscle as Kelly lets out another wicked sounding laugh.

"We've been fucking for years. When you're not looking, he comes onto me hard, sometimes I give in if I'm drunk enough. He fucked me for the first time the night before your wedding. He begged me to marry him instead, saying we'd run away together before he dumped his load inside me."

Shock ricochets around the table as Kelly continues.

"So, did he tell you? Is that why you tried to steal the only sliver of happiness I had in this life? Or did you hear us Friday night? I told him to stop moaning so goddamn loud."

"Wait, wait, wait. Wait. You're saying that you've been fucking my husband for fifteen years? You're saying that you fucked him as recently as Friday? Like this last Friday? Four days ago? With me and our children in the house, that's what you're saying?" Marissa stammers.

A vengeful smile spreads across Kelly's face as she nods.

"He told me that I was the best pussy he's ever had."

Oh god. When he was drunk, yammering in the rec room

with me. He wasn't talking about Marissa, he was confessing his affair with Kelly.

"After he told me that he was in love with me," she says with a raise of her eyebrow.

Marissa stares down at Tom, pure heartbreak in her eyes, her voice cracking as she speaks.

"Tom..."

He takes a sip of his juice, still not looking up at the train-wreck around us.

"I want a divorce," he says stoically.

A broken sound escapes Marissa as the hurt in her eyes transforms into something dangerous.

"You fucking WHORE!" she screams as she leaps across the table, smacking, scratching, and beating the absolute shit out of each other.

"You've ruined my life!" Marissa shouts.

"You've ruined mine! How could you fuck Logan?"

A sharp slap jerks Kelly's face to the side as Marissa laughs bitterly.

"How could I...How could you fuck my HUSBAND?"

"He always initiated. I'd never do that to you," Kelly defends.

Marissa's eyes widen in disbelief because, honestly, what kind of fucking excuse is that?

"What you did was so much worse," Kelly snarls as she shoves away from Marissa, standing to her feet. "My Logan would never have come onto you, which means you seduced him!"

Her moral compass is so fucking skewed it's incomprehensible.

"You stupid cunt, I never fucked Logan!" Marissa shouts.

Here we go.

"Yeah, right." Kelly laughs like she doesn't believe a word.

I see Tyson positioning himself between him and Kelly more as Marissa continues.

"Yeah. Right. Never. Those aren't my panties, and they aren't your panties, so I wonder who they could belong to," she says, giving Kelly a deadpan stare.

The fury in Kelly's eyes shifts for a moment, confusion clouding her gaze before understanding clicks in. Like something out of a horror movie, she slowly turns her head to face Arianna. Guilt is etched all over my sweet girl's face before an animalistic screech rips out of Kelly.

She dives for Arianna, landing a sharp slap across her cheek before Tyson holds her back, picking her up and throwing her over his shoulder. He walks her to the other side of the room where she rages like a wild animal.

I rush over to her, cupping her face tenderly as I examine where her mother struck her.

"We messed up so bad," she whispers softly.

"No, we didn't, Sparrow."

She opens her mouth to say something when Tyson screams.

"The bitch bit me!"

Kelly storms across the room towards her daughter as I intercept her, holding her by her arms.

"Kelly! Enough!"

She thrashes against my hold, vibrating with feral rage as I shake her harshly.

"I said enough! Do you hear me! You've done enough!"

"Me?" she gasps. "What about you! You've been fucking my daughter! How long? How long have you been fucking us both? Since we got married? Before? Did you leave me for her?"

"No, Kelly, we aren't all disgusting homewreckers like you!" Marissa shouts.

"Shut up!" Kelly screams before looking back at me.

"Arianna and I were together long after you and I divorced."

"But not long after you were inside me!" she snarls.

"Remember that, *Ari*. Remember when you walked in on your *boyfriend* inside your *mommy*?" she says, sneering every name as she gnashes her teeth.

Arianna looks like she's going to be sick as she looks away.

"If you're gonna be a slut, at least own it. You're fucking a man old enough to be your father. Hell, he was your father. Step up and claim your prize, you worthless fucking whore!"

"SHUT UP!" I thunder, loud enough to stun the entire room into silence. "Shut your fucking mouth right now. You are done. You are selfish, miserable, and ugly as fuck on the inside. You've betrayed your sister, happily it seems, for decades. You've attacked your daughter and reduced her to nothing her entire life. All you see is yourself, your goals, and your desires. No one else in the world matters besides you. That's why I left you. Not to mention you cheated on me. Sounds like it was more than once if you and Tom were fucking while we were married. Tom?" I ask for clarification.

The slimy bastard seems to have no shame as his eyes cut to me, and he gives a quick nod.

Thought so.

A horrified sob escapes Marissa as she runs off to the bathroom, slamming the door shut as she does. Tom sighs, standing to his feet and heading for the back porch. He's not even going to attempt to console his wife or apologize or anything. Real nice guy.

Tears are streaming down Kelly's face as she looks up at me hopelessly. I'm not finished with her yet, though.

"We are nothing, we've always been nothing. Even when we were married, clearly, it meant nothing. Do not call me, do not reach out to me. If you so much as take a step closer than three hundred yards to myself or Arianna, I will have you arrested on site. We will be filing a restraining order against you, today. Goodbye, Kelly. It's been a complete displeasure to know you."

She sobs, falling to her knees as she lays on the floor. I don't try to soften the blow, and I don't pay her an ounce of attention as I hold my hand out for Arianna. I'm surprised how quickly she takes it, lacing our fingers together as we make our way up the stairs.

When we get to the top, Brady and Melissa are staring at us with looks of concern and heartbreak. I give them sympathetic frowns as we move past them, heading for Arianna's room first.

Wordlessly, I begin helping her pack when Ty comes in, staring at his forearm with a frown.

"Fucking bitch. You think I could get rabies? Or whatever STD she no doubt has."

My stomach sours at that. I didn't consider STDs when I fucked her on the pool table. I should have, though, knowing her. Arianna and I share a worried look, and I rest my hand on her shoulder as I nod, letting her know I understand her fears and we'll take care of anything when we get back to Seattle.

Once Arianna is all packed, we grab mine and Tyson's things before heading downstairs. I look out the back window to see Tom and Marissa arguing before Marissa slaps him across the face. Good for her.

Kelly is still curled up into a ball, sobbing a puddle of tears on the floor. None of us give her a second look before we are out the door and heading to our cars. I hate that Arianna has to drive right now, given everything. With the state of things, though, I don't trust that her car would be safe here.

Tyson starts up his car while we load our bags. He comes around to hug Arianna, whispering something into her ear that

I miss. She hugs him tightly, nodding before giving him a watery smile. He returns it, taking her hand and pressing a gentle kiss to the back of it before getting in his car.

Arianna turns to me, and I immediately pull her into my arms.

"I'm so sorry. I know that was probably the worst case scenario."

"It's fine. I just want to go home."

I couldn't agree more. "I'm gonna take you home, Sparrow. Follow me."

She swallows, giving me a shaky nod before I lift her chin up, bending down to press my lips to hers.

Chapter Twenty-Five

Arianna

When Logan said that he was going to take me home, I thought he meant my apartment just off campus. No, apparently, he meant *his* home, which is a sprawling six bedroom, four bath mansion on a huge chunk of land. Sometimes I forget that Logan isn't just well off like my mom has been since she got into real estate. He's fucking wealthy.

We have spent almost every second since being back in Seattle in bed. We only left the house for the occasional takeout meal, and to get STD panels, luckily both of which came back clean. Our days consisted of, eating, showering, and copious amounts of sex.

It. Was. Perfect.

Now it's Sunday, though, and I have my first class at seven in the morning, which means I need to head back to my apartment and get all of my things together. Logan disappeared to his office a few minutes ago for an important phone call, so I decided to gather up my things and get ready to leave.

Once my bags are at the front door, I move down the marble floored hallway in search of him. I hear his voice muffled through the closed door and I slowly peek my head through.

"No, we're not going to take a plea bargain, and I'll tell you why, Gerry. As soon as he takes that plea—"

His words pause as he sees me.

I mouth to him that I'm going to go as I point to the door, and he frowns.

"One moment, Gerry," he says before setting the phone on his desk.

"Where are you going?" he asks.

"I have class tomorrow. I need to head to my apartment, get ready, and get to bed at a decent time."

Pushing to his feet, he moves away from his desk towards me. His dark hair is styled perfectly, a white button down shirt wrapping around every muscle he has. Muscles I've become extremely well acquainted with over the last seventy-two hours.

He hmphs at that, running his fingers through my hair as he turns his head to the side like he's in thought.

"You could always stay."

I smile at him, enjoying the feel of his hands on me.

"I wish I could, but I want some new clothes. I need my laptop. I haven't been to my apartment in almost ten days, Logan."

"We can bring it all over. There is more than enough room for you...I want you here."

My eyebrows raise. "You mean, like, you want me to move in...here...with you?"

He nods, his fingers burying deeper into my hair before tightening his grip. A surprised gasp escapes me as pleasure sparks inside me. Goddamnit, why does this man have to be so intoxicating? When he leans in close, his mouth ghosting over mine, I can hardly remember my own name, let alone what we were discussing.

Moving in. Right. With him. Is he fucking nuts?

"We just started...seeing each other, Logan. I can't move in with you."

"Why not?" he challenges easily. "Is it the house? I can sell it. I have a penthouse downtown that I rent out. We can move into it within the month if that's what you want. Or I can look into a new property, you can pick it out. Whatever you want."

I look at him like he's delusional.

"You can't buy a new house because of me or sell your old one. No, it's not the house. The house is lovely."

He frowns, his grip on my head loosening as he drops his hand by his side.

"Then what's the issue?"

"The issue is..." I'm left speechless for a moment as I try to process what he's saying. "I can't move in with you! We just started dating, if you can even call it that. I can't just give up my housing and hope this thing between us works out."

"It will," he cuts in. "Work out. Us."

"You don't know that, not for sure. In case you forgot, we have a lot going against us," I laugh humorlessly.

"I don't give a fuck about anything but what you think here," he says, touching my temple before his hand skates down to my chest. "And feel here."

The reminder of his words at the lake house do something to me. I feel my heart ache as if it were desperate for him to touch it. To cradle it in his hands and keep it safe and protected from now until forever. That's just a fantasy, though, right? That's not rational. It's not real life.

Right?

"Logan," I say on a soft whisper as I shake my head.

"Don't," he says, holding his hand over my heart as he presses his forehead to mine. "Don't sell us short, Sparrow.

We're on the verge of something great, something perfect. You just have to be brave enough to fly with me."

Am I crazy, or are his words actually wearing me down? Shit. No. I can't. I can't do this. I can't move in with a man on a whim, that's just so outrageous I couldn't even begin to list the ways. What if I'm his midlife crisis, what if I drop everything for him and he leaves me on the sidewalk in the cold when he gets tired of me?

The look in his eyes promises that he would never do those things, and I know it's stupid, but I believe it. I believe him. This pull, this...draw. It's the realest thing I've ever felt, and just seeing how off kilter it's thrown him over the last week, I think he feels the same.

"You're crazy," I say with a teasing laugh.

He smiles, though, because he already knows that I'm caving.

"I'm persistent."

"You're a tad manipulative," I counter.

His hand moves from my chest to my jaw, cupping it gently as he looks down at me reverently.

"Only when I'm doing what's best for us. You know that, right? You trust me to take care of you, to take care of us?"

My nod comes immediately. I trust him more than I've trusted any other person. Whether he has earned or coerced that trust, it's hard to say. Our entire relationship started with a lust drunk night and damn near every moment spent together has continued that way. Moments filled with tension, heat, and passion.

I mean, there are worse ways to live life.

"I do," I say.

Saying those words seems to physically do something to Logan. Like I've just given him the most precious gift he's ever received. Like he could die a happy man from this moment on.

He is the one who is always so in control, so dominant, but right now, I feel like the one with all of the influence, and it's an incredibly empowering moment.

"Then I'll call movers once I'm done with my call. Your things will be here tonight, ready for your classes in the morning, okay?"

I smile softly, my heart beating wildly in my chest as I prepare to agree to perhaps the craziest and stupidest thing I've ever done.

"Okay."

His lips come to mine and my chest immediately fills with butterflies. My arms wind around his neck when he breaks apart.

"We'll be celebrating properly soon. I need to finish this call. Come," he says easily.

I do, of course. I follow along willingly as he laces our fingers together and pulls me towards his desk. Taking a seat, he pats his lap gently, and I take the cue. I perch myself onto one of his legs and his hand reaches out, pulling my legs all the way over his lap so I'm curled up on him completely.

He presses a soft kiss to my forehead as he turns his phone onto speaker and begins mindlessly stroking the sensitive skin of my ankle. I rest my head against his chest and his other hand comes up, running his fingers through my hair as he begins speaking.

"Sorry about that. Where was I?" he asks.

An older sounding man begins talking, both falling into a heavy conversation about an upcoming trial. My mind quickly wanders off, lost in the feel and sound of his deep rumbling voice. I haven't heard from Aunt Marissa, not that I'd expect to. She's grieving a horrific betrayal, and who knows what's going on between her and Uncle Tom. By the sounds of it, he's not sorry or looking for reconciliation, which is disgusting because she deserves so much better.

I still can't believe my mother has been betraying her own sister for years. She cheated on Logan with...him? For years. I'm speechless. And then my mother had the audacity to be mad at Marissa because she thought she did the same with her ex-husband? It would have been better if she did! Of course, she can't see that, though. She's never in the wrong.

I realize that this weekend permanently cemented her out of my life, and I know I should be sad about that. Maybe one day I will be, but not today.

Since we left the lake house, I also haven't spoken to Ty. There was no real need, I guess. Logan and I have been more than a little preoccupied, but the reminder of him has me feeling the need to check-in. I didn't realize how much I adored him until this week. I missed him in my life, and I don't want another three years to go by before I see him next. Then again, if I'm living with his brother now, I'll bet that I'll be seeing him sooner than later. I hope things will be okay between us when everything...settles. Lines were blurred on that lake, things got messy, but I hope out of the rubble, that can be one relationship that's salvaged.

I glance up to see Logan already looking down at me, smiling softly as he talks on the phone. It still doesn't feel real. That I'm here, that we're together. The gravity of our situation is so heavy, you'd think I'd be suffocating. When in reality, I've never felt more free.

Chapter Twenty-Six

Arianna

I'm rushing into my advanced photography class at seven on the dot. The professor gives me a look but doesn't say anything as he shuts the door behind me. Cassi and Naomi wave at me from the corner where an empty seat is beside them.

Thank god.

They took this class because they thought it would be an easy pass. Depending on the surliness of our professor, I'm not sure how easy any of this is about to be.

"Dude, you live right across the street. How can you be the last person here?" Cassi laughs under her breath.

Shit. Yeah, we all really haven't caught up in...fuck too long.

"Uhm, yeah. So, I'm kind of not living there anymore."

"What do you mean?" Naomi whispers.

"I moved," I say, wondering if that will give them enough to drop it. Of course, it wouldn't, though.

"Where?" Cassi asks.

The professor begins introducing the class and expectations as I look to my best friends, quickly shaking my head as if to say not here. They look disappointed but drop it as we focus our attention up front.

As soon as class is dismissed, though, their questions pick right back up.

"Where did you move? When did you move?" Cassi asks.

"We could have helped you!" Naomi adds.

"So, uhm, remember your birthday?" I ask Cassi.

She freezes for a moment before nodding softly.

"Well," I continue. "I hooked up with someone."

"We know, and then you went back the next week, right?" Naomi asks.

"Yes, exactly. Well, that someone turned out not to be just anyone. He was...Logan."

"Logan?" Cassi frowns like she's trying to place the name.

"Cunningham," I add.

Understanding hits them both simultaneously before their jaws fall open.

"You fucked your stepdad?!" Cassi shrieks, earning a few less than savory looks from some of our peers.

I shoot Cassi an irritated look as we grab our bags, standing to our feet before rushing out of the class. As soon as we're in the quad, they pepper me with nonstop questions. Then, the floodgates open. I tell them everything about our nights together, him showing up on the trip, me and Ty, me and Logan, my mom and seemingly everyone, before I finally finish.

"So...you moved in with him?" Naomi asks.

"Yeah, yesterday."

"Are you crazy?" Cassi laughs, though her tone holds no judgment.

"I think so," I say with an eye roll.

Naomi smiles, rubbing my arm softly.

"Does he treat you well?"

I nod.

"Then we're happy for you," Cassi says.

I'm surprised. Not that my friends are unsupportive or critical, but I expected a little judgment. A few strong opinions or words of caution. Instead, they seem all for the huge age gap and inappropriate natured relationship.

"Thanks," I say suspiciously. "What ever happened with you two that night?"

"Hm?" Cassi asks.

"I know you both hooked up, we've all never shared details, though, which isn't like us. Now you know why I didn't share mine because, I mean, I wasn't exactly proud. Your turn bitches, spill."

Naomi gets a call as she looks down at her phone.

"Oh, got to take this. See you guys later!"

She's practically sprinting away, forcing Cassi and I to both look at her with suspicion. That is until my eyes turn to Cassi. She scrubs a hand down her face as she lets out a deep sigh.

"Okay, but you can't tell anyone."

"Like I ever would," I scoff.

"Okay."

I texted Logan when I was done with my classes for the day, and he said that he came home early and was waiting for me. It felt stupid to get excited over his next text, but when the butterflies began, they didn't stop the entire drive home.

Logan: Come home to me, Sparrow

Home. His home. He wants me to consider it my home but seeing as I "moved in" twenty-four hours ago, it's taking some getting used to.

When I park in the driveway, I unlock the front door with

the code that Logan programmed for me. This man wastes zero time when he wants something.

Shutting the door behind me, I drop my purse at the front entry table and begin winding through the large house in search of him. To no surprise, I find him in his office on a call.

"Uh huh," he says into his cell phone.

A smile spreads across his face, enveloping the surly frown that was taking up prior residence.

Giving me a quick wink, he continues speaking before holding out his hand for me, silently asking me to come to him. Of course, I do, crossing the room quickly before an idea comes to mind.

Instead of sitting in his lap, I drop to the floor. He looks down at me curiously, rubbing his hand over my head and down to my neck soothingly. I'm not planning on staying by his side, though. Crawling under his desk and between his legs, I situate myself at his feet before reaching for his belt. He grabs my hands quickly, delivering me a stern look as he speaks.

"I understand, but you have to give me more to work with than just 'I have no recollection.'"

Smiling sweetly at him, I continue working at his belt, pushing at his hands until he finally gives in, releasing my hands as I finally get his belt undone. Unzipping his slacks, I slip my hand in to find him already hard. I look at him with that same smile as I pull his cock out, his eyes narrowed and focused on me as I open my mouth and suck him down my throat.

His face tenses as his eyes roll into the back of his head.

"Yeah," he rasps through clenched teeth. "I'm listening," he says as I pull back up before pushing him down farther.

Of course, he couldn't let me take control for even a moment. His hand moves to the back of my head, forcing my head up and down in a rhythm he enjoys, and I love it. I love when he uses me like this, showing me exactly how to draw out the most amount of pleasure. I love when he tells me how good I am for him, how I do such a good job for him. I love it all. His touch, his attention, his words. I'm like a strung out addict desperate for just one more hit. One more will never be enough, though. I need everything he's willing to give me as often as he's willing to give it.

Logan begins face fucking me, his hips bucking as his hand forces me down further and further.

Involuntarily, I gag, and a light tap comes to my cheek. My eyes blink in shock as I look up to him to see him hold his finger over his lips, telling me to be quiet. I feel my pussy pulse because, again, some fucked up part of me likes that. He'd never hurt me, never do anything that caused me true pain, but he won't shy away from grabbing my attention, from correcting me when I need it, and I don't know why, but I find that so fucking hot.

Maybe chalk it up to daddy issues.

Nuzzling my cheek against his hand, curiosity sparks in his eyes as he gives me another tap on the cheek. I nod in response, swirling my tongue around his cock as he does it again and again, my pussy spasming with each tap.

Slipping my hand beneath my pants, I begin rubbing my clit when Logan delivers a harder tap this time, shaking his head no. I whimper in protest, desperate for touch, but do as he says. I take my hand out, and he snatches it up, sucking my fingers into his mouth and savoring the essence of me. I squirm at the sight, feeling more and more desperate by the second.

He releases my fingers as those chocolate-brown eyes stare straight into my soul.

"Sounds good. We'll talk soon," he says before ending the phone call.

Excitement stirs inside me when Logan lifts me up off the ground, pushing me onto his desk. He has my jeans pulled down, along with my panties, in two seconds flat and is running his tongue through me before I can even catch my breath.

"So wet for me, Sparrow," he murmurs against my sensitive flesh, his gaze locked on mine. "Do you get wet from pleasing me?"

"Yes," I pant.

"Yes, what?"

"Yes, Sir."

A sharp slap stings against my clit, and I cry out, pleasure ripping through me as my pussy aches.

"That's my good girl. You like it when I spank you, Sparrow? Like your sweet little cunt spanked?" he asks as he does it again.

My body bucks as a moan escapes me.

"Yes, Sir."

He leans over me, pushing his cock into me as his mouth covers mine. I gasp against his lips as he begins fucking me hard against the desk. When he pulls away, his hand pinches my cheeks together, forcing my lips to pout.

"Such a pretty face. You're beautiful, Sparrow, you know that? The most beautiful woman I've ever seen."

I moan in response, because all I can do right now is just feel. Logan's hand releases my cheeks, gently massaging one of them before he taps it. Like before, my pussy pulses and he groans.

"My woman likes it rough," he rasps.

I nod.

"More!" I beg. "Give me more, Sir. Please."

Rubbing my cheek a few times, he taps me again, hard enough to leave a sting behind before his hand is back, rubbing the sting away. A gasp rips out of me, and I squirm against him. I feel my orgasm just out of reach, my body violently trembling, desperate to fall over the edge.

Logan palms my cheek, warming it up once more before the hardest tap of them all comes. Just like that, I detonate. My vision blacks out briefly, and a scream I didn't know I was capable of escapes me. I fall apart on top of his desk as he groans out his release, his cock pulsing inside me as he pushes in every last drop.

When we catch our breaths, his touch is tender. He gently cradles my jaw as he examines my cheek, leaning down to press a feather light kiss against it. I close my eyes at the feeling as he places another and another, slowly covering every inch of skin with soft, kind kisses.

"Thank you, Sparrow," he murmurs against my skin.

"For what?" I ask softly.

He pulls back to look at me, shaking his head reverently.

"For trusting me so wholly. Your trust and obedience is a gift that I will never take for granted or waste."

I smile at that, nodding softly. "I know."

"I love you," he says next, causing my heart to slow and my stomach to clench.

My mouth opens as I attempt to gather some words, any words, but I come up short.

His other hand lifts until he's cradling my face gently as he speaks.

"It's okay if you don't say it, if you aren't ready to hear it. I do, though. I'm in love with you, and I'll be as patient as you need me to be until you're right there with me."

"Logan. I...we're moving so fast. We just got together and—"

"And I don't know about you, but it feels like I've been waiting a lifetime to find you," he finishes.

I stay quiet as he continues.

"It's illogical to think that I could love someone so soon, but I do, and I know it with every fiber of my being. I know it because when I'm with you, you're like...gravity. You center me, ground me. I feel a pull towards you like my very existence depends on it. I can be intense, I know that. I can be obsessive over what I want, I know that too. But this? Us? We're something special, Ari. Something once in a lifetime, and I don't intend on living a second of it not being one hundred percent honest with you."

His words are dizzying. I feel everything he feels. His confessions perfectly mirror the thoughts I've had in my mind but have been too scared to echo out loud. When I step back and look at everything with a clear head, it's absolutely insane, but when I shut out the noise and focus on what I feel, what I want, everything just...fits.

"How can I be in love with you too?" I ask in a soft whisper.

Leaning down once more, he presses his lips to mine, what feels like fireworks exploding inside me as he pulls back, resting his forehead against my own.

"Because this is fate at its most rare, Sparrow. Our paths crossed in the most unlikely and twisted ways, but they did so intentionally. Every second spent with you has only solidified that for me."

I nod as I lift my hand to his neck, holding him in place.

"I love you, Logan."

It was as if I just told him the meaning of life, the cure to all cancer, that all of his dreams were coming true in one moment. Euphoria washes over his face as he crushes his lips to mine once more, stealing the breath from my lungs, and I hope neither one of us ever comes up for air.

Chapter Twenty-Seven

Logan

I know I'm out of my goddamn mind. I have a twenty-one-year-old girlfriend who is still in college, is way out of my league, and oh, yeah, my ex-wife's daughter.

I don't care, though.

None of those little boxes are what Arianna fits into. She's like...air, forever constant and everlasting. She breathes life into me, shaking me from the existence I thought I wanted and introducing me to one I really want to have. I've been walking around numb to the world for longer than I'd care to realize. Longer than I probably have the capacity to realize. One night with her flipped my world upside down. Then it was two nights, then it was days. It was watching how kind she is to others, how passionate and creative she is. How beautiful she is to her core and out. I fell so goddamn fast, too fast, I know. There isn't any other way to explain it, though. I'm here, shaken to my core, for the only woman I shouldn't want, but the only one I do.

And she loves me too.

The high I felt when I watched those words escape her

lips? Unparalleled. I've never experienced a feeling like that in my entire life. Relief mixed with joy mixed with anxiety.

Would I be good enough to keep her happy? Strong enough to hold us together? Could I become the man she deserves? I'm not sure about that last one, but I'll fight until I'm bloody and weak every day of my life to attempt it.

I don't want her to think this is a lust fueled fling. I don't want her to wonder if I'm just love bombing her to make her pliant and vulnerable for me. Quite the opposite, actually. I love her fire. I love her fight. It's not a bratty mind game like what her mother used to play. She stands up for herself; she speaks her mind.

That's what makes her submission so sweet. It's a gift she's giving to me, and not lightly, either. To shed the tough exterior she tries to wear, the one she was forced to adapt to from a young age and allow herself to trust another person is easily one of the most difficult things I could ask of her, and she does it as simply as breathing. Like her soul knows mine better than we know each other. It's corny and crazy and maybe I'm totally overanalyzing everything, but I just know I need her, and I'll fight every day to make her as deliriously happy as she makes me.

I'm leaving the office, sending a text to Arianna that I want her ready for a date tonight. I'm taking her to the best little Italian restaurant in Seattle because my sweet Sparrow is long overdue for a proper date. I mean, we literally jumped straight over dating and went straight to living together and falling in love. We've been living together for two weeks, and I still haven't taken her on a proper date? Unacceptable.

As soon as I slide into my car, my phone rings. I'm surprised to see that it's Tyson. I haven't spoken to him since we left the lake house.

"Hello?"

"Hey, what are you doing?" Tyson asks.

"Just on my way home."

"Got any plans for the night? Was thinking we could grab a beer, watch a Crusaders game, or something."

We haven't gotten together to just hang out in a while. Months if I'm being honest. Tyson is always asking, but I'm always turning him down. I always have work, a business trip, or something that feels more important. I want to change that, though.

"I can't tonight. What about next week?" I offer.

"Hot date?" he teases with a light chuckle that dies quickly.

I don't respond because it isn't needed. He knows why I can't meet up with him tonight. Or at least has a suspicion. And his suspicion would be correct.

"You taking good care of our girl?" he asks.

"My girl," I snap.

A raspy laugh escapes him as he sighs.

"Man, you gotta stop being so easy to rile up when it comes to her. Some might consider it a weakness."

I let out a halfhearted grunt in response.

He's not wrong. Wish I could help it.

"What is she up to?" Tyson asks.

"She should be at the house," I say.

"Your house?"

"Our house," I correct.

Silence settles between us, and I sigh internally, awaiting the judgment he is no doubt ready to deliver.

"She moved in? Already?"

"Yeah, she did."

Another long pause comes, but I don't attempt to fill the silence before Tyson speaks again.

"If you guys are happy, then I'm happy for you."

I frown at that, taken off guard that he would be so...

supportive. I'm not sure why I consistently sell him short. He's always had my back, never not believed in me, and he seems to be the same with Arianna. My little brother turned out to be a great man.

"Thanks, Ty," I say softly, pulling up to my house.

Arianna's car is there, and though she already told me she was home, I still felt this unnecessary level of anxiety. Anytime she isn't with me, I feel it. It's already become extremely annoying, but again, I can't seem to help it. Until she is safely wrapped in my arms, I can't find any peace.

"Take care of her, Logan."

"I will," I promise before we hang up.

Looking up at the house, I see a silhouette pass the window before it backtracks. She looks down at me and smiles, waving excitedly in a way that makes me grin.

Fuck. I love that girl.

Reaching over to the passenger seat, I grab the bouquet of flowers that my secretary got from a flower shop downtown. Blooming Deals? Something like that. Roses felt too cliché, so I had her get an arrangement of hydrangeas. I remember how much she used to love to photograph the hydrangea bushes that were outside the house we lived in when I was married to Kelly.

As I step out of the car, hiding the bouquet behind my back, I don't even make it inside the house before the front door opens and a barefoot Arianna walks towards me. She's wearing a pair of jeans and a pretty black shirt that accentuates her curves perfectly.

"Hi," she smiles.

"Hi, Sparrow," I say as I pull her in with my free arm for a kiss, pressing my lips to hers before resting my forehead against her own.

"I got you something," I say as I show her the bouquet.

Her eyes widen and a sweet smile spreads across her face.

"For me? Logan," she says with a breathy voice as she takes the flowers, lifting it to her face to inhale. "I love hydrangeas."

"I know," I say with a small smile and a nod.

She lifts up onto her toes, placing a soft kiss against my cheek.

"Thank you."

"It's the least you deserve. We have two hours before our reservation tonight, so we better hurry because I plan to take up an hour and forty of that time."

Her eyes light up with excitement as I scoop her into my arms, kissing her as I walk us into the house and kick the door shut.

We definitely didn't make our reservation in time.

Luckily, the owner is an old friend of mine and was able to fit us in last minute. I pull out Arianna's chair for her as we sit underneath the Seattle sky, string lights covering the space above us as soft music plays from all around us.

A waiter comes over, lighting the candle at our table before rattling off the specials and promising to return soon. Arianna and I sit there staring at the menu for so long while she actively debates whether she wants the risotto or the chicken florentine.

"May I take your order?" the waiter asks.

Arianna's eyes widen in panic, clearly still undecided.

"We will take an order of the risotto and an order of the chicken florentine. Can we also get a bottle of Pinot Grigio? Whatever is best."

"Yes, sir," he says before taking our menus.

Arianna watches him walk away in disappointment.

"I didn't decide yet," she says.

I reach across the table, holding her hand in mine.

"I know, that's why I got both."

She smiles softly. "You're kind of the sweetest, has anyone ever told you that?"

"Never in my life." I laugh. "But I'm glad you think so."

Arianna nods as her eyes begin wandering around the space. It's elegant yet intimate. It's no wonder it's been rated one of Seattle's most romantic restaurants.

"I got you something," I say as I pull out the thin box from my jacket pocket.

"Logan!" she laughs with a smile. "You have to stop."

I frown as I set the box on the table.

"Why?"

"The flowers, the fancy dinner, the gifts. No need to butter me up, I'm already fucking you," she says with a smirk.

A chuckle escapes me as I shake my head.

"The flowers are nothing, a simple gesture to remind you that I was thinking about you today. The dinner is essential, I have to keep my girl fed. The gift, well, it's more for both of us than just you."

She tilts her head curiously as she lifts the top of the box off, revealing a white gold chain with two diamond encrusted heart ends.

"It's a necklace," I say.

"How does it go on?" she asks, clearly confused by the unique construction.

Standing from my seat, I round the table, gently taking the necklace out of the box as I begin wrapping it around her neck.

"I don't think you understand how in love with you I am, Sparrow. These things that you say are too much don't feel like enough. I don't deserve you. I'm painfully aware of that, but I will do everything from sunup to sundown, until my last breath, attempting to be worthy of your care, your affection, your love."

Her eyes shimmer with emotion as she looks up to me before down at the necklace. One heart sits higher than the other and she touches it gently.

"It's beautiful, how is this for you, though?"

My fingers grip the longer heart, yanking quickly as the rest of the chain tightens quickly around her throat, effectively turning the necklace into a leash and collar. Her eyes widen with surprise as her breath catches. I keep the diamond heart in my hand as I lower my face to hers and speak slowly.

"Because it keeps you exactly where I want you, no more than a step away from me. Look around, Sparrow. Do you see all these prying eyes? All these judgmental gazes?"

She swallows, taking an inventory of the looks we are getting because there are a lot. Mainly snooty rich people who aren't brave enough to actually go after what they want in life. Arianna and I have no such qualms, and neither of us is shy when it comes to putting on a show.

"Jealousy drips from them as they watch us. The men all want you, they envy me."

"And the women envy me," she says breathlessly, like that statement is somehow gratifying for her.

Her eyes swing back to me as she continues.

"They want this. A handsome, intelligent, strong man who will allow them to break apart into pieces. A man who will give them enough freedom to be an independent person, but enough boundaries to allow them a safe space to thrive. They want someone who will push them, break them, and then put them back together again."

I pull on the chain a little, tightening it slightly as I tilt my head and cup her face with my free hand.

"Is that what I am to you, Sparrow?"

She shakes her head in disbelief.

"More."

Pride swells my chest as I lean down, pressing my lips to hers. That pride only expands as I do, proving to everyone in this world and the next that this incredible, beautiful, amazing woman is mine, and I am hers.

When we break apart, a smile graces her face. One that is so breathtaking it sends my heart racing. I hold her face for several more seconds, shaking my head with reverence before I reach down and loosen the necklace, returning it to its original form.

As I take my seat, I notice Arianna touching the chain gently before a knowing smile crosses her face.

"Do we have any plans after dinner?"

Yes, but I'll change them in a heartbeat if she wants me to.

"What do you have in mind, Sparrow?"

Chapter Twenty-Eight

Arianna

Did you know that the club sells masks at the door if you don't have one? I didn't know that either, but when I told Logan that I wanted to go back, he asked for the check then and there and we were in the car within minutes. We got to the club, and after a quick exchange with the bouncer, Logan and I were slipping on our masks and walking down the familiar hallway.

His hand is resting on the small of my back, making sure I never move more than a pace or two away from him. I smile up at him as he looks down at me with a smile of his own, his hold on my back moving to my hip. I sink into his touch as we step out of the hallway and into the main room.

God. It feels like it's been a lifetime ago since I've been here, not a few weeks.

Everything has changed since I last stepped foot in here, absolutely everything. I never would have imagined the thing that would change the trajectory of my life would be going to a sex club.

My eyes roam around the room, taking in the people, the atmosphere. I swear it changes every night. Two men are making out on the couch to our left, while two women and a man are tangled up in a messy three-way makeout on the other. A man in his late fifties crawls by us on his hands and knees, a collar around his neck as a woman half his age walks him around the room, and it's just any other night for this place. There is no judgement, no stigmas. When you step through those doors, all prior notions of right and wrong fly out the window, and your desires are the only things that remain.

"Do you need a drink, Sparrow?" Logan asks, pulling me a little closer to him as he does.

I smile up at him, shaking my head.

"No, I want to remember everything vividly."

His other hand lifts to cup my cheek as he beams at me like that was the right answer. Wordlessly, he begins walking towards the stairs and I follow him happily. I don't ask where we're going, mainly because I don't care. We could use and experiment in every single room of this place and I would still never have enough of Logan.

He leads us down a hallway before stopping at a door. There is a green light beside it, which I assume means no one is inside. Logan pushes the door open, revealing a voyeur room nearly identical to the one we used our first night together, but the layout is flipped. Same furniture, same set up, same gorgeous people sitting in the viewing area, waiting for someone to entertain them.

"You know, for someone who is awfully possessive of me, you sure don't seem to mind sharing me," I tease as I face the crowd.

Logan comes up behind me, his hand wrapping around my throat possessively as he cranks my head back to face him.

"I enjoy showing you off, there is a difference."

I attempt to shrug, loving the simmering fire in his eyes right now.

"Strangers are watching me spread myself open for you and you love it."

A feral growl escapes him as he smashes his lips against mine. The kiss is so intense it nearly takes my breath away. When he pulls away, his feral snarl sends my pulse racing.

"Fuck yes, I do. I love showing others what I have, how precious my woman is. What a lucky fucking bastard I am."

It's weird that my heart flips at that, right? That shouldn't be sweet or romantic.

Somehow, it's both, though.

"What's that safe word of yours, Sparrow?" he asks.

"Banana," I say breathily, his hold on my throat flexing.

"Get yourself ready. On your back, legs open to them," he says as he moves over to the tools on the wall.

Anxiety swirls inside me as I make eye contact with a few voyeurs before lying down on the bed. My black dress bunches up easily, doing most of the work for me as I slowly begin parting my legs. I watch as each person's eyes darken with lust when Logan comes to stand beside me. He grabs the hem of the dress, pulling it up and over my knees before pushing my legs further apart. His hand slips down between my thighs, speaking to the crowd as he does.

"Isn't she the most beautiful thing you've ever seen?"

Several heads nod in response before Logan dips a finger inside me. I gasp at the intrusion and Logan groans.

"So fucking responsive for me. Always wet, Sparrow."

"Have you seen yourself? How could I not?" I tease.

Logan continues pumping a finger in and out of me before he pulls out completely. I whimper in protest as he gently pats my pussy.

"Hands and knees."

No further instruction is needed, and not an ounce of protest or hesitation comes from me. Quickly, I do as he says, arching my back as Logan quickly undresses himself. My dress is still bunched up around my hips, but something tells me he likes that. It's like we're just here for a quick dirty fuck. No time or planning put into it. Just a carnal need that needs to be satiated right here and now.

I feel Logan bury his face into my pussy, forcing a moan to escape me. His tongue flicks against me before dragging all the way through me, pausing on my ass. I squirm at the touch and his hand smacks the side of my ass.

"No moving. Stay still, Sparrow."

His tongue begins circling my asshole, and I can't help but wiggle softly. Logan pauses for a moment before grabbing something off the side table. A sharp yet solid smack comes out of nowhere, temporarily stealing my vision as my mouth opens on a gasp.

Whipping my head around, I see Logan holding a leather paddle in his hand. He pulls his hand back, smacking it against me once more.

"I said, no moving."

Normally, I always obey, never push the boundaries. Something in me is feeling a little too daring tonight, though. So, the next time he begins eating my ass, I grind myself against him, earning myself another smack while he continues licking me.

It's probably fucked up that I enjoy this pain the way I do. I can't explain it, and I don't really care to. All I know is that my pussy is fucking dripping right now.

"Be my good girl, and I'll keep using this on you. Clearly, punishment isn't the way to go with my dirty girl."

I still at his words before he bends down once again, running his tongue through me from front to back, testing me. I don't move a muscle as badly as I want to, and he praises me happily while massaging my ass cheek.

"There you go. Just like that. You're doing beautifully, Sparrow."

I melt at his words before he pulls away, rubbing the head of his cock against my pussy. It's enough to have me panting, but he doesn't apply enough pressure to actually slip inside me. I'm not able to help myself, I press myself against him, attempting to push him in, when another sharp slap from the paddle comes on the opposite cheek this time.

My back bows and a cry falls from my lips that quickly turns to a moan.

"We will be at this all night, Sparrow. Do not move and do not speak until I allow it. Patience is a beautiful thing, and I think it's time you learned that."

Pulling away from me completely, I swallow the whimper that attempts to escape me as he begins touching my back, his fingertips just barely grazing against my skin. It sends goose-bumps skating across my body before a gentle kiss is pressed to my upper thigh. He goes about this for what feels like hours. Soft, barely there touches and kisses ghost over my skin until he drags his cock up my inner thigh before pushing forward.

He doesn't push inside me, but instead rests his cock against my pussy lips. I feel his hand lift, winding up into my hair as the other takes hold of my hip. Slowly, he begins fucking me like this. I'd call it dry humping, but my pussy is leaking all over his cock, more than ready for him.

Logan tugs on my hair once, forcing my head back to meet his eyes.

"If this is all I'll ever give you, you'll say thank you. Do you understand? Speak."

"Yes, Sir," I pant.

"What do you say?" he asks as he continues thrusting himself against me.

"Thank you, Sir."

"That's my good little Sparrow," he says before he pulls back more on the last thrust and pushes inside me with a snap of his hips.

My vision spots, and I feel my mouth drop open in pleasure. I look to the voyeur window to see three men stroking themselves while one man eats a woman's pussy as she watches. It's such a powerful feeling to know that Logan and I together are enough to make half a dozen people hot. They have to touch themselves or their partner because we put on such a beautiful show.

"Fuck," Logan groans. "You're fucking soaked for me. Do you like it when I use the paddle on you?"

I nod my head desperately as a moan works its way out of me.

"Yes, Sir!"

He bends himself over my body, rumbling into my ear as he chuckles.

"Maybe we need some new toys for the house."

My head turns to look up at him as I excitedly whimper. He smirks at that, delivering me a sharp slap on the ass with his hand as he continues. It makes my pussy clench, so he does it again and again before I'm falling apart. I moan and squirm and wiggle against his cock before collapsing into a messy heap on the bed.

Logan runs a soothing hand up and down my back before pulling out of me and flipping me around. I land on my back against the bed before he pushes my legs up and over his shoulders as he slides into me.

I squirm at the feeling, my pussy feeling extremely sensitive as he begins fucking me slowly. I'm not sure we've ever fucked slowly before. It's usually a rushed, lust filled, in the moment kind of thing. This, though? This feels different.

"What are you doing?"

"Taking my time with you. Why, do you have somewhere to be?" he teases.

I smile and shake my head as I look up to see the room still filled with people, watching us intently.

"What about them? Aren't we supposed to be putting on a show for them?"

"They aren't here for a show. They are here to witness anything that happens between us in this room. They just watched me fuck you, now they are going to watch me make love to you."

My heart swells as his thrusts push in and out, slow and steady, his mouth running up and down my neck before moving across my face. Every touch, every movement from him is drowning with love. His deep brown eyes never leave my own. Soon, everything seems to fade away, like we are in our own world together. There is no club, no voyeurs, no outward worries or responsibilities. There is just Logan and I together, and right now, it feels like all I'll ever need.

I feel Logan's hand come to my pussy, his thumb rubbing slow circles against my clit. I gasp at the feeling, and he swallows the sound by covering my mouth with his. Our tongues tangle together, something about this hypnotic combination sending me tumbling over the edge, again.

This orgasm isn't as intense, but no less potent. It feels as natural and as easy as breathing. I feel my legs quiver, my pussy pulse, and a wave of euphoria wash over me from my head to my toes. I whimper against Logan, and I feel the moment that he finds the same pleasure. His deep groan practically rattles his chest as his cock swells inside of me, pushing his cum further and further until both of our bodies still.

When we pull apart, he smiles down at me, a heart-clenching, swoon-worthy smile. His hand lifts up to brush some hair out of my face so gently, I can barely feel his touch.

"I'm so in love with you, Sparrow."

My heart thrums at that. "I love you too."

Chapter Twenty-Nine

Logan

It's been six weeks since Arianna has moved in. You'd think that both of us would be settling in, getting used to the other, and the honeymoon phase would start to fade. You'd think.

Instead, every day I come home, she is either leaping into my arms, peppering me with kisses, or waiting for me on her knees. I swear to god, I'm the luckiest man in the goddamn world.

I bring her home flowers or a gift every day. She tells me it's excessive and unnecessary. Logically, I know it is, but I can't stop. I have more money than I could ever spend in one lifetime, and it would be a waste not to thoroughly spoil her rotten. She says I'm going to ruin her for all others, but that's entirely the point because as long as I'm still breathing, there will be no others. Ever.

My eyes glance at the new camera sitting on my desk. My assistant had to scour the internet for weeks before she found it. A 1923 Oskar Barnack o-Series Leica. Arianna had come home talking about it after her lecture one day and said she would love to see one in person. It held such a huge piece of history and was such a rarity that little to none are even on the market or believed to exist. The way her eyes lit up solidified that not only did she have to see it, she had to have it. My assistant checked with me three times before buying it, verifying that I wanted to spend over twelve million on a camera that wouldn't even be used. Just picturing that same excited gleam in her eyes is well worth the money and then some. Besides, the last time one went to auction, it went for over fourteen million several years ago, so this was a steal.

My phone rings on my desk, and I look to see that it's my assistant calling from her desk up front.

"Yes?"

"Uhm, Mr. Cunningham. I have Ms. Fulton here to see you."

"Let her in."

"Are you sure? I know you have that debrief coming up—"

"Louise, let her in now," I say sternly, shaking my head.

Arianna has come to visit me a few times at the office, and I told Lousie from day one that she has an all access pass to the building. She can come and go as she pleases. I don't know why she thinks she has any right to stop her, let alone argue with me over it.

Tucking the present into my drawer, I hide it for now. I want the moment to be perfect when I give it to her. Locking my computer, I feel myself straightening my tie and running my fingers through my hair like a kid picking up his date at prom. It's a pretty spot on feeling. Arianna puts me on edge in the best way. I'm always cool, controlled, and confident, but she throws me off kilter. She makes me really think about my actions, my words. I hyper fixate on every single conversation we have, and I have yet to, and will never stop, trying to make myself better for myself, but mainly for her.

I stand, smiling to greet her when my smile falls. A woman pushes into my office, her high heels eating up the space between us before she pushes her weight to one hip, her hand on the other as she smiles at me in a way that twists my stomach.

"Hi Logan," Kelly purrs.

Wrong Ms. Fulton, Louise.

Goddamnit.

"What are you doing here?"

She snorts out a laugh, eyes roaming around the room.

"Not very friendly today, I take it."

"To you? Never. Maybe I wasn't clear, but both Arianna and I want nothing to do with you. Get the fuck out of my office and stay away from the both of us."

Her face pinches at that as she gives me a disgusted look.

"I would, but it's not just us anymore," she says before resting a hand on her stomach.

My brows furrow as I stare at her. It takes longer than it should for her words to sink in.

"You're knocked up?"

She bristles at that as she snaps.

"No! I'm pregnant. Knocked up is something that happens to slutty teenagers."

"Well, you're an adulterous whore, so." I shrug.

She narrows her eyes at me.

"Well, this adulterous whore is carrying your baby."

My body goes cold, a chill running through my body, and I instantly have the urge to throw up.

"Bullshit."

"It's true!"

"Even if you are pregnant, which I severely doubt, there is no way it's mine. We fucked once in the last three years. God knows how many men have been inside you in the last three weeks."

She sneers at me, attempting and failing to keep her cool.

"It's your baby, Logan."

I raise my hands in bewilderment. "You literally admitted that you fucked Tom within days of me. It's probably his."

"I know that's what you'd hope, but Tom and I always used protection. You, however, came inside my cunt, and now your child is growing inside me."

Her tone seems like it's supposed to be upset or maybe even irritated. The winning grin on her face tells me that she feels nothing of the sort, though.

That nausea from before is hitting me full force. I can hear the blood pounding in my ears as she carries on. This can't be happening. She has to be lying. She doesn't look pregnant, she's a manipulative bitch.

As if she can read my thoughts, she reaches into her purse and pulls out a pregnancy test, setting it on my desk. The word pregnant glares at me as she sets down another. Pregnant. Kelly pulls out one more that looks like it hasn't been used yet as she waves it in front of me.

"I'm happy to take another in front of you if that's what it takes."

I feel my chest begin to heave, anger thrumming through my veins as I turn to my desk, hastily grabbing my briefcase, phone, and Arianna's present.

Fuck.

Arianna. This is going to kill her. It's killing me. What the fuck have I done?

"I want a paternity test immediately."

"Fine by me," Kelly says.

Shaking my head, I storm out of my office and down the hallway.

"Mr. Cunningham," Louise calls out, but I put my hand up to stop her.

If I talk to anyone except Arianna right now, I'm gonna blow the fuck up, and no one deserves that. This is my fuck up. I got shit faced drunk and fucked my ex. Without a condom. All because I was falling in love with her daughter, who kept pushing me away. Fuck, fuck, fuck.

When I get to my car, I type out a quick text to Arianna.

Me: Meet me at home as soon as you can.

Her response comes immediately.

Sparrow: What happened? Is everything okay?

No. Everything is fucked beyond belief. I don't want her to be scared and driving erratically, though.

Me: Everything is fine, Sparrow. Drive home to me as soon as you can.

Sparrow: On my way.

I'm sitting in the living room, my knee bouncing uncontrollably as I wait for her. I debated giving her the camera first, like it would somehow soften the blow. In reality, I know that's a terrible fucking idea, so I hid it away for now as I clench my fists together and wait.

When the front door opens, I don't feel ready for what comes next. Telling her feels like it's making it real, and it could very well not be. Maybe I'm overreacting. Maybe I should wait to say anything until the paternity test. I could be spiraling over nothing but a bullshit lie.

I can't do that, though. In our relationship, trust is the most important thing to the both of us. If I don't come to her with something like this immediately and she ever finds out...I'm not willing to risk that.

A concerned looking Arianna steps in the door, her hair up in a sleek ponytail I absolutely love. She's wearing a pair of jeans and a simple white t-shirt, but she makes the entire outfit look completely breathtaking.

"Hey, what's going on?" she asks with a frown.

I stand to my feet, wrapping my arms around her as I just hold her. We stand there for several seconds before I look down at her.

"What's going on, Logan?"

The fear in her voice tells me she knows it's something bad, and I'm not exactly downplaying it because it is bad. It feels like my entire life, our entire life, is crumbling around us.

"Kelly came to see me today."

She frowns at that, waiting for me to continue. Only, I can't. I struggle to find the words as I stare at our intertwined hands. I don't even remember grabbing them. Not surprising, though. I seek her out at every opportunity, every moment. This is no different despite the words tumbling out of my mouth.

"She's pregnant."

Arianna stills, unmovable like a statue, as her eyes bore into me. She blinks once, twice, before finally speaking.

"And the father?" she asks tightly.

"We're getting a test," I answer.

I don't know what I expect her reaction to be. Probably devastation and heartbreak like I'm currently feeling. It's not. It's anger. Pure blinding anger.

"What the FUCK, Logan!" she snarls, throwing my hands away from her as she moves to the other side of the room.

"How the fuck could this have happened? Did you fuck her without a condom?"

I look down at the floor, too ashamed to meet her eyes as she lets out a mocking laugh.

"Unfucking real. Cool, so my boyfriend knocked up my mom. Awesome."

"We don't even know if the baby is mine, Sparrow. It could be Tom's. It could be some random guy she hooked up with. I'm going to get a test done immediately and—"

"And what? Huh? What if the baby is yours, Logan? What's your plan?"

I'm at a loss for words, knowing nothing I can say will fix this.

"I haven't made it that far yet."

Her lip wobbles, and though there is still fire in her eyes, her voice is strained.

"So, you're saying that if the baby is yours, we're over."

I take two large steps, closing the distance between us in an instant.

"No! Fuck no. Never, Sparrow. No matter what happens, it doesn't change anything between us."

"But?" she says, pushing my hands away.

"But what?"

"I'm sensing a but there. If the baby is yours, you won't be with her, but…"

I sigh, running a hand through my hair as I look into her watery eyes.

"I won't punish the child. I'll support it, be a part of its life."

A choked laugh escapes her as a tear rolls down her face. I reach out to brush it off when she swats my hand away from her. She lifts her finger and opens her mouth like she's about to tear into me as more tears begin running down her face.

"I…you…"

All of her words die before she shakes her head and storms past me.

"Where are you going?" I ask.

"Wherever you're not!" she shouts.

Running my hands over my face and up into my hair, I pull hard as I shout.

"FUCK!"

When I look up, I realize that she's already out of the house and climbing into her car. Jogging after her, I reach the side of her car in seconds.

"Please don't drive, Ari. Not like this. I'll go. You can have time to think and process—"

"Process?!" she shouts. "There is nothing to process, Logan. You fucked my mother. You knocked her up. I'm not gonna stick around and play step-mommy to my fucking sibling!"

She shuts the door and starts the car as I grip the open window.

"Please, Sparrow. Just—"

"Do not call me that! This was a mistake, everything. I wish I could go back in time and never see you at that fucking club."

Hurt pierces through me, but I know she doesn't mean it.

"You don't mean that."

Her head turns to me, an impassive, icy stare covering her face as she glares.

"Yes, I do. I really do."

That hurt blooms into an overwhelming amount of pain. I push it down, though, focusing on her safety first and foremost as the car starts to move. I hold on to the open window as I start jogging.

"Arianna! Stop it! Get out of this fucking car."

"Fuck you!" she snarls before punching the gas.

I have to leap out of the way before she runs over my feet as she peels out of the driveway. I feel my heart break with every foot she drives. Part of me is ready to jump in the car and chase after her to make sure she's safe. The other part knows she needs the space.

"GODDAMNIT!"

Chapter Thirty

Arianna

I hit Facetime on the group chat, tears pouring down my face as I maneuver through the streets of Seattle. Cassi is the first to answer, her face filling the screen.

"Hey, babe! What's—"

Her words pause as she looks at me, her smile disappearing in an instant. The next moment, Naomi joins. Her equally waiting smile slipping away.

"What happened?" Naomi asks.

I begin word vomiting everything, sobbing in between breaths before I finish. Both look stunned, speechless, before Naomi speaks.

"Are you okay?"

"Come on, Nay, she's clearly not fucking okay!" Cassi scolds.

Naomi shoots a scathing look at her, and it catches me off guard. We never snap at each other like that, especially not to Naomi. She's the sweet cinnamon roll of the group, she doesn't look like it right now, though. Her eyes are dripping with irritation and what looks like judgment as she stares at the camera before speaking.

"I know you're not okay. What can I do?"

"Can I come over?" I sniff. "I gave up my fucking apartment for him. I have nowhere to go."

Naomi frowns as she nods. "You know you're welcome at my place, but I'm not there."

"Where are you?" Cassi asks.

Once again, Naomi gets a sharp look.

"I'm out of town, where are you, Cassi? That hotel room doesn't look familiar."

Now that I glance at the background behind Cassi, it does look like a hotel room. Cassi's face flushes a deep crimson.

"I'm in Boston."

"Visiting your sister?" I sniff.

A bitter laugh escapes from Naomi.

"The office will let you into my place, Ari. I'll call them. Stay as long as you need. I'll be back on Monday."

"Thank you."

"Once I'm back, I'll come over. We'll cry and eat and slash his tires, okay?" Cassi says.

I scoff halfheartedly, knowing that is how she shows her love.

We hang up shortly after, and I pull up to a light, turning on my blinker to take a right when I pause. I'm glad I have somewhere to go tonight, but I really don't want to go sit in my best friend's empty apartment. I want to talk to someone. I want to rage. I want to go numb.

An idea pops into my head as I quickly change lanes, pissing off the person behind me as they blare their horn before I head down East Pike Street. Before I know it, I'm parking, wiping the running mascara down my face, and stepping into the Cosmic Tavern. It's a local dive bar that's pretty popular and also happens to have the best bartender around.

Ty is behind the bar, a shaker tin in one hand as he pops the tab on a few beers with the other. His eyes move across the room, checking on everyone before he pauses. A huge smile spreads across his face as he sets the shaker down, rounding the bar top as he approaches me. I can see he wants to pull me in for a hug but stops short when he gets closer to me. His eyebrows knit together in concern as he looks me over.

"What's wrong?"

I swallow roughly, giving him a half smile.

"Can I get a drink?"

Ty stares at me for a few seconds before nodding, walking me over to a quiet corner of the bar top. It's a Friday but it's only four o'clock, so it seems things haven't taken off just yet. Sliding behind the bar, Ty grabs a glass, pouring a tequila shot before passing it to me.

"It's like you know me or something." I smile weakly before tossing it back.

I slide the glass back to him and he pours another shot. When I try to grab it, though, he holds his hand over it.

"Not until you tell me what's going on."

"Your brother knocked up my mom."

Ty's eyes widen and his mouth drops open. I push his hand to the side and take the shot, knocking it back with ease.

"Yeah, my sentiments exactly." I laugh bitterly.

"Wait, wait. How? When?"

"The lake house. Remember?"

"How does she know it's his, though? She's been a fucking whore. It could be Tom's or—"

"It doesn't matter, Ty!" I snap.

I stare down at the worn bar top as he speaks.

"No, it definitely does matter. She could be just trying to trap him. He needs to get a test before he does anything crazy."

I shrug. "He said he was going to."

"Okay." Ty exhales in relief.

"He also said that if he is the father, he wouldn't punish the kid. That he would be in their life."

Ty stares at me for a second, tilting his head to the side like he's confused.

"And that's bad?"

"Ty!" I shout. "Yeah, it's fucking bad."

He rests his forearms onto the counter as he looks at me.

"So you're upset with him because he's *not* a piece of shit? That he wouldn't ignore a child he fathered just because the mother is batshit?"

Well, when he puts it like that.

"No. I'm mad that he stuck his dick in my fucking mother in the first place."

Ty gives me a sympathetic look as he reaches out, covering my hand with his.

"I'm not saying this to be hurtful, babe, but you did tell him to do that. You pushed him away, and in a moment of weakness, he did what you said, what you told him you wanted."

I shove away his hand. "Seriously? You're siding with him?"

He stands up, holding his hands in the air in defense.

"I'm not on anyone's side. I'm just trying to give you some perspective. Was it a massive mistake? Absolutely. Should he have never even thought about touching her? Of course. Did he regret it and hasn't looked back since? You know the answer to that, Ari. He's so fucking crazy about you, and you are crazy about him. If, and right now, that's a big if, he is the father, you two will deal with it. Together."

I shake my head.

"No. I'm out of this equation. Us being together was a

mistake to begin with. Besides, if the baby is his, do you really think there is a chance in hell my mother will ever let him go? She'll demand they get married again, probably cut me out of his life forever. It's just...fucked, but maybe for the best," I shrug.

His lips tighten into a flat line.

"You don't mean that, Ari—"

"Yes, I do. I just...I don't want to talk about him anymore, Ty. My friends are out of town, I don't want to be alone. Can you just...can I have another drink?"

He tilts his head like he's contemplating something before he lets out a heavy breath.

"Alright, only if you drink water first and have some fries."

"Fine, whatever."

Ty nods, moving to get me a cup of water before tapping something onto the computer. French fries come out a few minutes later, and Ty hands them to me with another shot of tequila. The bar starts to fill up as the happy hour rush comes in. Soon there is a line wrapping around the building, which is pretty crazy for a dive bar. Ty completely dominates behind the bar, charming everyone he comes into contact with while slinging drinks like a pro. His eyes manage to come to mine no less than three times every minute, as if to make sure I haven't disappeared somewhere.

I've had a few more shots, and my head begins feeling light and floaty. Suddenly, I'm not nearly as stressed out or heartbroken over the fucked up situation that is my life. I feel myself begin to sway on the barstool to the music playing from the speakers before a body comes up beside me. The pungent smell of cheap cologne and cigarettes fills my nose, and I have to resist the gag building inside me as yellow teeth grin at me.

"What's a pretty little thing like you drinking alone for?"

"You're never alone when you're with Christ," I slur, letting out a raspy chuckle as I slump against the bar.

The man gives me a pitying laugh as he looks at my empty shot glass.

"You need another?"

"Yezs."

"No," Ty says, coming out of nowhere. "She's cut off."

"C'mon, man. She looks fine to me. I'll look after her, I promise."

His hand is heavy as it rests on my shoulder, and it sends a slimy feeling skating across my skin.

"Get your fucking hands off her," a deep voice rumbles from behind me.

My vision doubles as I turn to see Logan standing there, his tie loose and dangling around his neck, hair disheveled, and eyes pitch black with rage. He's so handsome. Why do the biggest assholes have to be so handsome? Why does such a pretty package have to break your heart so goddamn badly?

"Hey, man, I don't know who the fuck you think you are but—"

In a flash, Logan has the guy's head cracking against the bar top, his arms pinned behind his back as he presses against his temple.

"That's my fucking woman you're touching. So much as breathe in her goddamn direction again, and I'll bury you."

"Fuck yo—"

Logan cracks the guy's arm in a way that makes an echoing snap. He howls out in pain as Logan tosses him to the floor, his hands cupping my face instantly. I hear voices bickering, but it's too hard to keep my eyes open and focus.

"Was that necessary?"

"Very. How much has she had?"

"A lot."

"A lot? That's your fucking response?"

"Sorry, that doesn't sound like, 'Thank you, Ty for letting me know where my woman is even though I don't deserve to find or see her because I'm a fuck up.'"

"She told you."

"Fuck yeah, she did."

"Out, now!" a third voice echoes.

I'm able to force my eyes open enough to see a large security guard quickly escorting Logan out. He reaches for me, pulling me along a few steps before my legs give out. Shit, I'm more fucked up than I realize. Logan pauses, pulling away from the security guard before lifting me into his arms. I slump against him, and he hikes me up a little higher to keep me pinned against his chest before he carries me out.

The night air is cold and pricks at my skin as I shiver. Logan holds me closer like he's trying to protect me from it. Like he's capable of protecting me from anything when he's broken my fucking heart. Or maybe I broke it myself by ever opening myself up to someone who is so completely wrong for me.

I don't remember getting in the car or where I am. All I feel is the soft cushion of a mattress beneath me and a gentle kiss to my temple before everything goes truly black.

Chapter Thirty-One

Logan

I sat outside the spare bedroom all night, just in case she needed anything. I figured she wouldn't have felt comfortable sleeping in our bed, so I laid her down in one of the spare rooms before kissing her goodnight. I had every intention of going to bed to get some rest after I spent half the night trying to track her down. Then I just...didn't. Walking away from her felt like I was tearing a hole in my chest. So, I slid down the wall to the ground and I just sat, listened and waited.

Tyson is right. I'm a fuck up, and it's not something I can say I'm used to. One drunken mistake very well may have cost me the most precious thing I've ever been gifted in this life, and I don't know how to fix it. Well, that's not true. I do know how.

I already called in a favor with a friend at the hospital downtown. We are scheduled to go in and do a DNA test. When I texted Kelly that I would be picking her up and driving her to the hospital, she seemed irritated but agreed.

My phone buzzes in my pocket just as my eyelids become heavy. I blink them open quickly, pulling it out to see a new text.

Tyson: Did you get her home okay?

I tap out my reply.

Me: She's fine. Sleeping still.

The texting bubbles appear and disappear several times before a text comes through.

Tyson: Give her space, Logan. I know that's a foreign concept, but she needs it. You put her in a fucked up position, and you have to respect the fact that you don't get to control her feelings on this.

My gut twists at his words. Mainly because he's right. I want to handle everything, to sweep this to the side and do what's best for her, but it's not the right thing to do. It's not the right thing for her. She deserves to have her feelings, to hate my fucking guts if the worst comes to fruition. I hope she doesn't, though. I really hope it doesn't.

Jesus Christ, please don't let that baby be mine.

The door beside me opens before I jump to my feet. A groggy looking Arianna startles slightly, squinting at me as she looks around the hallway.

"How long have you been sitting outside the door?"

"How are you feeling?" I ask.

"All night, I take it?" she continues, her eyes roaming over my rumpled clothes and no doubt dark circled eyes. When her gaze comes back to me, there is a guarded look to her.

"I'm sorry. I shouldn't have left like that. I was mad and—"

"You have nothing to apologize for. You have every right to feel every emotion you do."

She looks surprised, blinking at me like she's never seen me before.

"My friend is going to let me stay with her for a little until I can figure out...what to do next."

I wince like I'm in physical pain at that. Because I am. This feels like the end before we even really began, and it's fucking agonizing.

"I have an appointment at the hospital today to run a paternity test," I say.

She raises her eyebrows.

"That was quick."

"I need to have all of the information as soon as possible."

Arianna nods and I can't help it, I cave. Closing the distance between us, I reach out, cupping her face in my hands. I'm prepared for her to push me away, but when she doesn't, I drag her closer until our bodies are flush.

"Give me the weekend. We'll do the test today, have the answers by tomorrow even if I have to camp out there all night. I'll do it. I just...will you stay? If the baby isn't mine, if I'm not a part of this mess...do you want to stay with me?"

I hate the way I sound. Pathetic, weak, desperate. Normally, I'd rather jump off a cliff than be perceived as any of those things. Right now, though, it really doesn't matter, because I am all of those and more.

She closes her eyes, letting out a heavy breath before looking at me once more.

"Logan, this thing between us–"

"Our relationship," I intervene.

"It's not practical."

"Why not?"

"For this very reason! If it was, we wouldn't even be put into this mess. We're...messy, unorthodox. We don't...fit."

I feel her attempt to pull out of my grasp, but I don't allow it, holding her tighter before pressing my lips to hers. At first, she resists me, but she quickly melts into my touch before I pull away, leaving her breathless as I grumble.

"The first two I'll agree with, but don't even pretend you mean the last. We fit, Sparrow, better than any two souls ever have, and you know it. You can tell me that you don't want to be with me, you can even tell me that you don't love me but don't stand there and try to convince me for one goddamn second that you weren't perfectly made for me and I for you, because I'll call you a fucking liar every time."

She blinks up at me, so much desperation splashed across her face as she nods. Tears spring to her eyes, and it guts me to see her like this.

"I just want things to go back to how they were, when life was perfect."

"It will, baby. I promise. No matter what I have to do, no matter what happens. I promise. Just say you'll stay, say you'll love me, and I'll handle the rest. Trust me."

Arianna doesn't speak for several seconds, her eyes flicking back and forth between mine. I see it the moment she makes up her mind, her eyes hardening with resolve as she forces herself onto her tiptoes, pressing her lips to mine. I welcome her instantly, savoring the embrace for as long as she'll allow it before she pulls away.

"Go get the test done, and we'll go from there."

"Together."

She agrees. "Together."

I asked Arianna if she wanted to come to the hospital, but she declined, mainly because she didn't want to be anywhere near her mother. Can't say I blame her choice. I pull up to Kelly's house, honking the horn before resting my hand on the steering wheel. A few minutes later, she comes strutting out in a black bodycon dress and a pair of stiletto heels.

I'm trying to remember why I decided driving her was a good idea. I figured if I didn't, she would come up with some bullshit excuse not to come, and if we don't have her DNA, we won't have the baby's, so it's kind of crucial.

She stands at the door and waits like it'll open itself. I laugh derisively, shaking my head as I face forward. Finally, she gets the hint, yanking the door open as she slides into the seat. The overwhelming scent of her perfume nearly suffocates me to the point that I roll down my window.

"Would it have killed you to come to the door?" she grumbles.

"Probably," I remark, putting the car in drive the second her seat belt is fastened.

"Jesus! What's with the rush?"

"I want to get this over with."

She shrugs, looking out the window as she speaks.

"It's a waste of time. I know the baby is yours, so the sooner you accept it, the better off we will all be."

I ignore her, maneuvering us through traffic before we enter downtown. She tries to start up a conversation several times, but she finally gives up after I stay silent.

When we pull up to the hospital, relief hits me as I drive towards the parking garage. Once I'm parked, I'm out of the car and heading inside. I hear the clicks of her heels pattering behind me as she attempts to catch up.

"Wait! Logan! I'm pregnant, you fucking dick. The least you could do is slow down or open a goddamn door!"

I roll my eyes at her dramatics as I step inside, heading for the nurse's station.

"Hi, I have an appointment with David Roberts."

The nurse nods, making a quick call before smiling.

"He's waiting for you in the lab. Follow the blue arrows down the hall, and you'll find your way."

"Thank you," I say, just as Kelly catches up to me.

I take off down the hallway, and she huffs in frustration

before following me once again. When we reach the lab, my old client stands from his seat in the waiting room as he shakes my hand.

"Logan."

"David, it's been a while."

"Not long enough." He laughs, probably reminiscing about how I narrowly got him to evade prison time for embezzling from this very hospital. The board of directors rarely questions the CFO, and he almost got away with it until someone tipped them off that the numbers are a little skewed. He's lucky we got a lenient judge and a disinterested jury to dismiss the case.

"Right this way," David says, gesturing down the hall into the lab.

I follow behind him where two lab techs are waiting, smiles on for the boss, clearly. Moving to one of the chairs, I take a seat as the tech does a cheek swab for me while they set up Kelly for a blood draw. I'm done in seconds and stand, checking my phone as I look to David.

"I'll get the results no later than tomorrow morning?"

"I will personally see to it."

Nodding at that, I clasp his hand once more.

"Sounds good. Thank you again."

"My pleasure, Logan."

I begin making my way out of the lab when a shrill voice calls out to me.

"Wait! Logan! Where are you going?"

"Home," I say, not bothering to turn around.

"What about me? You're my ride!"

Pausing, I look over my shoulder to see the tech taking her blood. Kelly's face is panicked, and she looks ready to bolt, needle in her arm and all.

"You have a phone, I'm sure you're capable of getting a ride to your house."

With that, I turn back around and make my way to the car, feeling not an ounce of guilt for leaving that manipulative bitch behind. Even if I am the father of her child, it will never change how I view her. I just wish I would have woken up like this years ago.

When I got home, I was surprised to find Arianna still there. I figured she would have left the instant I pulled out of the driveway. I half expected her to say that she would stay, that we would figure things out just to pacify me. A small bit of relief swelled in me when that appeared to not be the case.

She spent most of the day working on a paper while I caught up on some emails. Instead of handling that in my office, I decided to do it in the living room beside her. When I sat down, she didn't leave or tell me to go, so here I'll stay for as long as she'll allow it.

"Are you hungry?" I ask, glancing to see it's already seven at night.

She shrugs her shoulders, and I frown.

"What have you eaten today?"

Her blue eyes come to mine. "I had a piece of toast this morning."

"That's it?" I confirm.

She shrugs again. Unacceptable. Within the hour, I'm walking into the living room with five different delivery orders, the bags halfway up both my arms. I set them down on the table and her eyes widen.

"What the hell?"

"What do you want? I got street tacos, sushi, pizza, burgers, and gyros."

Arianna looks up at me like I'm crazy before reaching for the sushi. Good to know.

We begin eating in silence for several minutes before she speaks.

"Thank you."

I look up at her, hating the six feet of space between us.

"Of course. I need to be better about ensuring you eat, that's on me."

"Logan, you don't need to make sure I eat. I'm not incompetent," she says with a stern look.

"Incompetent isn't even in the same realm as you, Arianna. I do need to, though. I need to make sure you're taken care of in all ways, physically, and emotionally. And, no, I don't need to, I want to."

She gives me a sad smile, almost like she wants that too, but she isn't sure how to drop her guard. It fucking kills me how broken her trust is right now.

My phone buzzes in my pocket, my whole body going still when I pull it out.

"What?" she asks.

"It's the lab results," I say.

Her brows furrow as she sets her food down and scoots over to me. When her thigh presses against mine, it pulls my attention away from the phone. I feel one of her hands slip in mine, and I intertwine our fingers, looking at her and memorizing her perfect face in case it's the last time I ever see it.

Letting out a heavy exhale, I press a kiss to her forehead that she seems to sink into before I turn my attention back to the phone. As I navigate through the login process, I feel Arianna shaking beside me. Or maybe I'm the one that's shaking. Either way, the nerves are high, emotions are even higher, as I click on the test result that will easily determine our relationship and the rest of my life.

I click on the test result, waiting with bated breath as the spinning wheel of death circles and circles and circles.

"C'mon, c'mon, c'mon," Arianna mutters under her breath.

When the screen pops up and those words flash across the

screen, I'm in complete bewilderment. I blink hard several times as a stuttered breath escapes Arianna.

Probability of Paternity: 0%

My eyes move to Arianna's, both round with shock before she leaps into my arms. Relief floods through my body as the gravity of the words truly sinks in. Holding her tight in my arms, she pulls away slightly to look at me as I palm her jaw tenderly.

"I love you," she says.

"I love you more, Sparrow."

Chapter Thirty-Two

Arianna

Relief. Bliss. Pure unfiltered joy.

I can't even begin to come up with all the emotions that describe how I feel. The terror that was wreaking havoc inside me from the moment Logan left to run the test until the moment we read those results was agonizing. Of course I didn't eat all day, how could I when my stomach was in such tight knots?

Logan and I fell asleep wrapped around each other, him practically smothering me, per usual, and it was so fucking welcomed. I can't believe that nightmare is behind us. This leaves one huge burning question though, who is the father? Like Ty said, it really could be anyone, knowing my mother.

I hope for my Aunt Marissa's sake that it's not Tom's. She still hasn't spoken to me. I've reached out a few times and have been met with radio silence. I know she's not mad at me, per se. She's grieving, struggling with one of the worst betrayals a person could suffer through. She's allowed to not be okay. I miss her, though.

This morning, we woke up early and went straight to the

police station where we filed restraining orders against my mother. Mainly because an hour after the test results came in, Logan's phone began blowing up. Calls, voicemails, texts, each one more unhinged than the next. She sounded psychotic as she began to spiral, demanding there was a mistake, how no man could fill her the way he could. How this is all my fault, and she would make me pay for this. I knew she was just being desperate and delusional, but Logan was not accepting it. The emergency restraining order was put into place based on the text messages alone. We're on our way home to forget about this mess when he gets a call from the office.

"Hello? Yeah. What? Are you kidding? You're fucking kidding," he groans through the phone, wiping a hand down his face as he listens to the person on the other line.

"No! Fuck no. Hold him there, do not let him leave."

He hangs up shaking his head.

"FUCK!"

I frown, reaching a hand out to rest on his thigh. The muscle instantly relaxes at my touch, and he looks at me, swallowing down his irritation as one of his hands covers my own.

"Sorry, Sparrow. I have to go into the office."

I raise one shoulder as we pull up to the house. "It's okay. Everything alright?"

"Yeah, just a client trying to go rogue before his trial next week."

Nodding my head, he gives me an apologetic smile.

"Forgive me?"

"It's fine, Logan." I laugh. "Go handle work. I have a little more homework to take care of."

"Alright, but tonight we're celebrating," he says as he gets out of the car just to get my door for me.

"Yeah? What are we celebrating?" I laugh as he cups my

face with both of his hands, bending himself over so we're nose to nose.

"Our new beginning."

I smile at that before he presses his lips to mine. I'll never not melt at this man's touch. His soft lips pull at mine as my tongue tangles with his. He pulls away too soon for my liking, which he seems to echo if his frustrated growl is anything to go by.

"I'll be back in a few hours, max, okay?"

"Okay," I agree, making my way to the front door. I pause before going inside, waving to him. He returns the gesture, turning around before heading down the driveway.

I punch in my code into the keypad and the lock releases with a whir. I step inside the house, closing the door behind me as I drop my purse on the entry table. I'm kind of hungry, so I head for the kitchen to get a snack. At least I intended to. My feet pause, an unsettling feeling causing goosebumps to race down my spine as my head turns. I thought I just saw…

"Hello, Arianna," my mother says with a sinister grin.

She's sitting in the formal living room right off the entryway. Her legs are crossed, stiletto heels on her feet and a red dress that is far too revealing to be something she wears to work. She lifts the bottle of vodka in her hand to her mouth, taking two large gulps while keeping her eyes on me.

"What are you doing here?"

My mom doesn't respond, pushing herself to her feet before she staggers a few steps. I look down at the bottle to notice it's well over half gone. She's absolutely shit tanked.

"Aren't you pregnant? Not sure you should be drinking."

"Fuck offff," she snarls. "I drank plenty with you, although, you turned out to be a backstabbing little bitch, so maybe you're onto something." She cackles, taking another healthy swig as she stares at me, only one eye open as she continues.

"You ruined everythingss, you knows that? That I hate youz. That you costed me the first love of my life and now the second," she says with a disbelieving laugh. "Who *does* that?"

I shake my head at the sad drunk excuse of a mother before me.

"I didn't do anything to you. I'm sorry you fucked a dude that was such a loser he skipped town the moment responsibility came knocking. I'm sorry you're such a whore you can't stay faithful to one man and lost the only good one that ever looked your way."

I shrug like there is nothing else to say. She closes the distance between us faster than I'd have thought possible, her free hand cracking against my face, whipping my head to the side before snarling.

"You don't know how sorry you should be, little girl. You're about to find out, though," she says with a smile so evil it chills me to the bone. I barely have time to wince before she lifts up the bottle, smashing it over my head.

Blinding pain radiates from my head before I feel myself falling. A hard thump to the ground is the last thing I feel before darkness overtakes me.

Chapter Thirty-Three

Logan

It took less than an hour to talk my client out of completely torching this case. He's desperate to get home to his family in Boston and was willing to do whatever it took to get there. Even if that meant taking a plea that would ultimately call into question all sixty-two of his current family's businesses. As one of the most notorious organized crime bosses to this day, the DA would love to take him down any way they could, even at the risk of losing the bigger fish. Sometimes I feel slimy covering these criminal's asses. I never represent a murderer or rapist, that's a hard line that I draw. White collar crime, though...am I an asshole if I look the other way? Probably, but it keeps this firm afloat and allows us to do the work that actually matters, like pro bono cases for domestic violence victims, low-income families, and malpractice suits that take years to go through.

I contemplated stopping by the store to get Arianna some flowers and champagne because I meant it, we're celebrating tonight. We are both free from her mother, free to love openly, to have any kind of future that we desire, and I intend on making her choice to stay worth it. Instead of stopping at the store, though, I decided to just head home. I just want to be near her.

When I get to the house, I park my car before coming up to the front door. I punch in my code when I realize the door isn't actually locked. Shaking my head, I push the door open. I keep telling her to make sure she locks the thing after she comes inside.

Shutting the door behind me, I engage the lock before calling out for her.

"Ari!"

"In here!" another voice calls out.

I frown at the sound, following it to the formal living room. I stop short, in complete disbelief of what I'm seeing. Arianna is tied to a chair, slumped forward with blood dripping down her head and a dazed expression on her beautiful face.

"Logan," she slurs as Kelly stands behind her, wrapping a chunk of Arianna's hair in her fist, yanking her head up before pressing a kitchen knife to her neck.

"Welcome home, sweetheart," Kelly purrs.

The room reeks of alcohol, and I look down to see shattered glass and blood on the cream colored carpet.

"What are you doing, Kelly?" I ask stiffly.

"Just handling a little problem," she says as she drags the tip of the knife down Arianna's neck, over her chest, and down to her stomach. "I wasn't expecting you home so soon. Good thing I came prepared," she says, stepping away from the chair to show off her red lingerie set that she's currently wearing.

My eyes scan the room, thinking of what exactly I can do to get Kelly away from her.

"Look at me!" she snarls, and I snap my eyes to hers.

She preens at the attention, pushing out her tits as she speaks.

"That's better. Do you like what you see?"

I don't speak, gritting my jaw tightly. I notice Kelly sway slightly on her feet and my eyes narrow.

"Are you drunk?" I ask, trying to steer the conversation in a different direction.

"Not anymore." She shrugs. "Kinda coming down now."

"What about the baby?"

"You mean the baby you don't want?" she asks, tears springing to her eyes out of nowhere.

My god, she can change emotions at the drop of a hat.

"I didn't say that," I say, attempting to play off her mood swings.

She looks at me curiously as I take a step towards her. I feel Arianna's eyes on me, but I force myself not to look at her, focusing all of my attention on the crazy bitch with the knife.

"You wanted a paternity test!" she snaps, like she's attempting to keep her guard up.

I continue walking slowly, but Kelly is still on edge, digging the knife deeper into Arianna's side in a way that makes her wince.

"I did. I wanted to know if this baby was mine or if we'd have to try again," I say as I reach out for her, resting my hand on her stomach and rubbing it soothingly.

She seems to soften at my touch, the knife moving away from Arianna slightly, allowing me to breathe a little easier as I continue.

"You want to have a baby with me?" she asks desperately, like she's never wanted anything more.

"Of course, baby. You're the love of my life. I'm just so sorry I hurt you," I say as I cup the back of her neck, keeping her eyes pinned on me.

"You're mine." Kelly nods with a watery smile.

"I know, baby. I know. Everything you've done, everything you're doing. It's for us."

"Yes!"

"I know," I dip my chin, my thumb rubbing soft circles on the back of her neck as I keep her focus on me.

"I'll get rid of this baby, and we can start fresh," she says with a smile, a tear slipping down her face.

My gut twists at her words, at how I never saw the fucking crazy behind the mask. I don't let it show, though, forcing a genuine smile to spread across my face.

"That's all I want, Kelly."

I glance out of the corner of my eye to see that she's still holding the knife, though one of her arms has wound around my neck. Fucking hell. Sparrow, please forgive me.

Slipping my free hand around her waist, I smash her mouth to mine. She greets me eagerly, her tongue wrapping around mine like a fucking sea serpent as I hear the thud of the knife hit the carpet. Kelly's hands wrap around my neck, and I take the opportunity to lift her into the air. Her legs wrap around my waist as I begin carrying her across the room and into the foyer. I feel her teeth nip and pull against my lower lip, and I fake a groan as I slam her against the wall. She moans, grinding herself against me as I rest one of my hands on the wall.

Tearing my mouth away from hers, I cover her neck with kisses as I attempt to hit the emergency alarm on the keypad inside the doorway. Everything goes well until the enter button makes a beep. It's soft, almost silent, but her ear is centimeters from it. Immediately, she freezes. Pulling away from me, her calculated eyes narrow as she looks from me to the keypad, 911 flashing on the display.

Shit.

Kelly headbutts me, catching me off guard as I drop her with a thunk. She somehow recovers quicker than I do as she scrambles towards the living room, bending down to grab the knife.

"NO!" I shout, moments before the most haunting, gut-wrenching sound pierces the air.

My brain struggles to process the image of my Sparrow, wide-eyed and terrified, as she looks down at the knife sticking out of her abdomen.

A horrified gasp erupts from Arianna before she screams. That's all it takes.

I see red.

Letting out a roar that I'm fairly certain isn't human, I rush Kelly. She still holds the knife in her hand, her crazed eyes still on Arianna, which I use to my advantage. I tackle her to the couch, pinning her down by her throat as her eyes bulge in fear. Her nails begin clawing at me as her other hand attempts to stab me with the knife. I grapple with her for several seconds before I'm able to get a hold of her wrist, twisting it hard enough for her to let it go.

Her nails dig into my face, attempting to scratch my eyes out before I shove her deeper into the couch. Somehow, she's able to get her knee up and drives it straight into my balls. Pain radiates my entire body as I groan, falling off of her and onto the ground. The crazy fucking bitch stands to her feet, looking down at me with a disgusted look before her glare returns to Arianna.

Arianna looks at me, her face contorted in pain while her eyes bulge with panic. She will not hurt her further. She will not touch her. Reaching out for Kelly, I'm able to grip her ankle before I pull sharply. She topples over, unsteady from her buzz or these ridiculous fucking shoes, but not before she hits her head on the mahogany end table. Her skull makes a sickening crack before she collapses onto the ground.

Pushing myself up, I move over her limp body, not giving a

fuck whether she's alive or dead before I drop to Arianna's side. Her light blue shirt has a deep red stain that is only growing by the second. I press my hand against it, forcing a scream to erupt from her as I attempt to stop the bleeding.

"I know, Sparrow. I know. Keep breathing. Help is coming."

"Log-gan," she pants.

"I'm here, Ari. I'm here."

"I-I don't want to di-e."

Panic fills me as I shake my head.

"You won't! You hear me! You will not die. You and I, we have so much life to live, so many new heights to hit together. I still need to pick out the perfect ring, plan the perfect proposal. I need to hear you say that you'll marry me and watch you walk down the aisle in a white dress. I need to have babies with you and grow old with you. You and I? We're just getting started, okay?"

She smiles at that, her breathing becoming choppy.

"Okay."

"Okay?" I nod.

"Okay, I'll marry you. I'll have babies with you. Th-he works."

I feel a tear slip down my face as I let out a gasping laugh and give her a watery smile.

"Perfect, that was easy,"

Arianna chokes out a laugh, wincing at the end.

"Seattle PD, open up!" a shout calls out.

"In here! Hurry!" I call out.

Several loud pounding noises echo through the house before I hear the door splinter open. The security alarm goes off as heavy footsteps sound from the front door.

"Over here!" I yell again.

"Hands where we can see them!" a police officer yells.

"She's bleeding out! Help her! Save her!"

I watch him call in the scene on his radio as another officer comes over to us, untying Arianna before checking Kelly for a pulse.

"Make that two ambulances," he says to his partner.

"Help is here, Sparrow. You just have to hold on, okay? Just hold on."

She gives me a soft smile, but I see the life begin to drain out of her.

"No, no, no! Fuck! C'mon, Ari, baby. Stay with me. Don't leave me."

One of the cops rushes inside with a first aid kit, pulling out rolls of gauze that I quickly put against her before applying pressure once more. She's lost too much blood. She doesn't need gauze, she needs a doctor.

Thankfully, the sound of sirens rings out before four paramedics rush inside, two coming over to Arianna and two to Kelly. Carefully, they lift Arianna onto a stretcher, taking over holding her wound as they rush her off. I try to follow her when a cop stops me with a hand on my chest. I look down at his hand, pure fury running rampant inside me.

"Get your fucking hands off me."

"We have some questions, sir."

"Then ask them on the way to the hospital, that's my fucking fiancée!"

I don't care what Arianna says when she makes it out of this. She agreed to marry me, she's locked in now. She has to live because she promised. She has to be okay because we have a whole life to live.

The cops agree, thankfully. One stays behind while the other jumps into the car with me, immediately asking questions about what happened. I give him every shred of detail I can while my mind stays laser focused on the ambulance carrying my whole world in front of us.

When we get to the hospital, it feels like it takes forever to get to the nurse's station.

"Arianna Fulton, where is she?"

"Are you family?" she asks.

"Yes," I answer immediately.

Her fingers move across the keyboard, not fast enough if you ask me, before she looks at me.

"It looks like they took her up to surgery."

"She's alive?" I ask, like I need to hear the words.

"I can get someone to come out with an update if you'd like."

"Please," I rasp as I dig my hands into my hair and walk towards the wall, slumping down to the floor.

For hours I pray to God. I bargain, I threaten, I beg. I've never been a religious man, but in this moment, I'll say as many Hail Marys, do as many good deeds, promise anything in the whole fucking world if I can have Arianna back.

Chapter Thirty-Four

Arianna

Blinking my eyes open, I have a pounding headache and my stomach hurts. It takes me a second to understand where I am. A hospital. I'm in the hospital? Then, as if watching a movie trailer of a horror film, pieces begin flashing inside my mind. My mom with the bottle, with a knife. So much blood, so much bleeding, and then...nothing.

"Sparrow?" a panicked voice asks before I look to my side and see Logan beside me.

"Oh my god," he gasps, his shoulders shaking as he cries. I've never seen him cry before. Frowning, I reach my hand out to him, rubbing his back slightly as his head is pressed against my other hand resting on the bed.

"What's wrong? Are you okay?"

His head whips up, his rich brown eyes hidden behind a thick layer of tears.

"Am *I* okay? Ari, I thought I lost you."

My frown deepens. "Am I okay now?"

"You're doing well," a man says as he comes in from the hallway.

"I'm Dr. Parker, I was one of your surgeons today."

"Surgeon? I had surgery?"

He nods. "You came in with a ruptured spleen and a minor brain bleed."

A brain bleed? What the fuck? I don't even know how minor and brain bleed can be used in the same sentence.

"We were able to repair the damage to your spleen, and your brain bleed should heal on its own. We're going to keep you for a few days just to monitor you and baby."

It takes my fuzzy brain a second to process his words before I pause.

"Baby?"

The doctor looks down at his tablet.

"Yes, we monitored the fetal heart rate during surgery. Good heart rate and the ultrasound showed no free fluid or damage to the amniotic sac. It's truly amazing they made it. Babies in the first trimester with trauma like this to the abdomen usually don't."

"Whose baby?" Logan asks.

The doctor frowns. "You're only seven weeks along, but you're definitely pregnant. I'm sorry, did you not know?"

"Did our shocked expressions give it away?" Logan drawls sarcastically, and I wave him off.

"I'm pregnant? I...I'm gonna have a baby?"

He nods. "I'll have OB come down and talk to you, and a nurse will be in momentarily to get your vitals."

"Thank you," Logan says as I sit there in shock.

"Sparrow, are you alright?"

My head turns to him, incredulity no doubt all over my face.

"I'm gonna have a baby...I'm—"

"We, Ari. We are gonna have a baby," he says, pressing his lips to my hand before a wide smile spreads across his face.

I feel a matching one take over my own before Logan cups my face in his hands and kisses me.

"Don't give me that shit! We are her family. Fucking move before I throw your ass down this hallway!" a familiar voice screams.

Cassi and Naomi rush into the room, slamming the door shut like that will keep people out.

"Fucking bitch," Cassi mutters.

"Ari!" Naomi rushes, coming to my side. "How are you? How is she?" she asks Logan.

"What are you guys doing here?" I ask.

Cassi gives me a disbelieving look.

"When you get a call that your best friend is in surgery, you drop everything. We would have been here sooner, but I had difficulty tracking down Nay."

She gives Cassi a sharp look before turning back to me.

"What happened, babe? Are you okay?"

I nod. "I'm okay," I say as I notice Logan sink into the back of the room, allowing more space for my friends.

I begin telling them every detail, and they hang onto every word, their mouths falling further and further open until I look at Logan, wiggling my fingers for him to come closer. He does so with a small smile on his face as he bends down and presses a featherlight kiss to the top of my head.

"And that's not the craziest part," I say.

"How the fuck could your mom going psycho and trying to kill you not be the craziest part?" Cassi asks, eyes wide in shock.

"Well," I say as I look up at Logan. "We're having a baby."

Naomi gasps as Cassi's mouth drops.

"No way! We're gonna be aunties?"

I give them a tear streaked smile and they both hug me gently, kissing my cheek before they shake their heads.

"Wow, you've certainly been busy these last three months," Cassi says with a laugh.

Fuck, has it really only been three months since Cassi's birthday. I look up at Logan and he seems to be sharing my thoughts. It feels like it's been a lifetime already, and yet, not nearly long enough. I can't believe this is my life. That on a dime, everything changed.

One look. One touch. One night.

Epilogue

Logan

I'm holding Arianna's hands as we sit on the couch, awaiting her test results. She was discharged last week and has basically been on bedrest. I took a short leave from work to be here with her, and I wouldn't have it any other way.

That first day in the hospital was a flurry of doctors. The OB came in and told us that the baby appeared to be strong and healthy after performing an ultrasound on Arianna. I've never felt pure awe or more joy than when I heard that tiny heartbeat for the first time. Then, the image appeared on the screen, and there was our little gummy bear. Well, that's what Arianna calls it. It's fitting, since they really do look like a gummy bear in the sonogram.

Since then, she has been closely monitored as we approach the end of the first trimester because, unfortunately, she is at extreme risk for miscarriage. We've been taking it one day at a time, and as of yesterday, our little gummy bear was still doing great. She insisted on a paternity test since she was with Tyson and myself so close together. She discussed the dates with the OB, and I guess based on her cycle and when she was ovulating, the doctor assured her that it would be almost impossible for Tyson to be the father. Arianna insisted that a test would give her peace of mind, so we did it.

Her finger clicks on the paternity test, showing mine first.

Possibility of Paternity: 100%

She looks up at me with relief and I smile at her. Of course I wanted the baby to be mine more than anything, but there definitely would have been worse people to be the paternal father of my baby. There was never any question whether that baby was mine outside of DNA, but now that it is one hundred percent certain, it does alleviate a little bit of stress.

Arianna looks at the screen again, moving to the other test. While we were at it, we decided to find out what the baby's sex was. I told her I'd be happy with anything, which she agreed, but I know she's hoping for a boy. Maybe it's from the trauma of her childhood and upbringing, but I know she will be an incredible mother no matter what.

The screen pops open and Arianna's mouth drops as I smile.

A boy.

She leaps into my arms, and I hold her tight, smiling into her hair. Ten weeks down, thirty to go until we meet our little man. Arianna pulls away from me, tears in eyes as I hold up her hand, kissing her ring.

As soon as I knew she was okay and fell asleep, I left her with Cassi and Naomi before driving straight to the jewelry store and buying her the biggest ring they had in stock. Cassi and Naomi looked at me like I was crazy when I asked what kind of ring she would like before they helpfully pulled up inspiration pictures. I took those down to the store and walked away with a three and a half carat cushion cut. She deserves something much better, and while I'd custom order any ring she would like, this one could be a placeholder.

When she woke up the next morning, I was on my knee, sliding the ring onto her finger. She said that I was supposed to ask if she would marry me, which I pointed out she already agreed. Ultimately, she wanted a better memory, and I was happy to give that to her. I told her how much I loved her, how I can't fathom a moment without her, and that I want to spend forever by her side before she finally accepted.

I wanted to get married then and there, but she is insisting on waiting until the baby is born, which grates at me a little because I just want her to be mine in every way humanly possible. I understand, though. She wants the big wedding and the perfect dress, and with her body and energy levels changing with the pregnancy, that would be challenging. So, I'll wait, for her. Let's not pretend I wouldn't wait until the end of time for anything she wanted. I'd find a way to wrangle the moon and gift her the stars if she desired them.

Tyson came and visited Arianna in the hospital. He was so upset when I told him what happened and rushed right over. He also expressed a few choice words of what he would do to Kelly if he ever saw her again. I shared every single sentiment.

Neither of us will ever get the chance, considering Kelly is currently in King County Jail with no bail, thanks to a judge that I have a wonderful relationship with. She is facing twenty to thirty years in prison, but I'm pushing for life. I never want my fiancée or my child to ever walk this earth in fear of that psychotic bitch.

Last I heard, Tom has been trying everything to get her out, claiming to be her husband. I guess the dumb motherfucker made his choice and chose the nut job carrying his baby over his wife and children.

Marissa came and saw Arianna on one of her last days in the hospital. She apologized for not returning her calls and texts. She said she took off with the kids and just drove. They ended up in Montana in a little rundown town and just... processed. Now she is in the middle of divorcing Tom and attempting to take every cent he has, with the assistance of a colleague of mine. She's a fucking shark, and most of the men she goes up against end up completely penniless, so she's in good hands there.

Naomi and Cassi have been coming over to visit Arianna often. I don't get the details obviously, but I'm observant enough to put things together. Seems that both the girls also made...unique connections at the club that night and are dealing with the chaos that ensues. Thankfully, none of them are dealing with a psychotic, murderous mother, but still, I don't envy them or the men involved.

"We're gonna have a baby boy, Logan," Arianna smiles.

I hold her face in my hands, bringing her lips to mine as I nod.

"Yes, we are, Sparrow. You ready for it? A lifetime with me? A lifetime of being my love, my best friend, my partner, my Sub?"

She grins. "Heavy on that last one."

I smirk, pulling her in for another kiss. I never thought that I would be able to find happiness like this. I wasn't sure happiness like this even existed. To hold it, feel it, experience first hand. It's truly unfathomable that the love of my life was in plain sight for years. It's completely insane that everything shifted from One Night. One Night of Seduction turned into a lifetime of bliss.

Thank You

I know what you're thinking. Was that last twist completely necessary? It's a Katelyn Taylor book...of course emotional trauma with a twist out of left field is necessary!

Thank you so much for reading about Logan and Arianna's messy start! If you've been wondering what else happened that One Night, make sure you check out Cassi and Naomi's stories!

One Night Scandal is coming February 2026! (Cassi's story)

One Night Surrender is coming April 2026! (Naomi's story)

If you are looking for your next read, then look no further! Angsty, emotional, forbidden love with a scorching amount of spice is at your service below!

. . .

Gallows Hill Series – A dark academia reverse harem
    Deceit – Book 1
    Descent – Book 2
    Demise – Book 3

The Alphaletes Series – Interconnected football romance stories
    The Loyalties We Break
    The Walls We Break
    The Hearts We Break
    The Rules We Break

Stand Alones –
    Deliverance – An FF forbidden romance
    Gratify – A forbidden age gap
    Graves – An MFM stalker romance
    Jagged Harts – An MMA enemies to lovers

Acknowledgments

To my Alpha, Sara, thank you for everything you do! This book REALLY pushed me, and you know what that means. If I'm being challenged then I'm falling apart all over you. Faithfully with a smile on your face you always manage to hold me together when I feel as if I'm about to break. Your kindness, determination, loyalty and love are the only things that get me through sometimes and I hope you never forget how much I appreciate you!

To my Beta's, Elena, Arianna, Kelly, Blair and Sarah, I adore you all! Thank you all so much for your hardwork and attention to detail on this! Each of you provides such an incredible opinion, point of view and advice! So blessed to know and work along side wonderful people like you!

To my editors, Brittany and Slasher, literally you two are out here doing the lord's work. No one would even be able to understand my gibberish if it wasn't for you two. Thank you for always helping me create the most clear and proper wording without ever losing my voice. I love you both dearly!

To my street team and ARC readers, thank you all for your

support! Every page read, every review left, and every post made truly means the world. I'm not even a little shy to admit that I have hands down the best people behind me.

To my readers, whether this is your first book by me, or you've been by my side since day one, thank you. There are millions of authors out there, billions of books and you chose mine. Each one of you pushes me to write when my fingers ache, plot when my brain is mush and keep moving forward when I'm ready to give up. You all are the best readers anyone could ask for and I love each one of you desperately.